STOMP!

BY NICHOLAS VAN PELT
FROM TOM DOHERTY ASSOCIATES

The Mongoose Man
Stomp!

STOMP!

NICHOLAS VAN PELT

A TOM DOHERTY ASSOCIATES BOOK
NEW YORK

This is a work of fiction. All the characters and events portrayed in this novel are either fictitious or are used fictitiously.

STOMP!

Copyright © 1999 by Nicholas van Pelt

All rights reserved, including the right to reproduce this book, or portions thereof, in any form.

This book is printed on acid-free paper.

A Forge Book
Published by Tom Doherty Associates, Inc.
175 Fifth Avenue
New York, NY 10010

Forge® is a registered trademark of Tom Doherty Associates, Inc.

Designed by Lisa Pifher

Van Pelt, Nicholas.
    Stomp! / Nicholas van Pelt.—1st ed.
       p.   cm.
    "A Tom Doherty Associates book."
    ISBN 0-312-86525-2 (acid-free paper)
    I. Title.
PS3572.A422674S75   1999
813'.54—dc21   99-21855
                                            CIP

First Edition: June 1999

Printed in the United States of America

0 9 8 7 6 5 4 3 2 1

For Ray and Fanie Vannest
of Ravenswood, West Virginia.

From the dark horizon of my future a sort of slow, persistent breeze had been blowing toward me, all my life long, from the years that were to come. And on its way that breeze had leveled out all the ideas that people tried to foist on me in the equally unreal years I then was living through.

—from *The Stranger*, by Albert Camus

I.

A PLACE WHERE WIND BLOWS

ONE

YEARS LATER, I READ in the *Oregonian* that an adolescent male spends 80 percent of the time in the classroom thinking about sex. I believe that. In the classroom and out. The summer of 1957, the break between my sophomore and junior years at Umatilla High School, was a hormonal time for me, that's for sure. I was flat addicted to the nudist colony magazines in Anderson's Market, and there were days when I felt compelled to lope my goat four or five times a day in pursuit of elementary relief.

The first time I saw Angie Boudreau was about eight o'clock on a sweltering Thursday night in late August. It was one of those days with a languid, torpid feel about it. A storm was in the air. There would be the usual darkening clouds in the west, followed by a gusting wind, then the rolling of distant thunder. After that great bolts of lightning would light the streets above Umatilla, and the storm would be full upon us. I had a feeling, a vague expectation, that something more was going to happen besides the storm. Just what, I had no idea.

Even now, after all these years, my stomach twists at the memory. Her. She. The very pronouns are an aphrodisiac, soft and suggestive, sensual, carrying a soulful baggage that I was to discover is at the heart of being alive.

I was nearing the end of a three-week stretch of mopping

the floors and cleaning the toilets at Baker's, a drugstore and soda fountain that also served as a Greyhound bus stop. The swing shift fry cook, who ordinarily took care of those chores before he went home, was on his vacation. This was the day before the annual Great Stomp that marked the end of the summer for a group of us who had figured out there was more to life than watching "Ozzie and Harriet" or "Rawhide"; after my Friday chores, I would participate in my second stomp.

Baker's was on Sixth Street, the main drag of Umatilla, which ran parallel to the Oregon bank of the Columbia River. The soda fountain at Baker's, with rounded stainless-steel holders for the paper napkins, those salt-and-pepper shakers with raised checks on the glass, and a Wurlitzer jukebox, was one of those places that later came to be regarded as classics. In those days I dated everything by pop songs, and in the summer of 1957 if Debbie Reynolds wasn't singing "Tammy," it was Pat Boone writing his syrupy "Love Letters in the Sand." Or even worse Perry Como, Mr. Laid Back, singing "Round and Round" What puke! I liked The Diamonds' "Little Darlin' " and the Everly Brothers' "Bye Bye Love."

Little Darlin' Bo, bo-bo.
Little Darlin' Bo, bo-bo.
Where you? Oooh, oooh.
Boop, a boop, a boop, a boop, a boo.

They were playing a lot of Elvis Presley, and he was good too—"Don't Be Cruel" and "Heartbreak Hotel."

My boss, Percy Baker, a jowled, sour man with crewcut blond hair that was almost white and a pinched, determined mouth, watched me silently every night with eyes that looked like one of those on my dad's hogs—small and surrounded by a circle of bulging fat; pig's eyes, I called them. He resented the dollar an hour he was having to pay me, but he could hardly expect me to clean his place for free. He wasn't my first boss, so I knew they weren't all that way. August was watermelon month, and during the day I pitched melons for Albert Vincent, who wore a filthy fedora over his sun-tanned face and was a good guy, and I had had okay bosses when I had driven truck in the peas at Walla Walla and wheat outside of Pendleton—June and July jobs. Mr. Baker was the first boss I had had who wore a suit, complete with long-sleeved white shirt on the hottest days; he was to forever color my attitude toward people who wore neckties. He had decreed that the toilets be free and clean for the incoming buses, which was a sensible request, and in anticipation of the Spokane bus, I had started with them first.

I didn't know anything at all about women at the time, and—outside of my mom and older sister, who didn't count—cleaning those toilets was my first encounter with that remarkable gender, whose members could be simultaneously wonderful and perplexing in the extreme. I had assumed that males would be the slobs, what with drunks from the Silver Dollar bouncing it off the walls and whatever, but I found they were downright fastidious compared to the women, who were given to squatting on top of the toilet seats like huge, featherless birds to do whatever they had to do—leaving it to me to clean the lids. That's not to mention the wads of bloody yuch they left strewn about. Later, I reckoned the march of inflation by the poem scrawled on the inside of a pay stall on the men's side: *Here I sit all broken hearted, paid a nickel and only farted.*

Baker's Drugstore was situated on a slope. The main entrance on the upper level faced Sixth Street—the town's main drag; the buses parked in the rear of the building on the downhill side. This was where the toilets were located. The passengers had to walk up a long cement ramp topped with a black rubber mat to the fountain to order their hamburger or chicken fried steak with mashed potatoes and gravy. People who had anything drove a car and scorned buses. The passengers who got off the bus in Umatilla tended to be young and broke or on their way to somewhere better, middle-aged and broken, or old and trapped on a fixed income.

On that memorable night I was listening to KORD in Pasco, Washington, on my transistor radio while I cleaned the toilet. On the news the talk was of the new sack dress, a stupid-looking bag that, if past form held, would replace the current skirts and sweaters within a matter of months. It was amazing to me how everybody felt compelled to look, act, and think exactly the same. Then there was the enforced segregation of the high school in Little Rock, which was supposed to eventually usher in a new era of racial harmony. Sure it would. We were treated to more blather about how the surgeon general had found a link between cigarette smoking and lung cancer. Like we were supposed to believe people were walking around with their lungs pumped full of smoke without any consequences. Finally, there was the Russian launching of Sputnik, which had everybody talking about how that was a prelude to unstoppable rockets being aimed at us from the moon and was a wake-up call. Right. The big local story was about a rape and murder of a high school sophomore in Kennewick about twenty miles north of Umatilla. Wonderful.

Listening to Elvis sing "Heartbreak Hotel," I put the finishing touches on the women's john, which I put off for last—what with the seats and bloody yuch—when I heard the crunch of gravel, the hissing of air brakes, and the mellow lope of a diesel engine. The bus from Spokane was in. I gathered my mops and bucket and cleaning gear to one side so as not to get in the way of the passengers.

There were only a half-dozen Greyhound voyagers: a cowboy in a denim jacket and with flakes of dried cow shit on his jeans; a crewcut college student in chinos and a blue short-sleeved shirt with white stripes; a middle-aged man with a huge, red nose, carrying a bottle of something in a paper bag—Jim Beam, most likely—a fat lady with boobs big as Cadillac bumpers and the kind of gelatinous, veined legs that we called cottage cheese legs; a blue-haired crone with a bumped back and trembling hands; and the last passenger off the bus, a slender girl my age with copper-colored skin and long, sleek black hair.

I stared at her, transfixed. I couldn't help it. She had electric brown eyes that were almond shaped and set at an angle in her oval face—much like a cat's eyes. She had prominent cheekbones that gave her a vaguely Asian look, but all of that was secondary to her large, sensuous lips, the bottom one of which stopped just short of a suggestive droop.

She wasn't large, maybe five-three or five-four with an angular, rather than a rounded, figure. She wore sandals, jeans, and a nondescript light green blouse. And she had something that was avoided by all the proper girls in Umatilla: pierced ears. She wore a small ruby in each ear. Pierced ears! Oh scandal, scandal! In short, she was a flat-out exotic in Baker's Drugstore.

She had gotten two large, battered suitcases from the luggage bay and carried a rumpled paper bag that didn't have much in it—a paperback novel and a candy bar perhaps, not much more. This had to be a visit. It was hard to imagine she would be moving to a hole like Umatilla. Talk about end of the line.

She paused at the base of the ramp with her two suitcases and looked about uncertainly. She saw me standing there with my mops and bucket and cleaning gear and gave me a small, sympathetic smile.

I shrugged and said, "Hey, the toilets are clean at least. Gotta start somewhere. You want me to help you with those? I'm big and strong like Hopalong."

"That would be nice, thanks," she said.

I grabbed the suitcases and took them upstairs.

"There by the phone booth will do, thanks," she said.

While she made a phone call, I went downstairs to retrieve my wheeled bucket. Baker didn't like me dragging my smelly crap around when people were trying to eat, but for once he had gone home to his horse-faced wife, so I stashed mop, bucket, and Pine Sol on the side of the store that sold drugs and whatnot and was roped off and closed.

When I got back upstairs, all the passengers were at the counter ordering something to eat. I noticed that the woman with the cottage-cheese legs was reading a paperback edition of Grace Metalious's *Peyton Place*. I had my own copy with the pages bent at all the good spots; many was the time that, dry mouthed, I had polished my knob to a sheen in appreciation of Miss Metalious's sweaty prose. But the girl with the pierced ears wasn't at the counter. She stood alone by the heavy glass main door, looking out on the street, where the wind was beginning to gust. Her suitcases were not to be seen. She had apparently stashed them in a locker. She too had a paperback, only hers was *The Stranger* by Albert Camus, the French existentialist who had won the Nobel Prize in literature earlier in the year.

I should say here that I was a longtime runt who had just grown five inches in six months. I had spent the first two years at Umatilla High School regarded as rather like a mascot. Although my name was Ray, everybody called me Skeeter. See how little he is. No bigger than a mosquito. Ha, ha, ha. Unlike muscled jocks and class presidents, I lacked that aggressive, self-assured presence that scored dates to the prom and the rest of it. It was difficult to have a whole lot of masculine self-confidence with a girl's boobs poking you in the eye in the middle of a fox-trot—embarrassing for both me and the girl. Bobs and Jacks and Toms had girlfriends, not Skeeter Hawkins, who cleaned the toilets at Baker's. So it was that I had become an observer. Since I had spent all my time on the outside looking in, they might well have called me Watcher Hawkins.

I took a deep breath, prepared myself for a likely get-lost reaction, and went to stand by the black-haired girl. It took me a moment to realize that I was as tall she was—taller in fact. At long damn last. Outside, a gusting wind, the edge of a coming storm, sent a tumbleweed bounding down the street.

Despite my newfound height, I was amazed she didn't move

away. I said, "The guy on the beach. The sand. The heat. The boredom. The Arab. Decisions. Decisions. What do you think?"

She glanced briefly at her copy of *The Stranger,* then looked at me with her startling brown eyes, no doubt amazed that I had read the book. "I think he's trapped, like the rest of us." She paused, then gave my bucket a push with her toe. "Getting it done?"

Outside there was an ominous rumble of thunder. "Got the upstairs to go," I said.

"Looked pretty desolate coming downriver. What do you do around here for fun?"

I grinned. "Not a whole lot. Great Stomp tomorrow night. End of the summer." God, those lips. When she talked, those lips moved. That alone was almost enough to give me a boner.

She raised an eyebrow. "Great Stomp?"

"Mice. We stomp mice."

She giggled. "What?"

"Out on the desert. What we do, see, is . . ." I stopped. How was I to explain a Great Stomp? "You'd have to be there to understand," I said.

"I bet."

"People call them kangaroo rats, but they're really mice. They look like miniature kangaroos or wallabies. They don't run. They bound. Hard to get a clear bead on one when he's leaping this way and that."

"Sounds like great sport." She had a great smile.

Billy Karady came rumbling down the drag in his glistening black Cunt Wagon, a 1950 Mercury coupe. Karady's version was lowered all around and chopped; that is, the entire top had been lowered so that the windows and windshield were pillbox slits; this gave it a sleek, sinister look. The Mercury sported a souped-up engine with a three-quarter cam that made it gurgle malevolently when it idled—a sort of sinister, loping sound. When Karady dragged the gut, it was with a rumble that threatened to explode the second he punched the accelerator. A pair of furry black dice with white dots could be seen dangling from the rearview mirror.

Billy peered out at us as he rumbled past with the light reflecting off the trio of knifelike flippers of his hubcaps.

She said, "Who's that?"

"That's Billy Karady in his Cunt Wagon, begging your pardon.."

"Local big man?"

I nodded yes. "He's wondering if you'll fit on his backseat."

"No doubt. Never happen though."

"Oh?"

"Not my type." She glanced up at the clock behind the counter. Those lips moved again. Mmmm. "Can you take time off for a walk?"

I hesitated. A sudden flash lit her face, followed by a window-rattling crack of thunder. It was difficult for me to believe that a girl like that would ask me, Skeeter Hawkins, to go for a walk with her. "I better stay and do the drugstore side," I blurted out. "Besides, we'll be getting lightning and rain in a few minutes." I was immediately pissed at myself for remaining Skeeter, when I had a chance, at long last, to be plain old Ray. I was as tall as she was, for Christ's sake, and she had never heard anybody call me Skeeter. Only an unregenerated twit would turn down an invitation like that.

She seemed genuinely disappointed. "Well, suit yourself. Like you say, we all have to make decisions." With that, she pushed open the heavy glass door and stepped into the wind, which began whipping her black hair. She turned her head against the wind, rounded a corner, and was gone.

It began a downpour almost immediately, the wind slapping the rain hard against the glass front of Baker's. This was quickly followed by another flash and a long rumble of thunder.

I expected her to return momentarily, but she didn't.

I didn't do any work for thinking about her. All I could do was watch the clock, wondering how she had escaped the rain.

Where had she gone? I hadn't learned her name. I knew for a
fact that when I went to bed that night I'd conjure up her image
in my mind's eye and imagine what might have been. Even if
she didn't have a name, the imagining of her brown cat's eyes
and oval face would, inevitably, lead to an enthusiastic trotting
of my dog. I was glad I had read *The Stranger*; at the time, I
wasn't sure what it was all about, but it lingered in my memory
and was to remain there for years just like Angie stepping off
the bus on that August summer night and, in varying detail, all
that followed.

*The food on the riverboat—coffee, rice, beans, and fish, with
an occasional, curious boiled root thrown in for good measure—was as repetitious as the passing forest. I didn't mind the
food, actually. If I had been healthy, I would have relished
eating it. In my many travels, I had prided myself on eating
whatever the locals ate. But not this time. All I could do for
more than a week was lie in my hammock and wonder if I was
going to make it, if one morning they would find me dead. The
captain couldn't take my corpse downstream in this heat; the
crew would either bury me in a shallow grave in the forest or
dump me overboard for the piranhas.*

*Then, slowly, just when I thought I was doomed, that I
would likely die there on the river, I began to recover. I knew
intuitively that given enough time, my body would triumph.*

*Lying there one night, I listened as the catfish that sounded
like banjos serenaded a young Brazilian couple who were flirting from hammocks strung on the bow across from me. I gathered from the snatches of murmured Portuguese that they were
talking about the fun they would have when the boat got to
Santarem. It was sweet to watch them. A joy! The girl had olive
skin and large brown eyes.*

*There, on the huge river, with the boat's engine going ka-
churg, ka-churg, ka-churg, I remembered Angie's dusky eyes*

and dark skin and our meeting in the bus station in Umatilla, Oregon, in that long-ago summer day.

The Amazon was curiously without wind, but it had current; it flowed, as did blood and the wind. As an ultimate result of Angie's arrival that night, I had spent decades in self-imposed exile—plenty of time to think about currents, blood, and the wind. In The Stranger, Albert Camus's protagonist—facing execution for having murdered an Arab on an Algerian beach—felt his life had been dominated by a "a slow, persistent breeze" that blew "from the dark horizon" of his future. I understood this blowing from the future as a form of existential backdraft.

Over the years, I had concluded that Camus's insight had been both accurate and inaccurate—accurate about the effect of the metaphorical breeze, inaccurate about it being slow and persistent. In fact, each life had its highs and lows, hot spots and cold stretches; the wind sometimes stalled in terrible doldrums and other times came in surprising gusts. Having no idea at all where my odyssey would eventually end, I charted the gusts of memorable incident in my own life, noting the details in a journal. The most-telling incidents were widely scattered in time and place. I drifted as a windblown sailor, fleeing the unresolved mystery of my past.

Billy Karady was yet out there, pursuing me, implacable and unrelenting as the wind.

TWO

To UNDERSTAND WHAT HAPPENED late on the afternoon of the next day, the Friday of the Great Stomp, you need to understand the geography of Umatilla—especially the confluence of the Umatilla and Columbia rivers—which was about 180 miles east of Portland, Oregon. The Umatilla River started its journey from creeks and springs in the Blue Mountains some eighty to a hundred miles to the southeast. The river traveled just west of Hermiston, six miles south of Umatilla, and flowed northward as it entered the Columbia. The Umatilla River, the effective boundary of the western end of the town, was highest in May and June when the snow was melting in the Blues, but by August it had shrunk to a path of exposed basalt bedrock that was rank with the stench of dead fish.

It's critical to mention here that the west bank of the mouth of the Umatilla, surrounded by a stand of willow trees, was well packed by the determined butts of people fishing for small-mouth bass and catfish. There was a small, kidney-shaped clearing in the middle of these willows; owing to the frustrating lack of cover for groping and heavy breathing, this refuge had become littered with empty beer bottles, Twinkie wrappers, and used Trojans.

A hundred yards north of these willows was an old-fashioned railroad bridge. Until the government built McNary

Dam, the Union Pacific Railroad had been the chief source of jobs in Umatilla; at one time my maternal grandfather and my dad worked for the UP, and later my older brother and his firstborn son and my first cousin. For years, there had been a large brick roundhouse and a tangle of railroad tracks that ran through the middle of the town; in those days these tracks separated the sleepy north side, which flanked the Columbia, from the south side, where activities were centered around selling gasoline and Orange Crushes to motorists on their way to Portland. If you pumped gas in one of these stations, and stocked the pop machines, it was considered sport to open an Orange Crush, take a couple of swigs, and pee in the bottle before recapping it. Fun to imagine thirsty travelers drinking pee on their way to Portland.

A couple of hundred yards south of the railroad bridge was the car bridge that crossed the Umatilla into town. Those were the days before Interstate 84, and Highway 30 was the main run to Portland. As it passed through Umatilla, Highway 30 became Sixth Street, the main drag, where Baker's Drugstore was located.

A bumpy road of rounded basalt rocks ran from the western end of the car bridge, under the approach to the railroad bridge, to a parking circle by the willow grove. This parking circle was used both by fishermen and the heavy-breathers who had discarded the Trojans.

Umatilla, an early rendezvous of fur trappers, was originally called Umatilla Landing; long before the trappers arrived, it had been an Indian campground. This ancient campsite was marked by large banks of discarded mussel shells on both sides of the river that was named—like the town, the county, and the Indian reservation thirty miles to the southeast—for the Umatilla tribe. I was curious about the mussels because I couldn't find any in the river. I assumed that they had been eaten out of existence, or maybe destroyed by the power dams that the U.S. Army Corps of Engineers was erecting on the Columbia River—

McNary Dam a couple of miles above Umatilla being the latest.

In the late nineteenth century, Chinese laborers had run sluices on the Columbia River, where layers of gold-bearing black sand lay beneath sandbars. The Chinese miners bulked the population of Umatilla to a reported ten thousand, but by 1957 it was down to 406 stranded souls. There remained brass opium pipes, tiny glass mercury containers, and Chinese coins with holes in the middle to be found on the town side of the Umatilla River.

This history of Indians, fur trappers, and Chinese gold hunters had provided grist for my hobby, something to do between sessions of pounding my eager, but frustrated, pud. I was Skeeter, the squirt, but my ration of hormones was apparently as large as the rations of the early-maturing fullbacks and first basemen. It was my contention that while they grew their fancy muscles, I had gone straight to dick.

What kind of country was this, you ask? What did it look like? To be honest, it was one of the ugliest places in the United States. Had to be. It was semiarid desert, but not scenic desert like you see in the John Ford movies, what with the saguaro cacti and the neat rock formations. Here the cacti were pathetic, spiny little clumps the size of a fist, and even the sagebrush was stunted. There were precious few trees that were not planted—a few cottonwoods along the river maybe and a narrow strip of willows flanking the Columbia. The temperature could soar to 110 degrees Fahrenheit in the summer and dove to 28 below in the winter. It was hard to imagine the poor damn Chinese going to America to seek their fortunes and winding up in Umatilla.

The army stored nerve gas and biological warfare agents at the Umatilla Ordnance Depot, about twelve miles to the southwest. The distant, muffled *whump! whump! whump!* of munitions being exploded was as common on a summer day as the clicking and snapping of grasshoppers or the rattle of diesel rigs heading for Portland. At the Boardman Bombing Range, twenty miles to the west, the Air Force apparently used jackrabbits and coyotes for high-altitude practice. At the Hanford Nuclear Reactor, thirty miles to the north in Washington State, the people of the Manhattan Project had made the plutonium for the nuke that flattened Nagasaki. You can see, from all this cheery activity, how the real estate surrounding Umatilla was held in the very highest esteem by the folks back in Washington.

There was no work in the watermelons, which had petered out, so I decided to spend the Friday of the Great Stomp looking for arrowheads. I would have the weekend to sleep it off. On Monday afternoon, football practice would begin. I lived a little over a mile west of town, and that morning, I packed my sifting screen into my car, a brown and tan 1946, four-door sedan. Detroit had been busy building military vehicles during the war, and my car had that bulky rounded look that had become fashionable by 1940. The paint was oxidized. It had a fist-sized hole in the rear fender. I had bought the car by picking up pop and beer bottles along the highway, using the money to buy four weaner pigs that I raised until they were full-sized hogs; I swapped the hogs for the car, a hog itself. It was, by universal agreement, the ugliest car driven by any student at Umatilla High School. It was so bad, it was downright embarrassing. No other car came close.

I parked my Chev in a small stand of poplars at the base of a sand dune on the Columbia River; this was about a hundred yards from the parking turnaround by the willows at the mouth of the Umatilla. There was no road from the turnaround to the poplars, just two parallel tracks that I had left from earlier arrowhead expeditions. My sifter was a shallow box with a wire-screen bottom and with legs and handles. The screening process was simple enough; I used a folding GI trench shovel to fill the box with sand, then rocked the screen back and forth on its two legs to separate collectible goodies from the sand. I had copied my model from a *National Geographic* photograph of an archeologist at work, and it truly was a dandy.

While I was on the river sifting sand and looking for bird points, I knew that the Bobs, Jacks, and Toms, which was my generic term for the Billy Karadys of the world, would later be driving their girlfriends to the swimming hole just downstream from McNary Dam. While I pawed through the screenings, they would be lying on blankets frying their skin and trying to get an angle on the top of their girlfriends' swimming suits.

Over the summer I had heard many eager stories about glimpses of forbidden territory. For example, there were reports of nip sightings on a girl named Rosie, whose small, pointed boobs were inadequate to her ambitious swimsuit. This was a time when conical, hard bras were in fashion, and a year earlier there had been jokes that I was afraid to ask Rosie to dance for fear of getting an eye put out. Ha, ha, ha! Another suggestive claim was that wisps of wet black pubes clung to the thighs of a freshman named Susie when she emerged from the water, and so those occasions had evolved into a form of spectator sport. Bun creep on the swimsuit bottoms was always exciting, but was such a common occurrence that I suspected the girls, pretending innocence, used it as a form of torment. Look at these numbers and dream on, pal. Anyway, there would be none of that for me.

Later on, while I stayed home with my sister, mom, and father, who had multiple sclerosis, watching "Dragnet" on the box, the Bobs, Jacks, and Toms would be parked up in the buttes, listening to Buddy Holly on the radio and getting their fingers wet. Sometimes these muscled strutters would leave their hands unwashed so they could push them in front of the faces of their friends at school with a smug, check-this look. It was said the odor of pussy juice had a sweet, pungent quality that was unreal. Some held it was worse than rotten oysters. Others said it was sublime. Whether awful or grand, discussions of this mysterious secretion were always conducted with much har,

har, har guffawing. As if everybody was in on the secret. Right.

That morning, as I refilled the sifting box with my trench shovel, I wondered if I would graduate to Ray in my junior year—what with me now being five foot nine and obviously still growing—or if I would forever be Skeeter. I had noticed before school ended that a few civilized classmates were calling me Skeets, rather than Skeeter—a recognition, perhaps, that I had caught up with them. But fuck Skeeter and to hell with Skeets. I had endured that tiresome crappola too damn long— enough was enough. I wanted to be Ray Hawkins. It wouldn't be easy, I knew. The Bobs, Jacks, and Toms were territorial; they didn't want competition for getting their fingers wet, so they would continue the cutesy Skeeter horseshit. What self-respecting girl wanted to go to the Dairy Queen with someone named Skeeter who drove a car that looked like a prop in an old war movie?

I had hit upon two forms of guerrilla warfare that I suspected were also helping turn the corner. Some of the most callous offenders had zits. They tried to conceal these by troweling on the Clearasil, which was supposed to be skin colored, but actually looked like a thin film of dried mud. I'd never had zits, and it was great sport, whenever one of those self-important assholes called me Skeeter, to use my fingernails to squeeze goo from a pretend pimple. Fun to watch their faces color. At school dances most of the hulks stood around like stupes, waiting for a slow dance so they could tuck their hard-ons up under their belts. They froze in the face of the simplest rhythm, as though doing the fox-trot was somehow unmanly, and ended up looking like The Thing trying to grope a donkey. It was clear to me that a lot of girls wanted to actually dance, and so I worked all kinds of entertaining twirls, whirls, loops, and spins into the swing. I knew how to move with the music— couldn't stop it, in fact—and when the needle touched the groove of Gene Vincent, The Big Bopper, or Little Richard, I went into action, leaving the John Wayne wannabes watching from the sidelines, secretly fingering their inflamed pimples.

So that's where I was then, sifting sand at a bank of mussel shells about a hundred yards west of the mouth of the Umatilla. And that's what I was doing: screening for arrowheads; dreaming about graduating from Skeeter to Ray; contemplating nips, pubes, and mysterious smells—and periodically rocking my Louie. *Rocka my Louie to the bosom of Alicia. Oh, rocka my Louie.* Alicia being a girl in my class with these honking big sweater stretchers.

Well, okay. I thought about sex and the coming mouse stomp. On the eve of the Great Stomp, it was impossible not to think of the action ahead. The first few weeks of school would be dominated by stories of the stomp—who tallied how many mice and by what manner of action. The Goodie Goods would all pretend to be offended at such a crass ritual, but they were just sore because they never got invited—not that they would have accepted. As a five-foot-three-inch and ninety-six-pounder, I had scored my first mouse between my freshman and sophomore years. Now at five-nine and 130 pounds, I had enough size to knock my competition off balance in the clutch.

THREE

THE SKY ABOVE THE eastern Oregon desert was cloudless, a pale, nearly colorless blue that faded to a slice of white at the horizons. Across the broad, deep river were the beginnings of the Horse Heaven Hills. There were no trees or shrubs on the rounded hills and not a hint of green. They were the color of a weathered cow pie; my mother, whose oils had dominated the blue ribbons at the Umatilla County Fair for decades, would have rendered them with a mix of raw ochre and burnt umber. There were no more wild horses left in that equine paradise; when my mother was a girl the horses had been herded, kicking, eyes wild with fear, into corrals along the railroad on the Washington side of the river. There, whinnying, sweating, nostrils flaring, they were killed with ball peen hammers. The merciful use of rifles would have required ammunition, which was profit-squandering overhead. Their carcasses were winched aboard railroad boxcars and shipped off to be turned into leather and mink food. If that was heaven, I wanted no part of it.

I didn't want ny part of the world of the U.S. Army Corps of Engineers either. Before they had built McNary Dam, there had been a current in the river, and come June high water had flooded the willows. It was fun to build rafts and float around like Huck Finn in Mr. Twain's story. The Corps of Engineers had built a damn at The Dalles that had flooded the rapids where the Indians had netted their salmon. There would come a day, I knew, when they would succeed in putting one dam after another on the river until they were like giant, concrete beads. Just how anybody expected the salmon and steelhead to survive all that was beyond me.

But now, as I dug sand and struggled with my sifting screen, it was yet another innocent day of soaking up ultraviolet rays; without knowing it, I was sowing and nurturing the seeds of basal-cell carcinoma. But I was unconcerned with the fate of the wild horses or such things as cancer and death. I was at the beginning of my turn; the summers seemed to last forever; and there was no end for my cycle that I could imagine. I had no idea, none at all, that there would come a day when the summers would seem to pass in the blinking of an eye.

A few minutes after the noon siren blew across the Umatilla, I climbed the top of the sand dune to see if the wind had uncovered anything interesting; I had once found a wonderful pestle poking out of that dune. I briefly considered walking to Benson's Truck Stop on the west side of the car bridge to buy myself a Royal Crown cola, then decided to forget it; a ten-cent RC was six minutes of pitching twenty-pound striped klondikes. I drank some more water from my canteen and returned to work at the base of the dune. That's when I heard an approaching motor, which then fell silent, followed by the slamming of a door.

I found a bird-point made of brown flint. It had neat little serrated edges that had required a skilled craftsman—a real find. Then I uncovered a flat piece of basalt with a neatly chiseled edge. This was a scraper, commonplace along the river. This was the real deal, although nothing to excite a collector because it was easy enough to make one yourself.

About twenty minutes passed before another door slammed, followed by the distant *whump! whump! whump*! of exploding ammunition igloos at the Umatilla Ordnance Depot. The explosions stopped.

A couple of minutes later, I heard the scream. I didn't have to be told that this was the real deal. It had a scary quality about it that I'll never forget. Somebody was in big-time trouble.

I scrambled to the top of the sand dune. I yelled, "Hey!" as loud as I could, then, continuing, "Hey, hey, hey!" I sprinted toward the stand of willows. Up ahead, about a hundred yards from my ugly beast, Billy Karady had parked his sleek black Cunt Wagon beside my bulbous 46 four-door Chevrolet sedan. Compared to Karady's Merc, my vehicle was maximum ugly, a wheeled turd with windshield—a car for a farmer or an old fart.

Suddenly, as I got to within fifty yards of Billy's Cunt Wagon, still yelling wildly, the screaming ceased.

I stopped, filled with indecision. Something was wrong; there seemed no doubt about that. Should I go down to the willows and check things out? And do what? I had no desire to tangle with Billy Karady. I was no kind of hero. Stuff the guilt, I returned to my sifter and my work. I refilled the box and shifted the load. Nothing. But my mind wasn't on the arrowheads. I should have gone into the willows to see if whoever was doing the screaming was all right.

A good five minutes passed, maybe more. I heard another vehicle arrive. The engine fell silent. Who was the new arrival? My conscience was gnawing at me because I hadn't done more about the screaming. I returned to the top of the sand dune and saw Brian Mungo, the coach at Umatilla High School, about to climb into his green Ford pickup. When I say coach, I mean Coach, cap C. There were only 118 students in the four classes at Umatilla High School, and Mungo coached the Vikings in all sports—football, basketball, baseball, and track. He had a volunteer assistant in football, the plump Mr. Holmes, who taught eighth grade.

Coach Mungo glanced in my direction with a look of surprise on his face. Hadn't he seen my car before?

I crouched down in the sagebrush.

Looking at me, Mungo hopped quickly into the pickup, started the engine, and raced off, leaving a horsetail of dust. He hit the gravel road that led under the railroad bridge and in a few seconds was gone, leaving Billy Karady's car in the parking circle.

Still wondering about the terrible screaming, I decided it was better late than never. Sitting back and watching weren't good. I had a responsibility. I had to do something. I ran along the edge of the river. I had no idea what I expected to find; I just felt compelled to take a look.

Brushing away cobwebs, I eased carefully into the willows, but didn't see anything. I got to the kidney-shaped clearing when I felt a presence behind me. I turned, and there stood a man in a blue baseball cap and white tee shirt. This was Carl Sellers, who owned the local Shell station where my mother did business; Sellers, a rabid Viking supporter, was a longtime president of the Umatilla Boosters. "I heard screaming," I said.

"So did I," he said. "What happened?"

"Sounded like someone was in trouble, so I yelled."

"I heard you," he said. He gestured toward the river. "I was down there fishing for catfish."

I said, "I was screening for arrowheads." I pointed downriver. "That's when I heard the screaming. "I saw . . ." I started to say I saw a worried or concerned Coach Mungo getting into his Ford pickup, but I thought better of it. Sellers was Mr. Viking of Umatilla. I licked my lips. I said, "I saw Billy Karady's Merc parked in the turnaround."

No sooner had I got that sentence out of my mouth than I saw a pair of girl's underpants lying at the base of a willow tree. It didn't take a rocket scientist to suspect that they might have come from the girl who had screamed. I only had Sellers's word that he had been fishing, so I didn't say anything about those either.

Sellers's face was clouded with concern—for whom wasn't

clear. "You suppose we should try to find Billy?"

"I think so," I said.

Sellers led the way down the trail out of the willows, and behind his back, I stooped and quietly slipped the underpants into my hip pocket. The underpants had likely come from the girl who had screamed, but where had she gone?

We stepped out of the willows to the turnaround and found the good-looking, curly-haired Billy Karady, soaking with sweat, looking under the opened hood of his Merc. He looked up at us with that long face of his and his good-looking, square jaw. He had these eyes that tended to bore right through you like you were a piece of shit—that is, unless he wanted something from you. On this occasion, he seemed halfway human. He wiped grease from his hands with a rag. He gave us a self-deprecating grin and said, "Hey, Mr. Sellers! Skeeter!"

Sellers, clearing his throat, looked around.

Billy said, "Fucking fuel pump again. It's the filter, I think. Good old Benson's Truck Stop. They've got everything."

He mopped his brow with his forearm and walked around to the driver's side. He slipped in and the motor started up. He got out, grinning. "That was it. Hey, not bad."

Sellers glanced at me.

Billy said, "You two look like you've been swallowing live frogs. Something wrong?"

FOUR

ALTHOUGH WE TALKED ABOUT it off and on all year, the actual planning of a Great Stomp ordinarily began in early June when school let out and lasted until the agreed-upon night in late August. There was no formal initiation or captain or anything like that. Responsibility for the stomp was passed along informally from year to year from preceding generations of stompers, and as August approached, the participants informally negotiated the date among themselves. Nobody wanted to miss the action because of work, and everybody wanted as much moon as possible—a full moon produced the most mice. The little hoppers were nocturnal, and that was when they were out and about in number.

Most of the participants got to take part in two stomps— one between their sophomore and junior years, and the other between their junior and senior years. Occasionally, a lucky freshman got tapped, as had been my case. Everybody knew I had creamed the Goodie Goods in the Stanford-Binet exams given at the end of the eighth grade, but I was not a Goodie, and everybody knew it. My father had done time for making moonshine whiskey when he was younger, and I was his clone both in looks and attitude.

The question of the driver was an annual problem. Some-body had to drive, and it was agreed that it was best that the driver shouldn't drink. Usually a borderline Goodie Good would hint that his services were available; that way he could participate, and get to tell stories later—with the suggestion that he was a closet wild one—while officially retaining his cherry of not drinking beer. That was the case this year, when an amiable, curly-haired doof named Harold Helton, good old Responsible Harold, volunteered to drive.

I completed my final night of cleaning and mopping Baker's Drugstore at ten o'clock and went home to take a nap. Responsible Harold would pick me up at eleven thirty or twelve, and I knew from experience that I wouldn't get home until the sun came up. My bedroom, separate from my parents' tiny house, had once been a chicken coop. It had been spruced up with overlapping red shingles made of asphalt, topped with tarpaper, and insulated with newspapers; inside, a single lightbulb hung from the ceiling above the narrow bed. The door by the head of my bed opened onto an irrigation ditch above a cow pasture. Below the pasture lay the stand of willows on the banks of the Columbia. In the summer, I was able to open the door and pee into the ditch with a refreshing cool breeze on my balls; I was convinced that people forced to pee on porcelain all their lives had missed an elementary pleasure. True, the cows peed in the water, which also bred mosquitoes, and there was often fresh cow plop a few yards away from the door, but for me this was *eau de youth*. My makeshift bedroom was something else when the winter winds came whipping out of Canada, but that's another story.

I lay on my bed in my tennis shoes, jeans, and T-shirt, but couldn't sleep; this was partly out of anticipation of the stomp, and also because I couldn't take my mind off the screaming at the mouth of the Umatilla. There had been genuine terror in that scream. A young woman or girl had been in big-time trouble. I couldn't forget Coach Mungo either. He was clearly looking in the direction of my Chev. Was there a connection between the screaming and Coach Mungo?

Or was the connection between the screaming and Billy Karady?

The relationship between Coach Mungo and Billy Karady is germane at this point. Coach Mungo was much beloved in Umatilla, where he was universally regarded as the good guy of the western world, but Coach clearly preferred good athletes to pathetic wannabes. He wanted to win ball games, so that wasn't surprising. It certainly was no secret that Billy was one of his favorites. Give Billy a football, and he was transformed into a Viking in every sense of the word. He was fast and strong, and he loved to lower his head and flatten a would-be tackler. He had taken the Vikings to the district championship the previous year, and if the Vikings were ever to go to state, it was Billy Karady who would take us there. But more than that, he had gained one hundred or more yards per game for three straight years; four straight years would be an Oregon high school record, and nobody had to be told that Billy's senior year would be a countdown in the newspapers.

I switched on my lightbulb and took a good look at the panties I had grabbed. They were size five, of a brand called Mystique. There was a tear on the seam at one hip, suggesting they had been ripped from the wearer.

At a quarter to twelve, I heard a honking horn, and went outside to where Responsible Harold had arrived in an old Dodge pickup loaded with stompers who laughed and hooted as I piled aboard. Then we were off, headed for the desert above the irrigation canal near the top of the plateau that flanked the river. In another twenty years this desert plateau, irrigated by water pumped from the Columbia, would be used to grow potatoes for the McDonald's fast-food empire. But not then. Then it was a form of no man's land, a territory of sand, stunted sagebrush, annoying little cacti, an occasional coyote, and mice.

As we pushed off, there were twelve stompers in all, ten in the pickup's bed with the six cases of Olympia and two in the cab with Harold, who had brought along a thermos of black coffee to help keep him alert. It was a warm, cloudless night, with a fabulous ration of stars and a full moon. We were young and in our prime and full of ourselves, and life was good.

Responsible Harold hung a right at the west end of the bridge over the Umatilla and drove us uphill, across the irrigation canal and past the dump, which is when we yelled for Harold to stop the truck: it was time to draw names for the running boards. Harold had written the name of each stomper on a small piece of paper that he had put in a Boston Red Sox baseball cap. He drew two names from the cap. My friend Buddy Inskeep, a stocky, muscular kid who was a terrific fullback, catcher, and third baseman, got the choice left board by the driver, and Billy Karady, who was the starting tailback on the Vikings football team, drew the right. The windows of the doors were rolled down so the stompers on the running boards could hold on; Inskeep and Karady would get a head start when the first mouse was spotted, and Inskeep would give directions to the driver.

I should add here that Billy was his usual confident, take-charge self. If he'd done anything wrong that day, he didn't show any signs of it. I should also add that it was bum luck for the rest of us that Billy got the right board because he had stomped the most mice the previous year. Buddy Inskeep was strong, but not especially nifty, so it wouldn't take long for him to wind up in the back; the quick, aggressive Billy could hold his beer, and he had an amazing ability to anticipate a mouse's next jump. There were no trophies handed out for the most mice; at the same time nobody wanted to admit that Billy Karady was better than they at every damn thing from hitting a jump shot and swinging a Louisville slugger to smashing a mouse in the sand. The joke at school was that Billy was a secret investor in the company that made Trojan rubbers.

The rules of a Great Stomp were simple enough. Pushing, tripping, and holding the competition were entirely in order as long as they remained good-natured and didn't get out of hand.

When a mouse was drilled, everybody drank a celebratory Oly and had a good laugh, after which the successful stomper claimed the left running board. The displaced stomper took the opposite board, relegating that competitor to the rear. The choice of Olympia beer was not by accident. There were one to four dots on the back of each Oly label. These were thought to represent vats in Tumwater, Washington, where the beer was brewed, but more than that, myth held that if your label had four dots, you would get laid next time out. A four-dot label was highly prized.

With the draw completed, Harold aimed the pickup southwest into the desert. Umatilla was two or three miles behind us; the town of Hermiston was several miles to the southeast; the Umatilla Ordnance Depot was maybe ten miles dead ahead. We entered mouse country about a mile past the dump, so Buddy Inskeep and Billy Karady claimed their spots on the running boards. Those of us in the bed of the pickup pushed the six cases of Oly to the rear and crowded around the cab.

It was the driver's job to propel the pickup in a slow, zigzagging left-right, left-right pattern—avoiding patches of sand in which he might get stuck—until we spotted the ruby eyes of a mouse in the headlights. His responsibility was to then to keep the headlights on the fleeing mouse while the rest of us piled off the vehicle and set off in hot pursuit.

With Buddy giving directions, Responsible Harold started the sweep of headlights. In the back, we began banging on the top of the cab and yelling, telling Billy how we were going to cooperate in keeping him from the mice. Everyone wanted to be the one to spot the first mouse and shout the traditional call that accompanied each sighting.

I shouted and teased along with everybody else, momentarily forgetting the screaming that had haunted me all day. I knew why I couldn't forget it. Guilt, simple as that. Plain old guilt. I should have done something to check out the screaming, not just yell my stupid head off, but I hadn't. While God knows what was happening to a young woman, I had gone back to my arrowheads. I remembered *Moby Dick,* which Miss Davis had required us to read—a long, boring story about whaling with an asshole named Ahab all the time pacing the deck. At the beginning of the novel the narrator had introduced himself with the simple line, "Call me Ishmael." Well, after the episode on the river even the hated Skeeter was too good for me. Call me Chickenshit.

Five minutes later, we all spotted the first mouse pretty much simultaneously, but Jerry Lee on my left beat us to the resounding call.

"Fucker ho!" he shouted. "Mouse in sight!"

"Stomp the little bastard!" Buddy replied.

"Drill him!" Billy yelled.

Led by Buddy Inskeep and Billy Karady, we all piled off the pickup onto the desert and sprinted in the direction of the fleeing mouse.

The Great Stomp of 1957 was officially under way.

Despite all the talk and the rehashing of previous stomps, the passing of a year had made us all forget how truly difficult it was to drill a shifty mouse with the heel of your foot. The first mouse turned out to be a tough little scrapper. Even though we were clear eyed and sober, he was as shifty and elusive as the truth, hopping this way and that, and reversing himself as he ran the gauntlet of our feet. He was here, he was there. He was, he wasn't. Decisions, decisions, decisions. For a mouse, they came in a fury. He leaped, he bounded. He zigged, he zagged. He ran in circles. He stopped, he started. He was everywhere at once.

As we ran after the frantic mouse, tumbling over one another, we could hear Harold behind us, laughing, banging on the door with the palm of his hand, and shouting encouragement.

In the end, despite our most determined efforts, he escaped. Even Billy Karady hadn't been able to lay a foot on him, even a glancing blow. Where the mouse had gone was a mystery. Had he just slipped out of sight, unseen, and disappeared into the night? Had he found himself a hole or burrow that we hadn't seen? Was he hiding in the base of a sagebrush? Nobody knew. This was both humbling and frustrating because we were denied closure, and according to the rules, no Olympias were to be consumed until a mouse was stomped. On a Great Stomp, the Olys were earned.

Responsible Harold was not to be blamed for our failure. Shifting gears with aplomb, backing up quickly when the mouse reversed directions, he had done a superlative job of keeping our quarry in the headlights. Harold was to be respected for not drinking. That was his choice. Far more honorable to drink coffee than to be a loathsome soda popper. The universally despised soda popper was a disgusting wuss who pretended to be drinking, but secretly poured his beer on the ground so as to remain sober while everybody else was getting tanked. Not that anybody ever got caught committing that heinous offense, but there were plenty of good-natured accusations and equally good-natured, if heated, denials. If you wanted to go on a Great Stomp, you had to match everybody else beer for beer. If you were starting to get sick or knew you couldn't take any more, all you had to do was say so. Everybody understood. It was the pretenders who were losers. They did not understand honor.

We climbed back onto the truck, laughing at our failure, but determined to score the next mouse. A gentle breeze kicked up, flowing easily across the desert. Nobody who had grown up in Umatilla minded a little wind; the desert air smelled clean and fresh—with perhaps a touch of pungent sagebrush—as it swept over the sand. Buddy Inskeep gave Responsible Harold new instructions, telling him to drive into the wind. Although none of us had actually studied the habits of a kangaroo mouse in any systematic way—whether he depended primarily on his ears, eyes, or nose—it didn't make sense to come at him from upwind.

The second mouse was easier, which in itself was a lesson. All mice, like all truths, are different. That is, appearances are deceiving. Some are complicated. Others are simple. The first mouse had acted immediately and with resolve, giving his all to freedom's run; the second mouse made a couple of lackluster moves then simply froze, petrified, its tiny eyes points of ruby in the headlights. What to do? Where to go? Blink, blink. This poor damned mouse had no idea whatever. Clearly, he would have been Billy's had Billy not stepped into an animal burrow and pitched headlong into the sand. Buddy hurdled Billy and would have nailed the mouse, but he overran it in his excitement. Jerry Lee, who was directly in front of me, tripped over Billy, leaving it to Terry Lorence, the runner-up of the previous summer, to nail him.

It was, as Mr. Ernest Hemingway would have said, not a good mouse. But a mouse was a mouse, and we all hurried back to the pickup to open our first Oly. Not only was Billy a two-time champion, he had the ability to open a beer bottle with his teeth and fire the cap like a bullet with a snap of his fingers. Terry replaced Buddy on the left board. Buddy took Billy's spot, and Billy joined the rest of us in the back of the pickup. Billy had failed only because of an accident that could have happened to anybody. Lucky he had merely stepped onto a burrow and not a cactus clump. He remained confident, however. He was bigger and faster than the rest of us, and we didn't have to be told that he was determined to stomp more mice than the rest of us. He liked to compete, which is what made him a good athlete. He didn't want any damn tie either. A tie was a defeat.

One benefit of my recent growth was that, presumably, I would be able to drink more beer before I got the dreaded dizzies. Open beers in hand and on the alert for the possibility of a soda popper in our midst, we set off in pursuit of another mouse. Responsible Harold, driving with a plastic cup of coffee in one hand, followed the directions of Terry Lorence, who was feeling good, what with one stomped mouse, on the left board, and Billy Karady relegated to the rear.

Like Buddy, Terry aimed us into the wind.

I finished my beer, stashed the empty bottle in the open case, and returned to my spot on the cab. As I rode with the wind batting against my face, my mind returned to the screaming. The underpants I had grabbed could have been left over from a nocturnal union between consenting partners, but I didn't think so. The screaming plus the underpants added up to a possibility that was disconcerting in the extreme: rape. Somebody had been raped in the willows, or at least attacked with intent to rape—possibly by Billy Karady.

I knew I needed to tell someone about the incident. After all, Carl Sellers had heard the same thing as me. Coach Mungo was a special, revered figure in Umatilla, and it was difficult if not impossible to believe that he had done anything to make a young girl scream. Anybody else, but not Coach Mungo.

But what if Coach had just happened to be getting into his pickup, packing it in after another day of fishing. Carl Sellers had certainly been Johnny-on-the-spot.

And what had happened to the girl? Where had she gone?

That's not to mention Billy Karady and his clogged fuel filter.

I was jerked back to reality by the cry "Mouse ho!"

I saw a set of tiny ruby eyes in the beam of the left headlight. I vaulted off the pickup, losing my balance in the process. I scrambled to my feet and joined the chase well behind Terry, Buddy, and Billy Karady, who led the pack.

The leaping, bounding mouse zigged left and zagged right, barely escaping a foot with each terrified leap. Then it reversed itself and raced through a confusion of feet, coming straight at me, its tiny feet digging in furiously with each quick bound.

Then it took a hard left, straight into a pile of bleached bones where a cow had met its end. A good move by the mouse.

Tripping over ribs and shanks and vertebrae, we followed in a pack as it bounded through the bones. Within seconds there were laughing stompers sprawled everywhere amid the disintegrating bones.

I survived the melee at the head of the pack. I cleared the horned skull, and buried the frantic mouse with my left foot. It wasn't like the dead mouse had been suicidal or anything like that—more like it had inadvertently run under my foot. Also, it had almost made good its escape. I had clearly lucked out. But luck, as I was coming to realize, was sometimes as important as skill.

Billy Karady said, "Nice move." He used his teeth to open my bottle of Olympia. He spun the cap into the night with a snap of his fingers. "Little fucker was a hustler. You have to give it credit. Damn near wound up with a rib up my ass."

I took my spot on the board beside Responsible Harold, holding my beer in my left hand and the top of the door with my right. No mention of Skeets or Skeeter. Things were looking up.

Responsible Harold looked up at me and grinned. "Where to, Skeets?"

FIVE

I WAS DRINKING RUM *and coke in Kaiser's, an open-air bar in the center of a large patio on the edge of a cliff overlooking the Caribbean. This was outside Negril on the western tip of Jamaica. A mellow male voice with that lovely, lilting Jamaican accent called softly, "Yah, mon. You like smoke, mon?"*

I turned. Three Rastamen with great manes of natty dreads sat on the low stone wall at the top of the cliff. One of the Rastamen had a paper bag and a large, flat envelope.

The Rasta with the paper bag said, "Me be Fireboy. Me be the champion smokah in all of Jamaica, mon. You want smoke wid me?" He pulled a battered magazine from the envelope. "Ere, mon. You look at dis."

I walked over to the Rastamen and squatted by the Rasta with the magazine, which turned out to be an old issue of High Times. *I could hear the waves lapping at the rocks far below. The Rasta, holding the magazine reverently, as though it were the Dead Sea Scrolls, opened it for me to read.*

The article detailed a writer's search for the champion ganja smoker in Jamaica, and sure enough there was a photograph of Fireboy, who was declared the winner. Fireboy waited for me to finish reading the article, then said, "You want to challenge me, mon. All me ask is a few dollahs for de smoke."

I understood. Fireboy had used his unofficial crowning by

High Times *to become a professional smoker. Nothing wrong with that. This was to be a friendly challenge of a once-in-a-while smoker to a Jamaican champion, a moment Ernest Hemingway would have appreciated.*

This was to be a smoking contest then, as the Great Stomp had been a form of drinking contest. I said, "Sure man. I'm no soda popper."

Of the three Great Stomps in which I was to participate on the desert above Umatilla the 1957 stomp was the most memorable, and not because I drilled the most mice; I didn't. I got two. And not because Mr. Hundred-Yards-a-Game set any kind of record. He didn't. He got three mice of the thirteen that were squashed that night, tied with Jerry Lee, but it was a close call, and he never gave up trying. Therein lies the story, which is one of character revealed.

The first mouse escaped.

Terry Lorence got the second. A poor mouse.

I got the third. Not a bad hit.

A few minutes later, Larry Trimbath, who was holding on to the door with his left hand and trying to pee with his right, fell off the passenger-side running board. He landed on his back, which knocked the wind out of him. He continued to pee as he tried desperately to breathe, making weird, *hoooop! hoooop! hoooop!* sounds. By the time he was breathing again, he had soaked his pants and the front of his shirt. He was no quitter; although he was clearly reeling from the beer and the blow of hitting the ground, he reclaimed his board. We had gone no more than twenty yards when he fell off again; this time he passed out cold.

We gathered around poor Larry, discussing what we should do with him, when we discovered that he'd never bothered to put his prick back in his pants. Big problem. We all stood around him, laughing. Nobody wanted to put his dork back in, yuch. It seemed coarse to throw him in the back of the pickup with his doink poking out, but it was not just for aesthetic reasons that we wanted the stupid thing back in its place. The rest of us had to ride in the back with him. He still had beer working through his system. What if he peed again? Better he peed in his pants than us having to stand in it. It was a rough ride back there, with a whole lot of bouncing around.

The coffee-drinking Harold Helton turned out to be re-sourceful as well as responsible. He found a chunk of dried sagebrush, and, with the rest us whooping with amusement, used it to push Larry's limp snake back into his pants, treating it like it was a live cobra about to bite him; in truth it looked more like a sodden, pathetic little worm. Harold did this while holding his nose because Larry smelled like a bucket of urinal crystal. In the retelling over the coming months, the details of the story would swell in inverse relationship to the length and breadth of Larry Trimbath's teeny little pud.

We stowed the unconscious stomper in the back with his fly unzipped, and took our places.

Responsible Harold poked his head out of the window, looking worried. He yelled, "Is he going to be okay back there? Larry, can you hear me?"

Feeling poorly, Larry opened his eyes. He knew nobody wanted to have to interrupt the stomp to take him home. That would have been the ultimate humiliation, and he wanted no part of it. He looked up at us with a dazed expression on his face and made a barely audible croaking sound.

"He's just fine," I said.

Responsible Harold put the pickup into gear, and we were off again.

Jerry Lee got the fifth mouse, after which we had our annual pissing contest, which was part of the Great Stomp. One at a time we stepped into the headlights of the pickup and aimed it at the headlights so that the distance might be marked. The kids who had been circumcised had to squeeze their pipes and force the clear beer piss through the restricted passages. It turned out there were three of us with intact foreskins—Buddy Inskeep, Responsible Harold, and myself.

Nobody knew that I had been practicing every night for the year by looping a stream across the irrigation ditch behind my chicken coop bedroom. During numerous experiments, I had developed a new tactic.

Jerry Lee and Larry Trimbath and Terry Lorence and Buddy Inskeep and Billy Karady, even Responsible Harold, took their turns. Harold, firing used coffee, was in the lead when I stepped up and unveiled my new technique.

While the rest of them watched in amazement if not admiration, I squeezed the end of my foreskin with my left thumb and index finger, trapping the pee at the end of my hose. The skin balloon at the end of my Louis grew larger and larger until it was downright huge, and I could take it no longer.

Suddenly, I squeezed the balloon hard with my right hand, and a great bolt of piss shot out in a rush, splattering the bumper of the pickup. A whoop and a cheer went up. I was clearly champ. No question.

Then it was back to the chase. We spent the better part of an hour trying to find another mouse, which Terry Lorence stomped, his second score.

We stood around Terry's dead mouse, relieving ourselves of more beer pee and laughing as we opened another round. I was beginning to get a real buzz on. I noticed that Billy Karady, who had yet to drill a mouse, was unusually quiet as he ripped the top of his bottle with his teeth.

Buddy Inskeep suddenly went *urp!* and puked all over himself. It just shot out. We all jumped back so as not to get any on ourselves. Buddy dropped to his knees and vomited with a terrible sound, like he was turning himself inside out. *Whauuuugh! Whauuuugh! Whauuuugh!*

It took him a full five minutes to get it all up, or so it seemed. The poor bastard was pale and trembling, and it seemed impossible that he could have anything left inside. We helped him to his feet and half carried him to the rear of the pickup. We had no sooner got him and the tailgate back in place than he upchucked again, this time blasting the inert Larry Trimbath with an awful ration of pinkish goo studded with chunks of yellow.

Larry screamed, "Jesus Christ!" and started to vomit himself, which triggered another round from Buddy, and soon the two of them were having a barfing contest. Within minutes Buddy and Larry were lying weakly in a sour slick of vomit. Sweet corn was in season, and it was obvious that Buddy had pigged out at supper. The pink looked like strawberry ice cream to us. We pushed, or rather slid, the two valiant stompers to the back of the pickup and used the empty beer cases to form a makeshift barrier between them and the rest of us as though they were disgusting lepers.

It was after that episode that Billy Karady began a terrific comeback. The rest of us had lost our coordination and were fading fast, but not Billy. He got the next two mice in a row. The dreaded spins had started, and I could barely stand up, much less compete with one of the best halfbacks in the state.

Jerry Lee lucked out and got the eighth mouse with a spastic lurch that was similar to the luckout move I made on my first mouse. This moved him one ahead of Billy, but Billy seemed unconcerned. As we stood there, starting another beer, my spinning was clearly turning to the badass dizzies. I'd been around that block a couple of times. This was a prelude to bringing it up, I knew. No way I wanted to join the company of Buddy and Larry. I struggled to keep my equilibrium. If I could just hold down the vomit, I stood a chance of keeping it down.

Billy Karady, seeing I was getting woozy, gave me a solicitous look. "You gonna make it there, Skeets?"

I took a deep breath, concentrating.

Billy ripped the cap off with his teeth as usual. He held up the cap. "Watch this mother," he said. He fired the cap into the darkness with a snap of his finger.

Everybody watched his hand except me. I was doing my best not to join the company of Buddy Inskeep and Larry Trimbath. I didn't want to spend the rest of the night back there with them in the awful puke pit, so I was staring with determination at the ground.

Concentrate, I told myself. Concentrate, you can make it. That's when I saw Billy Karady holding his bottle of Oly by the side of his leg, pouring the contents, *ka-chug, ka-chug,* on the ground.

I gave Fireboy the U.S. equivalent of ten bucks in Jamaican dollars. Fireboy opened the bag and got out a bong made out of a two-liter plastic container that had once held liquid laundry detergent. The bowl on top of the container was an upside-down Red Stripe stubby with the bottom cut off. He grabbed a fistful of ganj from the bag and packed it tightly into the bowl.

"Me go first, mon. Set de count." He retrieved a small box of stick matches. Watching me with amused eyes, he lit up, taking a long, continuous draw.

I counted out loud, one, two, three. . . . I counted and counted and counted. . . .

The count seemed to last forever.

At fourteen seconds, Fireboy, a terrific champion, looked at me with triumphant eyes, then let it out slowly. "It be your turn, mon. Go for it."

I sat on the low stone wall and glanced down at the ocean far below. A Rasta sat on either side of me and put his arm around my waist.

Fireboy said, "We don't want you fallin' in de watah, mon."

I smiled. Fireboy lit a match and held the flame to the ganj. I inhaled as Fireboy counted. "One, mon. Two. Three . . ."

I inhaled and inhaled and inhaled until my lungs were on fire. On the count of nine, I couldn't take it any longer and spilled the smoke. Recovering from the giant hit, I sat, drifty, thankful for the Rastamen by my side.

"Not baad, mon. You be no cunt." Fireboy started packing more ganj into the bowl. "You be ready for another round, mon."

I grinned. "Me be ready." All that ganja on top of the rum. I was flying. I listened to the waves lapping in the vast darkness far, far below me. The lapping was both frightening and seductive. I drifted in faraway, contemplative zones. I entrusted my life to the Rastamen on either side of me. I liked them and trusted them. I was not afraid. Well, that's not entirely true, I traveled with the gnawing fear that one day Billy Karady would step out of the shadows. I remembered watching him secretly pour his Oly on the ground the night of the Great Stomp.

Fireboy looked puzzled as he readied another match. "Tell me, mon. Wat de fock is a soda poppah?"

SIX

I HAD CONSUMED EIGHT bottles of Oly, which was too damn much for someone my size, and I was still feeling poorly when Responsible Harold headed home in the wee hours of the morning. I had stomped two mice, which wasn't bad, and I had won the pissing competition. We still hadn't passed the dump yet, when I was aware of a flashing red light. A cop. Oh shit! What kind of cop would be cruising this godforsaken place at this time of night?

Responsible Harold pulled the pickup to the side of the road and called back. "Everybody be cool back there."

It was late to chuck the empty cases of beer, so we all sat on them, hoping the cop wouldn't see. Slim chance, but we had to try. I looked back at the dark blue car with the blinking light on top. A state cop. State cops always looked impressive, with their blue uniforms and neat little Smokey the Bear hats. Small-town cops could be ignorant shits, but not the Oregon State Police. They were educated, well-spoken, and respected, I'll give them that.

A gloom settled over the stompers. Sobering fast, we awaited our fate.

A half a minute later, a flashlight beam swept the rear of the pickup, and a voice said, "Evening."

"Evening," we all mumbled, more or less in unison.

The beam went from one face to the next, pausing momentarily on me.

The officer then stepped up to the cab. "Could I see your driver's license please? Take it out of your wallet."

"Yes, sir," Responsible Harold said. He dug for his wallet.

"Have you been drinking tonight?"

Harold said, "No sir. Just coffee."

"Let's hope so."

Harold gave him his license.

The cop shone his light on it. "Please get out of the pickup, Harold."

Harold got out.

I recognized the cop. He was Tom Agnopolous, one of a large family of Agnopolouses that lived just west of Umatilla.

Agnopolous said, "Okay, I want you to touch your nose with your right hand."

Harold touched his nose.

"With your left hand."

Harold did as he was told.

"Repeat after me: 'Peter Piper picked a peck of pickled peppers.' "

Without hesitation, Harold fired right back, "Peter Piper picked a peck of pickled peppers." He paused and said it again, faster. "Peter Piper picked a peck of pickled peppers."

Agnopolous allowed himself a grin.

Harold wasn't finished. He wanted to show this cop that by God all he had been drinking was coffee. "Peter Piper picked a pop of puckled pippers."

Agnopolous laughed out loud. "That's fast enough. Now I want you to walk to the center line and go straight down it, one foot after the other, until I tell you to stop."

Harold hopped nimbly onto the line and did as he was told, one foot after the other, a regular twinkle toes.

Agnopolous said, "Okay, you can come back now." He shined the light in the rear of the pickup, the beam stopping on the empty beer cases. He shook his head. "Been collecting bottles have you? Pick up a little spending money." In Oregon in 1957, bottles were returnables. These were good for a nickel apiece.

We didn't say anything.

"Or maybe it's the four-dot labels you're after."

Silence.

"What have you guys been doing besides drinking beer?"

Harold said, "Stomping mice."

Agnopolous furrowed his brows. "What?"

"End of the summer," Harold said.

Agnopolous shined his light at Billy Karady. "Who are you?"

"Billy Karady, sir."

"The halfback?"

"Yes, sir."

"Coach Mungo know you do this sort of thing?"

"No, sir."

"You figure on making state again with Olympia beer in your veins?"

"No, sir," Billy said. We were all contrite and respectful. Even hotshot Billy. Very, very contrite and respectful. It was our only hope.

Agnopolous turned and shined the light in my face. "And you. Who are you?"

I wondered why he had singled me out. "Ray Hawkins, sir."

He frowned. "I thought so." He thought for a moment, as though uncertain what to do. Umatilla was the smallest of small towns. Tom Agnopolous either knew us or of us or had gone to school with one of our brothers and sisters. Everybody knew everybody else in Umatilla. This was the way it was, and as far as we knew, it was the way it would always be. If Agnopolous took twelve of us in for drinking under age, news of the bust would rock Umatilla with the impact of Ike having his heart attack or the sinking of the *Andrea Doria*. We'd be front page news in the *Umatilla Sun,* and the Vikings would likely be deprived of their allstate halfback.

Agnopolous's responsibility extended beyond merely enforcing the law. He sighed. He'd made a decision. He said, "Okay, Harold, I want you to take these morons home. Start with the two who are passed out back there."

This is when I spoke up. "Mr. Agnopolous, something happened today that I believe I need to tell you about."

The light shined back in my face. "Ray?"

"Yes, sir. Me. Nothing to do with our mouse stomp, but I think it may be very important. I know you'll want to hear what I have to say." It was only then that I remembered Billy Karady was in the pickup, but to hell with it. I had already committed myself.

"You come with me, Ray." He rapped on the door of the pickup as I climbed out of the back. "On your way, Harold. You've got a load of drunks back there, so drive slowly. We don't want somebody to fall out and hurt himself."

"Yes, sir," Responsible Harold said with much gravity, and there was not a stomper among us who was not grateful that he was our driver.

I slipped onto the front seat of the squad car beside Tom Agnopolous, feeling maybe a little better, while we followed the pickup past the dump and over the irrigation canal. To our right, the dark blue was during pale. The sun would be coming up shortly. As we drove, I told Agnopolous what had happened that afternoon at the mouth of the Umatilla.

Tom Agnopolous listened to my story with interest. "What time did that happen?"

"I don't have a watch, so I don't know exactly. The noon siren blew in town, I remember that. A short while later I heard some booms from Ordnance. Then the screaming started. If the people at Ordnance keep a log of their detonations, you could figure out the time from that, couldn't you?"

He thought for a moment. "Yes, I probably could. Good thinking. And where are the underpants now?"

"I've got them back in my bedroom."

"The chicken coop."

"Why yes. No chickens anymore, though. Just me." I was surprised that he knew about my little shack, and he picked up on it.

He said, "My brother Jim sold your dad the asphalt siding."

"Ahh," I said.

He glanced to the right, where the sky was turning a faint orange. "You stomp any mice?"

"Got two. And I won the pissing contest."

He arched an eyebrow. "Oh?"

"Long-distance pissing. I've got a special technique."

"I see."

"You want me to demonstrate?"

He looked at me mildly. "I believe I'll pass. You mind going with me to the willows to take a look around? I need to get a better idea of what happened."

"Sure. No problem," I said.

We rode in silence to the stop sign at the west end of the bridge over the Umatilla. As he pulled to a stop, he said, "That your sister Gracie working in the Dairy Queen?"

Now I had an idea why he'd shown an interest in me. "You been eating your lunch at the DQ, have you?"

He grinned, but didn't say anything. He proceeded across the highway, and we started down the rocky road toward the railroad bridge and the willows beyond that. We passed under the end of the bridge with his tires rumbling on the rocks and stopped just short of the dirt turnaround by the willows. He got out and knelt down, looking at the tire prints.

Standing beside him, I said, "Whole lot of traffic in and out. Last night being a Friday and everything."

He stood and pointed in the direction of the cottonwoods by the sand dune. "And you had your Chev parked down there."

"That's right. Carl Sellers can confirm my story, except he didn't see Coach Mungo's pickup, only Billy's Cunt Wagon. Listen, that was genuine screaming. I've never heard anything like it except in the movies, and even then it's not real, if you know what I mean. This was spooky stuff."

"Shall we take a look around?"

"Sure," I said. I followed him around the turnaround and down the path into the willows. When we arrived in the clearing, he stopped. "Where did you find the underpants?"

"Over there," I said.

He took a look near the spot. "Nothing else?"

"That was it."

"And no sign of the girl?"

"None."

"Tell me, Ray, how many girls you think would take off and leave their underpants behind?"

"That depends on who's telling the story."

He smiled grimly. "I better take you home now. I'll want the underpants, and I don't want you to talk to anybody about this."

"Got it," I said.

I climbed back into his cruiser with him, and he backed it up the road so as not to disturb the confusion of tire prints on the dirt turnaround. I said, "Why don't you ask her out?"

He cleared his throat, but didn't say anything. Then he said, "Who's that?"

"Why, Gracie. You've got your eye on her. Why else would you mention her? It's been more than a year since Len ran off the road, but people won't have anything to do with her."

"You're a regular little Sherlock Holmes, aren't you? Has it been that long?"

Ahh, I was right. "How long is she supposed to play the

grieving widow? None of you assholes will have anything to do with her, begging your pardon. It's like she's a leper or something. I know she's bored sitting home watching the tube night after night."

Agnopolous didn't say anything.

"Do it," I said. "She's not skinny, really. Slender is the word. She's got a real body on her. You should see her in a swimsuit. You'd be amazed."

He pretended to be shocked that a little brother would be talking about his sister that way, but I knew he wanted to hear more. I said, "Not that I've been copping looks in secret or anything, but I'm around her all the time. A person would have to be blind not to notice those blouse stretchers of hers. But I'll bet you've been checking those out yourself, haven't you? Leaning over the counter at the DQ trying to get an angle."

He tried not to respond to that, but I knew I was right. We pulled to a stop at the highway. He hung a right and started west, toward my house.

"Lucky girl, having a little brother like you."

I ignored that one. "Just pull in there and order a cheeseburger, maybe hold the onions, and say, 'Hey Gracie, how about a movie?' You don't have to start with the buttes, that can wait until later." Here I was, Skeeter Hawkins, trying to set my sister up. I didn't care how I sounded. I felt sorry for poor Gracie; bad enough that her husband got killed, now she was being treated like a pariah. "I know it might seem weird, me trying to give advice to a state cop and everything, but you can't be all bad."

He burst out laughing.

"Husband dead more than a year. No kids to cramp your style. Go for it."

"Should I tell her you recommended her blouse stretchers?"

"Go ahead if you want. She knows she's got 'em. Strikes me that it'd be a damn shame to let 'em go to waste."

He pulled to a stop in front of my house. "Get out of here

now, you little salesman. You got any Alka Seltzer around?"

"Maybe in the house."

"You might take a couple of tablets in a tall glass of water and pop two or three aspirin before you try to sleep. The shape you're in, you're going to need something, believe me."

I wanted to tell him that Billy Karady was a soda popper, but decided that could wait until later. I said, "I'll go get the underpants. Be right back."

SEVEN

FOR YEARS, THE UMATILLA Vikings had played six-man football, which was a kind of track meet with pads, what with everybody except the center being eligible for a pass. Then the Corps of Engineers built McNary Dam. For several years both the grade school and high school were bursting at the seams with the sons and daughters of construction workers, and the Vikings were promoted to regular football. This was a source of immense pride to the residents of Umatilla.

However, when the dam was finished, the construction workers moved on to their next job, and the town shrunk back to nothing. Umatilla High School, with a faculty of eight and a student body hovering around a hundred students, covered the state requirements for English, history, math, and science, and that was it. Girls had shorthand or home economics for an elective; the boys got to risk their fingers in shop. That was it. There were no foreign languages or any of that fancy stuff. The trouble was, nobody wanted to go back to six-man football.

Therein lay the problem.

The rule handed down by the state athletic moguls was that a school had to field enough players to at least scrimmage at practice. That meant twenty-two bodies. Tough to come by at Umatilla. The Vikings plunged into terrible times, and three years earlier had played an entire season with only nineteen players, including squirts and uncoordinated fat boys. Coach Mungo simply fielded what he regarded as his eleven best athletes, and they played both offense and defense.

Threatened with demotion for three years running, the school had replied by nearly requiring all males with a pulse to turn out for the team. This wasn't official or anything. That was against the state rules. But if you were undersized, as I had been my first two years, or just plain no good, which was also likely in my case, it was felt the least you could do was to demonstrate a little school spirit; this meant holding a tackling dummy or letting the regulars run over you while they practiced their offense. Slow but small, that was the book on Skeeter Hawkins. I probably set a Guinness record for getting the wind knocked out of me.

In Umatilla, it didn't make any difference how much you had grown over the summer or whether you now had a beard like a lumberjack; once the book was in on you—whether it was by teachers, the coach, or girls—that was it. You were stuck with that identity no matter what. Growth was not allowed because it screwed up stereotypes that helped make all decisions automatic.

There were a few exceptions to the unwritten rule of turning out for football; for example, Gerard, who displayed extreme feminine mannerisms. Gerard was well liked, but just different. Nobody wanted to be cruel, but life had to be difficult for him in a place like Umatilla. Gerard, like me, was a favorite of Miss Davis, the English teacher. His interest was in poetry, mine was in prose. Having read all about Ernest Hemingway, who had once been a reporter for the *Kansas City Star* and a foreign correspondent, I thought the way to become an author was to first become a newspaper reporter. It was in pursuit of one day becoming a newspaper reporter that I became the only male student in the shorthand class.

The Monday following the Great Stomp, Coach Mungo began his two-a-days. This meant calisthenics and running in the morning, plus more calisthenics and running in the afternoon. On Tuesday we would be stiff and sore, but Mungo would keep us at it until we got in shape. Bulked up to a manly 130 pounds, I showed up for the tryouts—which was a curious word, since nobody was rejected. The season officially started when we all lined up so Doc Ford could push our balls up inside us and make us cough, after which he pronounced us fit and we were issued a uniform and a playbook.

This year, after two years as a quarterback of last, laughable resort and defensive halfback at practice, I was to sit on the bench as a reserve end and defensive halfback. By participating in this ritual, I was demonstrating my school spirit; I was a full-fledged Umatilla Viking. The reason Coach Mungo made me a reserve end was obvious enough. Coach didn't believe in passing. The Vikings ran a multiple formation, changing from the newfangled T-formation to Coach's favorite, made famous by Frank Leahy at Notre Dame. The Notre Dame box was a single wing with a balanced line. The idea was to amass as many blockers as possible in front of the tailback, in this case Billy Karady, or the fullback.

As I was pulling on my pads, I noticed Coach Mungo looking at me. I caught his eye.

He said, "Looks like you've been filling out there, Ray. Going to bang a few heads this year."

Ray, he'd called me. Never before had he called me Ray. This was the first time. It was difficult to believe he was sizing me up for the first team. Me? Bang a few heads? Ordinarily, I would have been swelled with pride, but not now. Now, I wondered.

"Up to 130 pounds," I said.

As I walked down the sidewalk toward our practice field, my cleats rattling *ka-clunk, ka-clunk* on the concrete, I found myself walking beside Billy Karady.

He said, "Hey, there champ, ready for it?"

"I'll do my damnedest," I said.

"You put some real moves on those mice out there. Maybe this'll be your year."

My year. Right. The truth was Billy Karady didn't want anybody to have a good year except himself. As far as I was concerned, he had revealed himself on the stomp. Now I knew what he was.

I wondered, as I stepped off the sidewalk and onto the grass, if Tom Agnopolous had interviewed Carl Sellers and what he had learned.

Behind me, I heard Coach Mungo clap his hands and yell, "Come on everybody, hustle up. We've got work to do."

EIGHT

COACH BRIAN MUNGO, A tall, quiet, soft-spoken veteran of World War II, had been captured by the Japanese following the fall of Corregidor in the Philippines, and was a survivor of the infamous Death March on the Bataan Peninsula. He had spent the duration of the war in a Japanese prison camp, and the stories of the atrocities he had suffered were horrendous. He didn't run around volunteering these stories—he was no professional prisoner of war—but if you asked him, he sometimes would tell you a story. Other times, he politely declined. He never recalled his experiences with relish. That they had been awful, twisting experiences was clear from the faraway, almost glazed look in his eye in the telling.

In one of the stories that stuck with me vividly—told as we waited for the rain to clear before the start of a baseball game— was about an incident in which he and his fellow prisoners were eating a meatless broth. A Japanese guard incensed by an infraction of the rules bludgeoned one of his comrades so viciously that his skull split open and his brains went flying. A fleck of gray landed in Mungo's bowl. He sat staring at the fleck, knowing what it likely was. He was also starving, a living skeleton from lack of protein. As the Japanese dragged the body away, he consumed the rest of his bowl, fleck of gray and all. He said he never knew whether he was too hungry, too weak, or too indifferent to get rid of whatever it was that had landed in his bowl.

When he told this story with a distracted look on his face, casually checking the clouds, we all knew it was the truth.

No matter what his role in the events of the months that followed, or more specifically what he was, it was always difficult to judge him harshly.

Coach had been a high school athlete at Yakima, Washington, before entering the army, and on his return went to college on the GI Bill and was an end on the football team at Central Washington State College in Ellensburg. After that, he had become a high school coach. After a disastrous season at Caldwell, Idaho, he wound up in Umatilla—high school coach hell. He coached all four sports at Umatilla—football, basketball, baseball, and track—with only one assistant, that in football. As a permanent resident of the bench and a forever watcher, even I was able to deduce that he knew nothing whatever about basketball and was a lousy baseball coach. All he did in track was turn everybody loose to do whatever he wanted. His passion was football.

Coach Mungo, who was in his late thirties, lived in an apartment in the bottom of a brick building across the street from Baker's Drugstore. The top level, facing Umatilla's main drag, was occupied by a hardware store. He was six feet, four inches tall, and whereas he emerged from the war a walking skeleton, he now looked fit and muscular. He had short, kinky red hair with only a narrow island on top. By nature neat and tidy, he always looked like he had been tumble-dried and carefully pressed. He had a long, morose face with a cleft or dimple on his chin. He peered down on us through odd, green eyes as though examining us through a microscope. He wore round spectacles with thick, flesh-colored plastic rims.

Coach liked boys, which was likely why he had chosen to become a coach. We all thought he was a good guy and wanted him to approve of us, including me. He hadn't been in Umatilla more than a year before his apartment became a hangout for students who didn't have anything to do—these were usually starters in one sport or another and his favorites. Billy Karady, for example, was a regular. His athletes, including my friend Buddy Inskeep, were constantly in and out of the apartment.

It was difficult for me to become a member of that fraternity of visitors because I was no athlete. It wasn't that Coach didn't like me or anything; my not getting to play was not a judgment of me as a person; I just wasn't any good. I tried; oh, how I tried. I never gave up, never quit. At the school assembly after the completion of each season of sport, Coach made little speeches about all of his players. Of me, he said I had more heart and tried harder than anybody in school. I knew that was my reward for never actually getting into a game. I always swelled with pride when he said it. I was the skeeter with unstoppable wings. A natural assholete, I called myself.

I went to Coach's apartment only once, with Buddy, and what I saw amazed and puzzled me.

It was in early July. I was in Umatilla between driving pea truck for Dutch Van Elst out of Walla Walla and driving wheat truck for Dewey Purcell out of Holdman. We stepped into Coach's small living room, which was filled with barbells and weights of various sizes. So now I knew why he looked so fit and trim. He was listening to classical music on his record player.

He poked his head around the corner from his kitchen. "You guys want a Coke?"

"Sure," Buddy said.

Listening to the music, I nodded yes. I had never listened to violins and timpani before. I knew only The Platters, Elvis Presley, and Perry Como.

Watching me, Coach smiled. "That's Prokofiev. You like it?"

I did, as a matter of fact. "Prick-a-which?" I said.

"Sergei Prokofiev. A Russian composer." He headed for the refrigerator.

That's when I saw the huge pile of magazines in the corner. I went to check them out. They were muscle magazines featuring beefy guys with oiled lats, abs, and the rest of it. I had never seen anything like it. I could understand Coach's interest in working out, but why in hell he would want to collect muscle magazines was beyond me. Female bumpers and buns, I could understand. Guys showing off their stupid muscles was just plain dumb. Who the hell cared?

NINE

AFTER THAT FIRST DAY of practice, all showered and feeling pooped, but a good kind of pooped, I was about to climb into the Wheeled Turd when a girl behind me said, "Hey, you. Mr. Toilet Man. What're you up to?"

I turned, and there was the girl with the lips and almond-shaped brown eyes and pierced ears who had come in on the bus on Friday night. She was going to school in Umatilla. I could hardly believe it. I bet the people in the office and teachers couldn't believe it either. She was not wearing the unofficial uniform of girls at Umatilla, a skirt and sweater with an artificial collar called a dickey—the skirt being the prescribed length of halfway between the knees and ankle. Nor was she wearing white bucks with her socks rolled in a ball around her ankles. That outfit, or a variation of it, was worn by every girl in school. This costume might well have been decreed by some mysterious federal office back in Washington; it was always the same: sweater; dickey; long skirt; white bucks; rolled socks.

None of that for the girl with the lips and pierced ears. She was wearing white sandals, and a loose red-and-blue-striped cotton shirt over the outside of some tight white pants called Capris. I bet every male who laid eyes on her wanted to hike those shirttails up to see what the Capris looked like molded around her butt. This outfit was topped off by dangling earrings with small red ceramic balls at the bottom. At Umatilla High School, this was the fashion equivalent of a duck's ass haircut for the boys. It spelled bad girl. Or rebellious girl. Or something.

"You," I said.

"Me."

I heard an engine fire up and glanced at Billy Karady, who was sitting in his Cunt Wagon watching us. I was suddenly embarrassed by my wheeled turd.

"Your name is Ray Hawkins, and you're a junior."

Aware that Billy was still watching, I said, "I waited for you to come back at the bus station."

"I . . ." She started to say something more, but hesitated.

I let her off the hook. "And you are?"

"Took you long enough to ask. Angie Boudreau. I'm a junior too," she said. She smiled at me with her eyes as well as her face.

Angie Boudreau. It was hard not to stare at her lips when she talked. I felt a rush in my stomach. I could hardly breathe. "How on earth did you wind up in Umatilla?"

"I'm from Sunburst, Montana, about ten miles from the Canadian border and ninety miles south of Lethbridge in Alberta Province. My folks split up, and my mother ran off with a fertilizer salesman."

"I see. What about your father?"

"After a year, he took off too. He's a Sioux, which is how I get this skin and these eyes. He used to be a guide for big game hunters. He's probably in Alaska by now. So here I am, living with my sister and her husband."

I could hear the mellow *ka, lug, lug, lug, lug* loping of Billy's engine. Mr. Machismo. Why in the fuck didn't he go on his way and leave me alone? But I knew what was bothering him. Angie was new in school and so unclaimed territory. What in the hell was a sexy half-breed girl with pierced ears and tight Capris doing talking to Skeeter Hawkins! It wasn't done.

My hands literally began to tremble. My mouth was dry. I licked my lips. "They say I've got the ugliest car in school. What do you think?"

She laughed. "Does it get you there and back?"

"It does that, I guess. The Wheeled Turd, I call it."

"There you go. What more do you need?"

Billy pulled out onto the street with a spinning of wheels that sent gravel flying. He eased slowly past, watching us, then, with an annoyed look on his face, fishtailed down the street, tires squealing.

Angie glanced mildly after him, then turned back to me. "I saw them practicing football. You been to football practice?"

"Sure. I'm a Viking."

"You don't look like much of a Viking to me."

I chanted:

Loot and pillage. Loot and pillage.
We're the Vikings from Umatilla Village.

She said, "We were the Thundering Herd where I came from. Bison was the idea."

I figured I might as well get it over with. I said, "The truth is, I never get to play. I was so small my first two years that people called me Skeeter. I just hate it, I have to tell you."

"You're no Skeeter now. No crewcut either."

Had to get that one over with too. Wasn't easy. "That's because my mom cuts my hair. She doesn't do crewcuts."

"Good for her." Angie studied me for a moment, then smiled, "Well?"

I blinked. "Well what?" I said stupidly.

"Are you going to offer to take me home, or are you going to just stand there?"

This was the second time she had offered me an invitation. The first time I had stood there like a dumb shit, locked in my Skeeter mode. No way in hell I was going to just stand there a second time. Screw that Watcher Hawkins crap. No reason I had to remain on the sidelines forever. I denied it.

I hustled around to the passenger's side and opened the door for her. I thought momentarily of inviting her for an ice-cream cone at the DQ, then thought better of it. My sister, Gracie, was working the window, and when I got home I would have to put up with the razzing.

Angie Boudreau had taken the nickname and haircut in stride. I wondered if I should tell her I had to milk cows before and after school. Driving a wheeled turd was embarrassing enough; having to milk cows was something else again.

I fired up the Terrible Turd and eased it onto the street. I said, "You ever hear of Happy Canyon?"

She blinked. She hadn't.

I said, "It's a show they have every year at the Pendleton Round-Up. They have a huge stage big enough to accommodate wagon trains and cowboys and Indians fighting it out—a re-creation of the settling of the West. It's coming up in a couple of days. After the show, Brenda Lee will be singing in the National Guard Armory next door." She'd said her father was a Sioux. I was momentarily embarrassed. "If you don't mind the sight of a whole bunch of redskins biting the dust. It's got a lot of that. . . ."

She grinned. "I can take it. I'm half white-eyes remember. Can you get us tickets?"

"Happy Canyon's been sold out for months, but I've got a cousin who's one of the directors."

"You've also got a date," she said.

All right! I said, "My father was once on a Round-Up post-card. He was atop a bucking bronc. A horse named Angel." I hesitated. Having a crippled father, like driving the Wheeled Turd and having to milk cows, was not cool. It was important for me to let this girl with those almond-shaped eyes and wonderful lips know that I was proud of him.

TEN

ANGIE'S SISTER AND BROTHER-IN-LAW, Pamela and Paul Remillard, lived in a modest two-bedroom, red-brick house in a development of eight or ten residences on the sandy hill just south of town, across the Umatilla River. This was just below the irrigation canal we had passed over going to and from the Great Stomp.

I showed up at the appointed hour, and Pamela answered the door. Pamela, a plump, big-butted version of Angie, eyed me with a smile; she was curious about her sister's new boyfriend. She said, "Angie's still getting ready. She'll be right out."

Just like Gracie. Were all women like this, I wondered? I said, "No problem."

Paul Remillard, a chinless, big-beaked man with a five o'clock shadow, caught my eye and grinned. Get used to it, his grin said; my education in women was just beginning.

Pamela glanced outside at my car and looked momentarily puzzled.

Seeing this, I said, "The Wheeled Turd, I call it. Bought pigs with pop bottle money and swapped hogs for the Turd. I like to pretend it was Ike's staff car during the war."

Paul said, "I think she expected to see you in a sleek black Merc."

That sounded like Billy Karady's car, but I didn't say anything.

Pamela and Paul were watching "Bonanza." Their cocker spaniel, a neutered male named Buster, began humping my left foot, while their son, Tony, a slimy-faced two-year-old, started gumming my right thigh. I wanted to kick Buster through the window but restrained myself. Pamela gave the dog a swat with a rolled-up newspaper but made no effort to restrain Tony. "Damn dog," she said.

"Trying to knock up your foot," Paul said.

Pamela glared at him.

"Dogs are dogs," I said. I hated barkers, growlers, and humpers; dogs that slept all the time were okay.

"Tony certainly likes you," Pamela said. She was a proud mom, and in her eyes Tony the teether could do no wrong.

Paul said, "He thinks your leg is a bone."

I pretended not to mind Tony's chewing or the fact that he was soaking my leg with slobber. "Cute kid," I said. "Husky." The truth was he was an obvious clone of his father: chinless and big beaked.

Pamela said, "Paul pitched one year for the Walla Walla Bears." This was a source of pride to her also and impressive to me, I admit. The Bears were a Class-A team owned by the New York Yankees.

"I wasn't Whitey Ford, but I sent my share of batters to the pines."

"Struck 'em out. Okay," I said.

He grimaced. "Almost okay. The Yankee scouts want all their young pitchers to be like Whitey Ford. It's not good enough to have a decent fastball and a change-up to go with it, and maybe a forkball to get 'em to hit a ball on the ground. No, no, no. We were expected to have everything if we wanted to make it to the bigs. We're talking the American League here, small parks and big sluggers."

"What did you need?"

"More deception. In the National League, with all those big parks and bunting and hit and run, you can survive on a fastball. I needed a better curve. I had one, but it kept hanging on me." He sighed. "You can't hang your curves, even in Class-A ball. It's like handing the batter a beach ball. As soon as Tony's big enough, I'm going to have him fielding ground balls. I want him to be a position player."

In order not to have to talk about Buster's humping, Tony's teething, baseball, or the weather, I pretended to be interested in "Bonanza." The television Cartwrights, who lived on a Nevada ranch called The Ponderosa, were too damn Goodie Good for my taste: Big, gullible, good-natured Hoss. The handsome young Goodie Good, Little Joe. The intellectual Adam. The thoughtful patriarch, Ben Cartwright. We were all supposed to be like the Cartwrights. A nation of pious, thoughtful, respectful Goodie Goods. I was only sixteen years old, and I knew that was dreamsville crappola. But the worst, the absolute worst of the International Conspiracy of Wannabe Goodie Goods, was a program called "Father Knows Best," in which Robert Young never, but never knew best. His daughter knew best maybe, or his wife, but never poor old dad. The dumb bastard only thought he did. The myth of dad being in charge had become a national joke. The women ran everything because they had what men wanted. It didn't take Einstein to figure that out.

Suddenly, Angie's sister popped to her feet. "Say, how would you like to look at our photo album?"

This was a ritual I hated. You go to the house of somebody you've never met, and suddenly they pull out this album of plastic-covered photographs, and you're supposed to pretend to be interested in drooling old farts and dirty little kids whom you'd never seen. I wanted to say, *Photo albums are cemeteries, lady; I'd just as soon peer up a donkey's ass.* It didn't make a damn whether the beloved farts and cute kids were still living or not; the ones in the pictures were all dead, moved on to new incarnations. But this was Angie's sister, after all. I wanted her to be on my side. To politely study a book of dead identities was a form of test or initiation, and I was determined to see it through with as much enthusiasm as I could manage. I had my eye on a prize with lips like Brigitte Bardot's. I said, "Sure, I'd like that."

Knowing I was a horny hypocrite, Paul scooted over to make room for me on the sofa. He'd been in my shoes once himself and understood the drill. Now it was my turn. This little torment was just the first of many locks I had to open before my pony could get some genuine action. If I was to get my end in, I had to play pretend.

Angie's sister, filled with bubbly energy, spread the photo album on the coffee table in front of us.

"See, there's Angie as a baby," she said.

I found myself looking at a large-eyed baby that as far as I was concerned had little or nothing to do with the sexy Angie who had stepped off the bus from Spokane. The baby didn't do a whole bunch for me. I suppose baby Angie was cute and everything, but I didn't care what was under her diapers at age ten months. I sure as hell wanted to check out the territory now; all I could think about was getting the grown-up Angie into the buttes and onto the backseat of the Wheeled Turd. I grinned at the picture, prepared to maintain the grin until my cheeks ached if necessary.

"Ready?"

I turned. Rescued! There stood Angie wearing black leotards and an old sweatshirt, and with her long black hair combed to a sheen and hanging to the small of her back. Even with the sweatshirt, I could see she had a fine pair of headlights. Couldn't hide 'em.

Her sister, disappointed that she wasn't going to get to test my ability to maintain an artificial smile, cast a disapproving look at the leotards. It's obvious she didn't understand her younger sister, but had given up on trying to change her. "You two be back before midnight, and be good."

Angie said, "Before midnight?" She rolled her eyes. "Pam, we're going to a Brenda Lee concert after Happy Canyon. Give us a break."

Her sister frowned.

"If you can't be good, be careful," Paul said. He winked at me.

His wife gave him a look that said, *Knock it off, asshole.*

Angie and I made good our escape, and a few minutes later got into the Wheeled Turd. She popped to my side like a magnet, and we were off. We were alone. I had a tank full of gas. The stars were out. Life was ours to enjoy. The warmth of her thigh and the smell of her perfume were overwhelming.

I tuned in to KORD out of Pasco, and we were off to Pendleton. We were sailing happily along on Highway 30, flanked by fields of wheat stubble and summer fallow, when we got the splendid news that a freshman at Hermiston High School had been found raped and murdered, her nude body left in a watermelon patch just outside of town. A spokesman for the Oregon State Police said the details of the crime led them to believe it was the same killer who earlier had murdered two girls near Kennewick, Washington.

Out of the corner of my eye, I saw Angie bite her lower lip. She tried not to look my way, but she did. She couldn't help herself. Something was chewing at her. Just what it was, I had no idea.

ELEVEN

THE COVERED STAGE FOR Happy Canyon was fifty yards wide, and the spectators sat in bleachers to watch the pageant, which began with whole families of costumed Indians passing across the stage on foot. In the beginning, this was their place. Indians on ponies then chased a small herd of bison across stage; they erected teepees and got campfires going on stages with women cooking and children running about playing. Fur trappers strode onto the huge stage wearing coonskin caps and moccasins and the rest of it. They held a trading rendezvous and swapped whiskey to the Indians for fur. The Indians proceeded to get rip-roaring drunk.

Then the first wagon trains arrived on the old Oregon Trail that ran right by Pendleton. The stage at Happy Canyon was filled with prairie schooners.

After that cowboys and Indians did battle, firing blanks, falling off their horses, and dying in splendid action that filled the air with smoke. The people staging the battle scenes had been doing it for years, and several horses had been trained to drop to their knees as if they'd been shot and toppled onto their sides so their riders could continue firing away while using their bodies for shields. The cowboys were about to be taken under by the Indians when the cavalry showed up, bugles blowing, to save their hides.

Finally, white man and Indian sat around the campfire and smoked the peace pipe. "From where the sun now stands I shall fight no more forever," Chief Joseph said after he had failed to lead the Nez Perce into Canada. Stirring words, right up there with Abe Lincoln's at Gettysburg. All this might have been Happy Canyon for the white eyes, but it wasn't hot damn for the redskins. Angie was clearly on the side of the redskins, and I was too.

After the show was over, we adjourned to the National Guard Armory, which was next door, and the interior of the armory, a large basketball court with a stage at one end, was packed. A small area in the middle of the court was reserved for dancing, but it was obvious that the muscled stupes were interested only in getting the Brenda Lee crap out of the way so they could get on with the business of finding somewhere to park.

The lead singer of the warm-up band did a passable imitation of Elvis Presley singing "Don't Be Cruel." I started moving to the music, couldn't help it. I said, "What do you say let's do it? Let's dance."

Angie said, "Okay!"

Never mind that their dates might want to dance, no self-respecting stupe wanted to be first on the floor. The stupes had to be told it was okay to dance and not just stand around. The entire herd had to move, or they weren't about to budge. A slow dance was okay, what with warm bazoongies to press up against, but the stupes weren't so hot for rock and roll. However, once Angie and I started dancing, another couple took the floor, then another—a triumph of female will. It was the girls who wanted to dance, not the stupes.

Angie liked to dance, and we were good together. We had danced several songs when we noticed a stir at one end of the room. Brenda Lee had made an appearance at the edge of the circle, where she stood with two older men, possibly her manager and father. She wanted to watch the dancing before she did her thing. Did she want to dance too?

As if reading my mind, Angie said. "Why don't you dance with Brenda Lee?"

I laughed. "Sure. Just walk right up there."

"It's not like you're going to rip her clothes off or anything. She's human like everybody else."

It would never have occurred to me to ask Brenda Lee to dance, but I was beginning to learn that Angie Boudreau was an uninhibited free spirit of a kind that I had never met. She was unintimidated. If it was out there, she wanted to try it, and she was encouraging me to do the same thing.

Angie said, "Why do you suppose she's standing there? I bet she's made appearances in dozens of places like this around the country, and nobody has ever asked her to dance. Why not ask her? The worst that can happen is that she'll say no. That won't kill you, will it? You won't wilt from embarrassment."

She was right of course. Let the stupes stand around with their mouths open. Here was a chance for me to take a major step toward breaking my Skeeter Hawkins persona. I had always been treated like Skeeter, so I had come to think like Skeeter. But Skeeter Hawkins wasn't writ in stone.

The lead singer said, "Well, here's one we hope you like. A little tune by The Big Bopper."

I knew which song he was likely talking about, and I liked it a lot.

I said, "Okay, here goes."

"Do it," Angie said.

I strode right up to Brenda Lee and said, "Would you like to dance? Please don't say 'I'm sorry.' " That was a reference to the lyrics of one of her hit songs, "I'm Sorry."

I'm sorry, oh so sorry.

The older men flanking her smiled. They weren't unfriendly at all and did nothing at all to discourage me. She laughed. "Sure. I'd love to dance."

Angie was right. Brenda Lee was a flesh-and-blood human being, same as everybody else. And she was smaller than me. I looked down on her. Yes! As we stepped out onto the floor, she said, "I've been watching you and your girlfriend. You can really dance."

"Thank you," I said.

"Sexy lady. Lucky you."

"She's half-Sioux. Yes, I am lucky."

The lead singer sounded just like The Big Bopper himself.

Chantilly lace, a pretty face,
A ponytail, a hanging down,
Makes the world go round, round, round.
Oh, baby, you know what I like.

The stupes and their girlfriends all applauded as I guided Brenda Lee past Angie Boudreau, who was having a good time. Brenda Lee was a soulful little pop singer, and she knew how to dance, but the truth was Angie was better looking and sexier. Man, oh, man, did I ever feel good about myself.

Holding both her hands, I spun Brenda Lee around so that her back was to me and her arms were wrapped around her sides. I held her tightly, feeling good—looking at Angie watching us—then spun her around, guiding her forcefully with my hand. She responded like a sports car with a big grin on her face. Yes!

It didn't occur to me that Brenda Lee was in a fragile zone of good looks and fame that dissolved with each passing month. One day it would pass, and her identity as the perky pop singer with the soulful voice would be lost forever. It was only later that I understood that she very likely thought about it a lot; in fact, the fading zone was probably on her mind when she agreed to dance with me.

•   •   •

Later, as Angie Boudreau and I waited in line to leave the parking lot outside the National Guard Armory, somebody rapped on my window. Without thinking or looking, I rolled down the window. Billy Karady, red eyed and with boozy breath, peered into the car, looking meaner than hell. "You think you're pretty hot stuff, do you, Skeeter? Dancing with Brenda Lee."

He caught me alongside the face with a quick left jab, slamming me against Angie, who was as surprised as I was. Damn near took my face off. Then, before I could do anything, he grabbed me by the throat and yanked me back.

With my left hand, I rolled up the window, cranking as fast as I could. This was an instinctive reaction. What followed was completely unplanned.

Billy tried to pull his hand back, but the top of the window had closed on his wrist. He couldn't withdraw his hand. I had him trapped. I punched the lock.

I tasted something warm and salty. My nose was bleeding. I wiped at the blood with the back of my right hand. I was bleeding like a stuck pig. My face was throbbing, and my lip was stinging.

In front of me, the traffic was clearing. I tilted my head back and mopped the blood again. There was blood all over the place—on my hands, my shirt, and my lap. I ran the tip of my tongue over the left side of my lip, which was swelling fast.

Billy said, "Let go of my hand, you little son of a bitch."

It occurred to me that I was then in charge and then some. Let him bray and swear. What could he do with his hand stuck in my window? I put the Wheeled Turd into low gear and started forward.

Only then did Billy realize what a fix he was in. "Hey, let go of my goddamn hand."

I had him trotting.

"Open this damn window."

"Fuck you." I stopped the Turd, still in gear but with the clutch to the floor. I looked at him mildly. My nose was so stopped with blood I had to breathe through my mouth. "What do you suppose would happen to your wrist and hand if I popped this clutch?"

"I said, 'let go,' dammit!"

"Oh, you did? Really? I could rip your hand from the end of your arm, couldn't I? Or your shoulder from its socket?" I was furious and suddenly pumped with adrenaline. If ever Skeeter had was behind me, it was then. I was pissed-off Ray Hawkins, defending my turf and my honor.

Angie said, "Don't, Ray."

I popped the clutch and sent the Turd forward, nearly yanking Billy Karady off his feet.

"Don't do it, Ray," Angie said.

Talk about a reversal of fortune. I popped the clutch again, harder. The adrenaline was pumping! Boy, oh boy, was it ever pumping. Billy Karady was completely at my mercy. I rolled the window up tighter so as not to lose him. I said, "Go ahead, hotshot. Yank your stupid hand."

"You could ruin his arm, Ray. It's not worth it."

She was right, of course. I said, "We're going for a little walk, Billy. Stay up with me, and keep your mouth shut, and I'll let you go with your arm intact. Give me shit, and I swear to God, I'll rip it off its socket. You hear me, Prick with Ears?"

He looked stricken. He opened his mouth, then closed it.

With that, I started forward again, slower this time. With Billy Karady running to keep up, I drove out of the parking lot. At the edge of the road out of town, I let him loose and took off. By the time he got back to his Cunt Wagon, I'd have a head start.

Just past the bridge over the Umatilla River on the outskirts of Pendleton, I hung a right for the longer way back to Umatilla—a road that wound through hilly wheat country. It was hard to celebrate the fun of having danced with Brenda Lee knowing that I had locked horns with Billy Karady for reasons that I didn't understand. Why in hell had he slugged me in the face? I hadn't done anything to him.

Suddenly, I started shaking. Couldn't stop. A wave of anxiety washed through my stomach as Angie Boudreau gripped my hand tightly. We both knew we hadn't seen the last of Billy Karady.

TWELVE

MOM, DAD, AND I all tried to be cool, like nothing was happening, but we all knew this was a big night for Gracie. It had been more than a year since her husband, Len, tanked after a night of shooting pool at the Midway Tavern in Hermiston, had sailed off the highway in his new Ford and landed upside down in the Umatilla River, drowning himself in the process. We had all liked Len. Now he was pushing up daisies in the cemetery up by the dump. Not to be disrespectful, but at long last, Gracie was getting on with her life. She had a date with the state cop Tom Agnopolous. We all wanted it to be a success.

In Umatilla in 1957, dating was primarily a teenage ritual. In those days, when you were married, you were married, so there wasn't a lot of horsing around by older people. There was the inevitable side action, the grist of scandal and gossip, but that was it. Gracie was a twenty-two-year-old widow, and Tom was closing in on thirty, which made things a trifle awkward. Easy enough to lay down the law for high school kids. This was different. The inevitable question on everybody's mind was just what in hell were they going to do? They could go have a chicken fried steak at the Snappy Snake in Hermiston. They could have a drink at the Three Cs in Umatilla. They could go to the finger bowl near Hermiston, which is what we called the outdoor theater, but it didn't get dark enough for the first movie until half past nine. They could go park in the buttes to grope one another. That was about it.

The rest of us waited for "The Ed Sullivan Show" to begin while Gracie lingered in the toilet, doing whatever females do to get themselves ready. If she came out early, she would subject herself to my alleged wit, and she didn't want that. So she stayed inside, waiting me out.

Tom Agnopolous was right on time, which I had predicted. I answered his rap at the door. He stood there, looking vaguely uncomfortable, but he had scouted the territory by befriending me; he had an inside man, and that made things easier for him.

"Hey, Ray," he said.

"Come on in. Gracie's still hogging the john doing her thing. Seems like she's been in there since "Death Valley Days"! The rest of us have to go outside if we want to take a leak. Real hard on my dad."

"Ray!" my mother said.

To me, softly, Agnopolous said, "When I get back, the two of us will go for a ride. We need to talk."

"No problem," I said.

My father struggled to put on the aluminum crutches that fit on the end of the arms, but Agnopolous raced to his chair to shake his hand.

"Mr. Hawkins," he said. "Tom Agnopolous."

"Pleased to meet you, Mr. Agnopolous."

I said, "Maybe Tom would like to see the family photo album. There's a picture of baby Gracie in there flashing her buns."

Agnopolous gave me a mild look.

"I'll get Gracie," I said.

While I headed for the john, Agnopolous made small talk with my parents and pretended to be interested in our tiny living room, which was undistinguished except for a modest bay window overlooking the railroad tracks and Highway 30. The living room was covered with my mother's oil paintings. The old man walking alone. The outhouse. The farmhouse in winter. My mother had won so many blue ribbons at the Umatilla County Fair that she'd made a quilt out of them. There was the black-and-white tube, the old couch, two easy chairs, and an oil stove.

I banged loudly on the toilet door. "Gracie, the big stud with the badge is here showing off his muscles."

The door opened. Gracie, wearing a long skirt and sweater with white dickey, plus white bucks and rolled socks, glared at me. "You!"

Behind me, my mother said, "Ray!"

"You smell like a French whorehouse," I said.

Gracie pushed me. "Snot."

My mother said, "Ray!" Everybody knew my tormenting Gracie was my way of telling her I loved her and wished the best for her. That didn't make it any easier for her.

Gracie followed me into the tiny bedroom, where everybody was pretending to watch Ed Sullivan introduce his guests.

I said to Agnopolous, "Didn't I tell you, Tom? Stretchers."

Gracie gave me a look. "You two been talking? When?"

Agnopolous said, "I was taking a routine swing down by the willows at the mouth of the Umatilla when he was packing his screen."

Gracie looked me with her head cocked and her eyes narrowed; she was suspicious. "What does he mean, 'stretchers'?"

Agnopolous cleared his throat. He said to my mom and dad, "We won't be gone long. Thought we'd get something to eat at Snappy Pete's, then go for a drive."

Gracie knew "stretchers" meant something or Agnopolous would have answered her question. She glared at me.

I said, "Are you going to use handcuffs on her?"

"Is that what you do with that little friend of yours?" Gracie cocked her head.

I looked chagrined. Why was it that other people could have a date and it was no big deal? But Skeeter Hawkins? I opened my mouth to reply, but my mother intervened.

"Ray!" She was losing her patience fast.

Agnopolous opened the door. "See you all later, then," he said cheerfully.

Gracie was having none of it. Her face went tight. "You damn little barbarian!" she snarled. She'd plumb tilted.

"I'm a Umatilla Viking," I said. "Rape and pillage."

"Loot and pillage," Gracie said.

"Oh yeah, that's it. Loot and pillage."

My mother said, "Ray!" This time she stood up. She had had enough.

With Tom Agnopolous off to do his thing with Gracie, I grabbed a couple of peaches in the small orchard behind our house and retreated to The Coop, which was what I called my bedroom shack; after all, it had once literally housed roosting chickens at night. I peed in the irrigation ditch and sat on the bed with the door open, eating my peaches and thinking. A train *ka-bump-ka-bump*ed its way by the front of the house on its way to Portland. There was a slight incline on Highway 30 opposite the house, where I had once witnessed a horrible four-car crash, and the big diesel rigs made an obnoxious rattling sound on the downhill side. There was nothing to do but wait. Once I finished the peaches, I started thinking about Angie Boudreau, which made me horny as all get out.

Dreaming of Angie the day before, I had yanked my noodle five times. I thought the poor thing was going to fall off. I had long since learned that a single mental image grew stale with repeated jacks, and this was true even of Angie, hot as she was. I knew I should give the poor girl a break for one night, so I could refresh the fantasy of checking out those warm puppies on her chest and peeling off her white Capris. Waiting for Tom and Gracie to get back from their date, I slid my collection of magazines from under my bed.

I didn't dig *Health & Sunshine,* which offered nudists wandering around with black patches over their private parts. Who cared about little kids or potbellied males? I wanted boobs and buns, which were to be found in such magazines as *Wink, Sir, Titter, Eyeful,* and *Flirt.*

Which beauty would I ravish while I waited? There was one model, Diane Webber, who appeared in scores of my magazines. It was astonishing how many spreads she commanded. She was everywhere and with good reason. Besides having a great body, she had an open-eyed, innocent face and an obvious knack for the kind of sexy art shots then in fashion. Despite being in nearly every nudie magazine ever conceived, she had still swung a centerfold *Playboy* layout in the May 1955 issue. But I wasn't in a mood for Sweet Diane. I thumbed through my old loves—sensational every one—until I settled on a spread featuring the actress Mame Van Doren wearing see-through lingerie—or almost see-through. Mame, like Jayne Mansfield, was a Marilyn Monroe wannabe. Jayne sported boomers that were so outlandish as to be antisexy in my opinion. Mame had all the equipment, including reasonable wahzoos, but lacked Marilyn's natural sexiness.

I had reread *The Stranger* after meeting Angie, although I still didn't understand it completely. On the other hand, she probably didn't either. I put my copy on the floor by my bed in case I was interrupted midpull.

I was flipping through the Mame Van Doren spread, baring her remarkable cantaloupes—this with my dog in a gentle, long-distance trot—when there came a banging on the the door.

Jesus! I damn near went through the roof.

"Ray." A man's voice. Agnopolous.

"Yes," I croaked. Mr. Clever. I threw Mame Van Doren under the bed and used my knees to make a tent out of the covers. It was the only way to buy time while my dog calmed down. Being careful to keep my concealing tent intact, I leaned over and opened the door.

"Is everything okay in here?" He looked about, suppressing a smile.

"Just reading a book," I said, doing my best to be cool. My mouth was dry.

He arched an eyebrow. "Mickey Spillane?"

"Albert Camus."

He furrowed his brows. "Never heard of him."

I picked up *The Stranger* and gave it to him.

He turned the paperback in his hands, looking puzzled. "Who's he?"

"A Frenchman," I said.

"Good as Mickey Spillane?"

"Different."

"Got some good parts, does it?" He smiled knowingly, and started flipping through the pages looking for the good stuff. "Is this a murder mystery or what?"

I said, " 'Or what' probably describes it best. There's a murder in it. And plenty of mystery in a different kind of way."

"Oh?"

"Its about a man in Algeria, a certain Monsieur Meursault, who kills an Arab on the beach. The French court convicts him essentially because he hadn't cried at his mother's funeral. He didn't show remorse. After his conviction, he sits around in his cell waiting to be executed. While he waits, he mulls everything over—his life and what it has meant and so forth. Then a priest comes in and gets all bent out of shape because Meursault won't call him Father. Meursault shouts at him and kicks him out, after which he thinks about the wind."

"The wind?"

"Blowing at him from his future. He has passed his life in one way, whereas it might have turned out totally different, depending."

"Depending on what? Not shooting the Arab?"

"Depending on his choices. Shooting the Arab was one of them. A bad one it turned out. He chose X, where he might have picked Y or Z, so there he is, waiting to die."

Agnopolous had no idea what I was talking about. He shook his head, looking at me like I was a trifle touched. "You want to go for a drive and talk?"

I said, "Sure." I popped up, wanting to get going.

Agnopolous spotted the corner of the magazine poking out from under the bed, still open to Mame Van Doren. He stopped and picked it up. "Man, old Mame's got a real pair on her, doesn't she?" He wasn't fooled. He knew what I had been doing.

Mame Van Doren, formerly the girlfriend of the Boston Red Sox outfielder Tony Conigliero, was returning from a trip to Vietnam, where she had entertained the troops with her presence and visited her new love, an army officer. I was then a twenty-eight-year-old reporter for Honolulu's morning daily newspaper. My city editor dispatched me to Waikiki Beach to join the reporters and photographers who been lured by the prospect of suggestive gossip and the sexy Miss Van Doren.

We gathered around Miss Van Doren, who posed for some cheesecake before she fielded questions. She was no longer an ingenue, but still sexier than all get out in a bikini. The eternal pursuit of attention had to be a tiresome chore for her. An aging jock arrived at work to find his locker cleared out; a sexpot, old meat in her midthirties, had found the checkout rags had moved on to younger women. It was easy to appreciate the feminist impatience with woman as sex object. It occurred to me, watching the photographers do their thing, that Miss Van Doren was far smaller than she had seemed in the magazines, and she had a hint of vulnerability about her that I somehow hadn't expected.

Where was the lead in a sexpot clinging to the flying fickle finger, hoping that something would happen to rejuvenate her career? Baseball bats? Big guns?

Holding my pad and pencil in my right hand, I twisted the tail of my handlebar mustache with my left thumb and forefinger. It didn't seem Mame Van Doren had anything to say that would entertain my readers. Who really cared if she had a boyfriend who was an officer in Vietnam? Marilyn Monroe had once been married to Joe DiMaggio. Being the ex-girlfriend of Tony Conigliero didn't cut it. They were both Italian-American baseball players, but Tony wasn't in Joe's league. There was a pause in the questions. The other reporters were frustrated.

I said, "I was really anxious to come down here today. You and I are old lovers ourselves, as it turns out."

She blinked. "We are?"

"From the magazines. You can't imagine the hot times we've had. My oh my!" I rolled my eyes.

Mame Van Doren liked to have fun, and she was flattered. She gave me a big, sexy smile. "Oooooh! Say, I like your mustache. Does it tickle?"

I could hear the whir of television cameras. "Depends on where I put it." Grinning, I leered and twisted the tail again.

A photographer caught Van Doren's naughty laugh in a delightful picture that would make the wire services.

It occurred to me as I was flirting with Mame Van Doren that what at first appeared to be coincidences were not that at all. Miss Van Doren, whose remarkable image had moved me to lope my goat as a teenager, was part of the existential wind that had fascinated me since I was seventeen years old. I lived bedeviled by a headwind from the future and the a tailwind from the past, carrying with it visions of a vengeful Billy Karady. This tailwind, fear, was ever present in my life.

I slid into Tom Agnopolous's new Ford, and we set off down Highway 30 toward Irrigon and Jackson. Agnopolous seemed in a good mood, so he must have a good time with Gracie. Good for him. And good for her.

He said, "Gracie never let up about that 'stretchers' crack of yours."

I grinned. I knew she wouldn't. "Did you tell her?"

He looked amused. "Had to. She wouldn't give up."

I grinned. "What did she say?"

"She was furious."

"Pretend furious. Can't admit she was flattered. She's female."

"I expect you're going to catch holy hell in the morning."

"By the way, I had another encounter with Billy Karady."

"Oh?"

"Following the Brenda Lee concert in Pendleton."

Agnopolous raised an eyebrow. "You took your girl to Happy Canyon, did you?"

This was just a question. Agnopolous had brains enough not to make a big deal out of the fact that I had a girlfriend same as everybody else. I liked him for that. "Angie Boudreau is her name. She doesn't mind riding in the Turd."

"The turd?"

"Wheeled Turd. My Chev. Cap *W*, cap *T*. This is The Coop, Cap *T*, cap *C*."

He smiled. "I see."

Omitting no detail, I told him about Billy Karady's having tried to break my face in the parking lot outside the National Guard Armory.

He burst out laughing. "Trapped his hand in the window? Good thinking."

"Good thinking had nothing to do with it. I was lucky."

Agnopolous shook his head. "I believe I'd have found it hard not to rip his arm off."

I looked chagrined. "If Angie and better sense hadn't prevailed, I probably would have. I've never done anything to Billy Karady to make him act like that. Something's wrong with him, big-time."

Agnopolous thought a moment, then said, "I took a look

around the willows again but didn't find anything more."

It was this connection between the screaming and Billy's behavior that had me worried too. "Did you talk to Carl Sellers?"

"Yes, I did. He said it never happened."

I was dumbfounded. "He what?"

"He says he doesn't know what you're talking about."

I said, "Mr. Viking. He doesn't want to get Billy Karady in trouble. Did you talk to him before or after they found the girl in Hermiston?"

"Before and after. He denied it happened both times."

"He didn't want to admit he lied to you the first time. Do you honestly think I would make something like that up out of whole cloth? Why? Why would I do that?"

Agnopolous looked at me. "I can't imagine."

"What if Billy Karady killed those girls and does it again? Does Sellers want that on his conscience? Jesus!"

Agnopolous looked resigned. "People don't think about things like that when they lie to you. They just wish they had been somewhere else. Sellers owns a gas station, and you're a sixteen-year-old kid."

"Who're people going to believe? I've thought about that. But it happened. It did. You should have heard that girl! My God! Hook me up to a lie detector, and ask me what happened. I didn't make that up. I'm not lying." My voice was rising. How could Sellers lie like that? It was incredible.

Agnopolous put his hand out. "Easy, easy. I believe you, Ray, I really do."

He slowed up as we entered Irrigon, which wasn't much more than a couple of fruit stands, a gas station, and a tiny grocery store that sold worms on the side.

"Now what happens?" I said.

"I think if Billy or Brian Mungo raped somebody and the girl doesn't press charges, there's nothing we can do. Girls who are raped are reluctant to press charges. Can't say as I always blame them." We passed the gas station and grocery store, downtown Irrigon.

"Girls who are raped and murdered can't press charges either."

He sighed. "There's that too."

"What about the girl who screamed?"

"What about her?"

"Why don't you find her? See what she has to say. Do you think you can do that?"

Agnopolous shook his head. "Not an easy assignment, all things considered." We were through Irrigon, and he speeded up again.

I said, "What if it's the same asshole who raped and murdered the girls in Kennewick and Hermiston, and I interrupted him in the middle of his fun?"

Agnopolous didn't answer. He drove in silence for a while, then said, "That possibility has occurred to us, yes."

"The guy on the radio was saying you people are holding back details so as not to foul up your investigation. Do any of those details fit with the killer being Billy Karady?"

"I can't tell you what they are, but yes, they fit with the murderer being Billy. But they don't prove it. They suggest."

"Suggest?"

"Correct. They could be coincidental. We lifted some of Billy's prints from the door handle of his Mercury, but we couldn't find them on anything at the crime scenes. On the other hand we didn't find anybody else's prints either."

"Wonderful." Again we rode in silence. Then, I said, "Maybe Carl Sellers was the one who caused the screaming. You ever thought of that?"

He checked his rearview mirror. "Yes, we've thought of that." He said nothing for a while, then said, "Billy Karady appears to have a thing for your friend Angie. Why is that, do you suppose?"

I said, "Easy enough to figure out. Take a look at her."

"Good-looking?"

"Hot," I said. "Why she would be attracted to me is an open question, I admit."

"Hot as your sister?"

I rolled my eyes. "No offense to you and my sister and everything, but hey. No comparison. Gracie's got a body on her, but she's not in Angie's league. Angie's got this face on her. And lips." I groaned.

He smiled. "Maybe Billy's just jealous. If he's a psychopath, we've got a real problem on our hands."

A rush of anxiety coursed through my stomach. "Yes, we do. Did you have those underpants checked yet? What did they tell you?"

"They're made and marketed in Canada."

"Canada?"

A speeding car whipped around Agnopolous. "Jesus, would you look at that? It's amazing the shit I see when I'm not in my cruiser."

THIRTEEN

NOBODY IN HIGH SCHOOL wanted to ride the school bus home, and the next day I began the wonderful routine of taking Angie Boudreau home after I got off football practice. All day in class and afterward, in football practice, I looked forward to this five-minute ride, and each day it became more relaxed and comfortable. Her sister spent every afternoon watching "Guiding Light" at a friend's house, and her brother-in-law wasn't home from work, so the house was empty. I couldn't go inside, however. I had to go home and milk three cows.

The Wheeled Turd was easy on gas. That didn't make up for its astonishing ugliness, the oxidized paint, or the hole in the fender, but it made it possible for me to show Angie Boudreau the countryside on what was our second real date after the fiasco following the Brenda Lee concert.

"Where to?" I said.

"Wherever." She put her hand on my knee.

"Okay. The grand tour then."

About thirty miles east of Umatilla, the Columbia River flowed west from the north, becoming the border between Oregon and Washington. For the better part of twenty miles it was flanked by high rimrock on both sides, then it flattened to the ugly terrain that was called high desert in the Zane Gray westerns. The only relief from the desert of bounding jackrabbits and nocturnal mice was an occasional outcropping of lava rimrock. There wasn't much to show her, but I did my best.

I took her to a place called Box Canyon, where my father had hidden his whiskey still in 1931. It was here that my father, atop a lava cliff above the still, had fired a high-powered rifle at the feet of Deputy Sheriff Bert Nation. He had made moonshine whiskey for the better part of ten years before they caught him later that year. He'd also been a bronco buster and horse trader; I wanted Angie to know that although he was now crippled, he'd once had a real pair.

I took her to a place outside of Hermiston where the fossil remains of prehistoric beasts were to be found; I had a substantial collection of perfect little bones and teeth.

Finally, I dragged the gut of Umatilla; on the outskirts of town, I passed Billy Karady going in the other direction in his polished black Cunt Wagon.

"Shall we head for the buttes?" I said. An outcropping between Umatilla and Hermiston was known locally as the buttes.

"What's there to see in the buttes?"

"Not a whole lot. Nothing to do there except neck or pop jackrabbits with a .22."

"We have a .22?"

I shrugged. "No."

She squeezed my thigh. "Good. Let's go."

I took what was called the "old road" to Hermiston; that is, the road flanking the Umatilla, and about a mile out of town hung a left. I saw headlights in my rearview mirror, but didn't think anything of it.

We found a good place to park, and finally, at long last, I turned and kissed her, feeling her warm body against me. She slipped her tongue into my mouth, and it was like I was being softly, sweetly electrocuted. I had never experienced anything like it. Never. It was exciting beyond anything in my wildest dreams, and Angie almost immediately began to pant. It never occurred to me that this shocking thrill could possibly recede with repetition. No, no, no! Within seconds, I was hard as a rock and had to straighten so I could tuck the excited Mr. Dick up under my belt. I tried to be casual about this, but I knew Angie wasn't fooled.

A half a minute later, I slid my hand up under her sweater while she twisted to unsnap her bra. I slid my hand over her warm breast, and in that instant I passionately, fervently believed that I belonged to Angie Boudreau heart and soul until the end of time. I could hardly believe the feeling. Wow!

"You like that?" she whispered.

I groaned loudly. "Do I like it? Jesus!"

We kissed again, then I took a deep breath. "No further tonight. Let's save it. Space it out. Deliberately drive ourselves crazy."

She gave me a hug. "I agree. No hurry. More romantic that way. Good thinking."

A half hour later, with my nuts aching with frustrated hormones, I fired up the Wheeled Trud to take Angie home.

As we started down the road out of the buttes, I saw headlights behind us. Were we being followed?

Angie was aware of the headlights too. "Who is that?"

The headlights were a malevolent presence. "I don't know," I said.

"We were being watched back there, weren't we?"

"Oh, I don't think so." I licked my lips—couldn't help it. I checked the rearview mirror—couldn't help that either.

She looked back at the headlights again.

I said, "Billy Karady?"

She scooted closer to me, if that was possible.

I said, "Your sister was surprised at the Wheeled Turd. She expected me to show up in a fancy black Mercury."

Angie said, "That's because he's been cruising by our house."

We were now on the main drag, and in my mirror, under the streetlights, I saw Billy Karady's fabled Cunt Wagon, riding low and with mere slits for windows. For Angie and me, it might as well have been Lucifer himself dragging the gut of our lives, tormenting us. There was no understanding his obsession. It just was. We were locked with him in a test of wills. We didn't try to fool ourselves that anybody would be intervening on our behalf. There was him, and there was us. Nobody else.

FOURTEEN

AFTER I HAD MILKED the cows the next morning, I began a daily drill of picking up Angie Boudreau on my way to school. Before the end of the week, knowledge of these before-and-after-school pickups made us, officially, an item. The girls in the white bucks and dickeys were likely curious at Angie's taste and maybe secretly envied her for having courage enough to express herself while they moved about in a sweatered herd; the boys were overtly bewildered that Skeeter Hawkins had scored the exotic new girl in school. None of this bothered Angie and me; we existed in a zone that was different than theirs. Or so we flattered ourselves.

One afternoon, three days following the incident in the buttes, Billy Karady followed us home from school. I remembered what Tom Agnopolous had said. Maybe Billy was just jealous. But what if he was a psychopath? If he was, we had a real problem on our hands. I went inside for a few minutes until he was gone. My getting home late made my mom sore as hell because if the cows went too long between milkings, they suffered, and the milk began draining from their tits onto the ground.

I hated milking cows, but the addition of Angie to my life made this chore more bearable; at least I had something to think about while I yanked tits in the morning with my breath coming in frosty puffs. The cows knew I didn't like milking them, so they gave me a hard time every way they could. The minute I sat down on the stool up would come their tails as a form of editorial comment. They just didn't piss. They PISSSSSSED! Out it came in a rushing splat, while I dove for cover, taking my bucket with me.

The way to stop a cow unloading a dump of wet crap—maximum yucko!—was to milk with my head jammed between her stomach and the bone at the top of her right leg—the one closest to me. She couldn't get into position to move her bowels without moving this bone.

My mother said the cows didn't like me because my fingernails were too long. That wasn't it. I kept my fingernails trimmed. I just didn't like milking cows. Who in his right mind did? The cows didn't like me. It was tit for tat. Fair enough. I gave them their stupid damned oats, after which they chewed their cuds stoically while I milked away with my head jammed in front of their leg bones.

As the days grew shorter and colder over the next three weeks, I began scouting the railroad tracks, watching for Russ. If Russ showed, I wouldn't have to hurry home to milk, and I would feel better about leaving Angie alone until her sister returned from watching the soaps with her neighbor.

Russ. It had been ten years since this cheerful little hobo had shown up at our farm one cold December afternoon, asking my mother for work in exchange for something to eat. He ended up spending the winter, living in the tiny, dank basement under the house. Never mind that he talked to himself and read the newspapers out loud and loaded his coffee with enough sugar to choke a horse, he slowly became part of the family. He conducted some of these interior conversations at the supper table, and bit by bit, we learned little snippets of his past. We learned that he was a navy veteran who was originally from Iowa. He had a tattoo on his shoulder that said Storm; he once said that was his last name, although we were never certain. Russ earned his keep by milking the cows, washing the dishes, and fixing lunch for my father while my mother was away working in the school cafeteria. There were other bonuses too. Whenever I killed a duck or a goose and brought it home, Russ snatched it immediately and cleaned it. As far as I was concerned, having to clean the kill was the worst part of hunting.

Every once in a while Russ would say to my mother, "Missus, I believe I would like some spending money today."

To this request, she always gave him a few bucks so he could walk to Umatilla and buy some Snickers and Mars Bars and a green tin of Velvet tobacco or a red tin of Prince Albert. This was Russ's big splurge. In a jolly ritual we all liked to watch, he carefully tore a piece of newspaper, which he used to roll a giant cigarette. The end of the paper burst into a flame when he lit it, sending him—and any of us who were watching—into fits of laughter.

When spring came following his first appearance and the Chinook winds had melted away the snow, he told my mother one day that he would be moving on. She bought him some good shoes, stocked a satchel with warm clothes, gave him a hundred dollars, and sent him on his way.

The next year, come late November and the weather turned cold, Gracie spotted him walking back and forth on the railroad tracks in front of our house. Again we took him in. He spent the winter, and, as before, hit the road come warm weather. Thus he established a pattern. Russ showed up in the fall and walked to and fro on the railroad until someone spotted him. After six or seven months of good food and tobacco splurges, he left in the spring with serviceable shoes, warm clothes, and a hundred bucks in his pocket. He loved the road, but was getting too old to travel in the winter.

So it had gone for ten years, with him showing up earlier and earlier each year, so that a late-September appearance, which I was hoping for, was not out of the question.

•   •   •

Angie Boudreau and I were young and passionate, and we both liked to read. It was fun to talk about the thoughts and speculations of Camus's protagonist while he waited to be executed. What, we asked ourselves, did they all mean? Did any of Monsieur Meursault's ruminations have anything to do with us, or was it just a lot of crappola written by a Frenchman with too much time on his hands?

The San Francisco police had arrested a poet named Allen Ginsberg for reading his poem "Howl," which they claimed was obscene, and this was much in the news as we began our investigation of existentialism—going so far as to order books from the Umatilla County Library in Pendleton. Both Angie and I wanted most desperately to lay our hands on a copy of "Howl." Then we read an article in *Time* magazine about the "Beats"—poets, artists, and intellectuals who hung out in Lawrence Ferlinghetti's City Lights Bookstore in San Francisco. We learned that the term *beat* came from "beaten down."

The Beats had the herd harrumphing and tut-tutting, so we concluded "Howl" had to be interesting. Arrest a man for reading a poem? What could a single poem possibly say that would threaten the republic? Even though we hadn't read the offending verse, we knew the authorities were essentially stupid to arrest Allen Ginsberg, whoever he was, in the City Lights Bookstore in San Francisco, wherever that was. If they hadn't busted Ginsberg, our curiosity wouldn't have been raised, would it? Dumb puds.

Compared to San Francisco, Umatilla was Moonbase Alpha. Talk about beaten down. Angie and I immediately expanded our reading from existentialism to include Zen Buddhism, another philosophy popular among the Beats. We did not pursue our interest as a form of display. It never occurred to us to call ourselves Beats. We were simply curious about the fuss and went about our investigation in a private way. Nobody except the school librarian knew what we were up to.

We found existentialism to be an impossible muddle. The very same people who claimed life was specific and individual then attempted to describe their philosophy in lingo that leaked into a gassy zone of the abstract. The texts were sprinkled with complicated definitions of absurdity, agony, angst, alienation, dread, despair, and ennui—all part of the wonderful heritage of the committed existentialist. That's not to mention Being, as distinguished from Being-in-Itself and Being-for-Itself. Jean-Paul Sartre rambled on at great, impossible length about how man was condemned to freedom, which meant choice, which he could never escape, and how not choosing was a form of choosing. A man exists only in terms of his flowing experience. To be free is to choose one's own living and dying. Et cetera.

What was all that crappola?

It was then, at the tender age of seventeen, that I began to suspect that politics was often at the heart of intellectual reputations. Both Albert Camus and Jean-Paul Sartre were active in the French Resistance during World War II. I began to wonder if all the fuss over Dashiell Hammet had as much to do with the quality of his fiction as it did with his telling the House Committee on Unamerican Activities to bugger off.

There were two existentialist insights I considered as a result of our investigation that I knew would stay with me, if only tucked away in my subconscious.

One was that life was a web of choice that, over time, defined an individual; a man created himself by his choices, and there was no retreating from these choices. To follow the herd without question was to act in bad faith and was inauthentic.

For me a concern with good and bad faith and the authentic and inauthentic in personal choice meant that I could logically accept part of the existentialist philosophy without accepting the entire swamp of the obscure and impossible; to accept it all would be the philosophical equivalent of wearing a crewcut and chinos with a buckle in the back. For existentialist Christians, the authentic religious experience was a personal relationship with God—not the entire dogma of a church.

I was also impressed by the existentialist trilogy of daunting, frustrating facts of human existence that were unknowable. As far as I was concerned, they were obvious and elementary.

The first unknowable was ultimate origin. The religionists believed gods started everything. The scientists, searching the heavens with their telescopes, believed the explanation lay in physics. In fact, no one knew or likely could know.

The second mystery was circumstance. How was it that an individual arrived in a single place at a specific time? The paths of an individual's life were constantly changed by circumstances over which he or she had no control. Russ the hobo, having shown up looking for something to eat, had stayed for the winter—a fork in the road of his life. He had taken it, and now he wintered every year in Umatilla. Angie's brother-in-law might have taken a job on another construction project, and there would have never been a meeting at Baker's Drugstore, much less all that followed.

To the unknown of circumstance, I assigned my presence on the Columbia River when I had heard the girl scream. I still didn't know who the girl was or why she had screamed, but the incident had some unknown meaning that haunted me. I should add here that for reasons that were unclear even to myself, I had yet to mention the episode to Angie. One reason was that I was likely embarrassed by my cowardice. Beyond that, I don't know why.

The third unknowable was fate. What was the end of the story? It was impossible to know the end, either of history or of a single life. We would all be shoveled under one day, but beyond that, what?

To fate, I privately added the ending to the story that had begun with the screaming. Another was Billy Karady's fixation on Angie.

Angie and I talked about forks and the unknown consequences of paths taken and paths ignored. We didn't regard any
of this speculation as depressing in any way. We were not tormented by angst. We did not wallow in ennui. We were young
and in love and having fun exploring ideas. As the man said,
the joy of youth is in their delight, so we skipped over all the
depressing horseshit and concentrated on what we understood.

We both found Zen to be similarly obscure and perplexing,
but still fun. We managed to come up with our answers to some
famously tough questions asked by Zen masters of their ap-
prentices.

What is the sound of one hand clapping?

Foolish question.

What causes unhappiness?

Desire.

How can one eliminate unhappiness?

Eliminate desire.

Speaking of desire, the next two sessions in the buttes were
given over to necking, a sublime form of mutual torture. This
gave me a nearly permanent case of painful blue balls. There
were times when my throbbing nuts, swollen from a rush of
hormones, felt like medicine balls being struck by lightning. My
gentleman was getting increasingly restless. Such frustration he
had never known. Ahh, but such sweet, sweet frustration it was.

*One Friday in the fall of 1969, the editors of Honolulu's morn-
ing newspaper learned through bar gossip that the afternoon
paper was scheduled to publish a show-off series—beginning
the following Monday—on the waves of hippies that had been
arriving in Hawaii. The flower children were getting off the
plane in numbers, drawn by rumors of Maui Wowie and Kona
Gold and the prospect of running nude on isolated beaches,
presumably with their pubes decorated with orchids.*

My city editor knew the competition would concentrate on

numbers. How many hippies were on welfare. How many on food stamps. How many had VD. How much all this was cost-ing the taxpayers. How many had burned their draft cards. How many were, horror, smoking pot. Et cetera. He called me to the city desk and said, "Ray, I want you to go down to Waikiki and talk to these hippies. Tell our readers what they're saying and doing. We'll start our series on Sunday." He looked amused.

"What?"

"Go talk to these kids. Listen to them. Numbers don't mean anything except to accountants."

Conventional wisdom had it that the hippie movement had sprung from the aftermath of the assassination of John F. Ken-nedy, the urban riots by black Americans, and the foolishness of the Vietnam War. I wondered if it might not be more com-plicated than that. Had not the seeds been sown a decade earlier by Allen Ginsberg, William Burroughs, Jack Kerouac, and the rest of them? The San Francisco Chronicle *columnist Herb Caen had coined the term* Beatnik *in 1958. A year later, the Beatnik parody Maynard G. Krebs appeared in the television series "The Many Loves of Dobie Gillis."*

Later, as I sat down at a typewriter to begin the first of a series of vignettes, remembering Angie and our introduction to the Beats, my stomach twisted with melancholy. I glanced at my notes, thought a moment, and started typing:

You're standing on the sidewalk outside the Mauna Kea Hotel, where a group of excited little old ladies in flowered muu-muus are unpiling from a tour van. Up the sidewalk come two plump adolescent girls with pale white skin, wearing see-through fishnet blouses and gauzy, nearly transparent bloom-ers—trousers of a kind worn by harem girls in B movies—under which large buns, succulent with cellulite, protrude from insuf-ficient underpants. The fishnet blouses and the undersized pant-ies are fashionably matched in red. Seeing this, the tourist ladies nearly lose their dentures. You try not to stare as the girls pass by, boobs bouncing, pink nipples poking through the fishnet.

The girls are followed closely by a long-haired, barefoot young man wearing earrings and a bone in his nose. He catches you scoping the passing young buns. "Groovy!" he says.

You grin and step into the shade to talk with him. He's obviously stoned. He tells you his name is Traveling Jack from Sacramento, and he's been doing some trucking.

I paused in my work, wondering: like, was this the end of authentic Bohemians in America—spiked by the dagger of public myth, leaving only posturing and bad faith? I wear a dickey and white bucks; I am a good girl too. I wear sandals and no bra; I am a hippie too.

I immediately reminded myself that it was unbecoming to actually give a damn if they were authentic or inauthentic. Why should I care? They were simply enjoying being young. In fact, I thought, the day I became so boorish as to resent the pleasures of youth, I would know that I had at last achieved that unpleasant status that nobody admired: a cranky old geezer who lived forever in the past.

I also thought: what if I should whip out my pad and pencil to interview a visitor to Hawaii and it turned out to be Billy Karady?

That night I began my first novel. I figured if I could earn my living writing fiction, I wouldn't have to stay in harm's way, would I? I could live abroad, where I could relax. I would write under a pseudonym. I once heard a writer say if he had a nickel for every newspaper reporter who had an unpublished novel tucked way in a drawer somewhere, that he'd be rich beyond his wildest dreams. I figured nothing ventured, nothing gained. I would try and see what happened.

FIFTEEN

IT WAS THE SECOND week of October, and I was warming up the Wheeled Turd; I saw a solitary figure headed west on the railroad tracks in front of the house. He was wearing a dark blue pea coat and a stocking cap and walked with his arms clutching a package to his chest. He glanced once at our house, then kept walking. I should have picked him up immediately to give him some relief, but the sun was warming quickly, and another ten minutes wouldn't hurt. He wasn't going anywhere but back and forth. I wanted Angie to see his return.

I hurried out of the driveway and drove to her sister's brick house on the south side of town to pick her up, but on the way to school I turned left at the west end of the bridge over the Umatilla.

Angie looked momentarily confused. "Where are we going?" she asked.

"To pick up a gentleman of the road," I said.

"Russ?"

I grinned. "He made it. One more round." Then for reasons that I can't explain—and not that I was to be relieved from the chore of having to milk—I began to get emotional. My chin began to bob, and I fought back the tears. "He did it. He survived."

Triumph! Yes!

Angie understood. She said, "Go get him. Hurry. It's cold out there."

When I got to the house, Russ, still hunkered from the cold, his breath coming in frosty puffs, was walking east, toward Umatilla.

I parked the Wheeled Turd by the side of the road that ran by the front of our house and hurried out onto the right-of-way to meet him.

"Russ!" I called.

He looked up, recognizing me immediately. His face was a stubble of beard. He had never called me by my name, and I never knew for uncertain if he even knew it. He brightened. "Morning!"

From a distance, the pea coat had looked warm enough. Up close I saw that it was tattered and patched, as were his trousers. He was a walking ragman. He looked gaunt and tired. How he had managed to survive was beyond me. I said, "Kind of cold out here, isn't it, Russ?"

He said, "Yes, it is. You don't suppose the missus would have some coffee on?"

"If she doesn't, she'll put some on," I said. "Here, let me carry that." I took his package, and he followed me off the right-of-way.

Behind me, he said, "Cows been milked this morning?"

I glanced back, and he was grinning. He might have been a little scrambled upstairs, what with all the time talking to himself out loud, but he wasn't crazy.

When we got to the Wheeled Turd, I said, "Russ, I would like you to meet my friend Angie."

"Ma'am," he said, doffing his stocking cap from his bald head.

I reached into the glove compartment and retrieved a green tin of Velvet tobacco and gave it to him.

He took it and turned it in his hand, admiring it. "Thank you. I believe I could use a smoke."

We continued on toward the house with Russ murmuring to himself. I didn't understand what he said, but two words were clear enough: "Pretty girl." He continued his mumbling, saying, "Texarkana," then after more mumbles, "big old trees," then burst into one of his curious fits of laughter.

Beginning with our third session of parking in the buttes, Angie Boudreau and I added another subject to our curriculum, sex. She said, "You know, Ray, I've been thinking a lot about this since the other night. We males and females are complementary—something nobody wants to admit."

"Complementary."

"I bet I want just about everything you want."

"Really?" I thought of some of the bizarre fantasies to which I had trotted my pony.

"Our plumbing is complementary, and so are our imaginations. It's an official unofficial secret."

"An official unofficial secret." I thought about that.

"That's right. Everybody knows the truth, but it's verboten to say so directly. We're all supposed to run our lives by an agreed-upon lie."

"And that lie is?"

"That you males are terrible beasts, driven by sex and dark secrets, and we females are pure and everything."

"Stanley Kowalski and Blanche DuBois."

"There you go. If we try to have any fun, we're Eve biting the apple." She gave me a wry smile. "But the apple we bite has to be your idea, not mine. You have to be the aggressor."

"Why is that?"

"I don't know. It just is."

It soon became clear to me that females were sexually more complicated than we males. Getting Angie's engine started and keeping it humming required that attention be paid to emotions as well as to physical knobs and buttons. Angie just didn't lie back on the front seat of the Turd and let me fumble and bumble along in a form of on-the-job training. No, no, no. We explored sex together just as we explored the ideas that we'd been reading about. Angie was unembarrassed. She was determined to pursue the truth, and she was convinced that her body was something to be enjoyed, not some mystical Temple of Evil. She spoke up. She told me what to do and why, for which I was grateful.

I learned to take my time. I learned of the great pleasure females took in having their puppies cuddled and fondled, which was sport for me too. And she taught me what to do with the wonderful little pearl above the fleecy gates. I had heard several hotshot studs, Billy Karady among them, brag about "finger fucking" their girlfriends, offering by way of proof their hands allegedly still pungent with the telltale aroma. Judging from what I'd learned from Angie, pity their poor girlfriends—treated to the excitement of being humped by a middle finger. Whoopie do!

One night, after I had stroked her pearl until she popped her cookies, Angie, gripping Eager Dick tightly with her fist, whispered. "Do what you want to do, Ray. Don't wait for me to ask."

I hesitated. I knew what I wanted to do, but I still hadn't had the nerve to score some Trojans, which I knew I should use. I didn't want to endure another round of blue balls, that was a fact.

"It's your turn. Don't be embarrassed," she said.

I put my hand on the back of her head and gripped her black hair. There were apples and then again apples.

She obviously got the idea. "Yes," she whispered.

I was uncertain.

"Let's go for it," she said.

I gave her head the slightest nudge, and she went down on me, sucking with abandon. Her mouth was warm and hot and tight, and I could feel her teeth at the base of my wand. I damn near went through the roof.

A couple of minutes later, I groaned and exploded in her mouth, but she wasn't appalled. On the contrary, she squeezed me as hard as she could, her body soft and eager against mine.

When we came up for air, I said, "God, that was good."

"Was it ever!" she said.

"You didn't mind?"

"Mind?" She sounded astonished. "Why on earth should I mind? Fun making you squirm like that."

A few minutes later, holding one another, my hand cupping one of her warm puppies, I said, "I think we need to make a run to Walla Walla."

"What's in Walla Walla?" she asked.

"A wagon by the railroad tracks where they sell popcorn and rubbers."

"I agree. We should definitely go to Walla Walla," she said. Walla Walla was fifty miles away.

I could tell from her voice that she was wondering why Walla Walla. I said, "The popcorn wagon is open all night. They also have three whorehouses in Walla Walla. The Ritz, the Waldorf, and the Astoria."

"The what?"

"It's because of the farmworkers in the peas, asparagus, and onions. The city fathers are not stupid."

She laughed. "I guess not. I don't suppose they sell a whole lot of popcorn in the middle of the night."

"You want to go shopping tonight?"

She squeezed me again and sat up, putting on her bra. "Let's do it. This is getting frustrating."

I asked, "Ready for graduation?"

"I think so."

I fired up the Wheeled Turd.

• • •

Angie Boudreau and I were hand in hand and thigh to thigh as I got the Wheeled Turd rolling at a steady fifty-five up the Columbia River. A half hour later, with the reservoir above McNary Dam on our left, we entered the twenty-mile stretch of desert gorge between Cold Springs and Wallula, where the Columbia turned west from south.

At Wallula, I turned east over a narrow, rolling highway that followed the Walla Walla River. A little over an hour and a half later, I pulled to a stop at a small white popcorn wagon by some railroad tracks. It was two o'clock in the morning. The wagon had a popper, a cooler of cold pop, and a small shelf of candy bars. That was it.

When I got out of the car, the clerk, a crewcut young man in his early twenties, got off his stool and put down a magazine. I bet he loped his goat a bunch—nothing to do but sell condoms to people who were actually getting it. I walked to the service window and pretended to be looking at the candy bars. My mouth was dry.

The clerk looked past me at Angie. He wasn't fooled.

I licked my lips. "Two bags of popcorn and a half-dozen Trojans, please."

"Regular or extra sensitive?"

"Extra sensitive."

"Lubricated or dry?"

"Uh, lubricated."

"Smooth tip or safety reservoir?"

What I had thought would be a simple score was like buying a new Ford. I thought, *Just give me the damn rubbers, asshole.* "Right, right. Safety reservoir."

He knew he had me going, the bastard. He turned, ever so casually, and began scooping the popcorn into paper bags. Then he looked at me, raising an eyebrow. "You sure a half dozen is enough?"

I was grateful for that question. "Better make that a dozen," I said.

He glanced at Angie again. "Good thinking."

At last I was able to pay for the popcorn and the rubbers and escape the clerk, who was getting on my nerves.

We had gotten no farther than a block when a red light began blinking behind me. A cop.

I said, "Aw shit." The cop must have been watching the popcorn wagon.

A Walla Walla policeman made his appearance at the window. "Good morning," he said cheerfully. "You been drinking?" He shined a flashlight around the inside of the car.

"No sir," I said.

"May I see your driver's license, please? Take it out of your wallet."

I did as I was told.

He could tell I hadn't been drinking. He glanced at the license and gave it back to me. "Long way from Umatilla, Ray."

"My girlfriend and I had a hankering for popcorn," I said.

He eyed Angie. Unless he had stainless-steel balls, he had to be envious. "They do sell good popcorn back there; that's a fact. Well, be careful on your way back."

"Being careful is why we drove all this way."

He grinned. The Walla Walla police didn't care about rubbers. In fact, they encouraged them, which was why the popcorn wagon was allowed to stay in business. They just didn't want teenage kids driving off the road.

When we got going again, Angie said, "You mentioned that Walla Walla has three whorehouses."

"The Ritz, the Waldorf, and the Astoria."

"You been to one of those places?"

"Once," I said.

Angie was at once surprised and curious. "You have? Really? Tell me about it."

"Well, last summer I was driving in the peas for Dutch Van Elst, who owns a few thousand acres just outside of town. I say a few thousand, maybe not that many, but a lot of peas—hundreds of acres for sure. I only had a learner's permit, but nobody cared. We stayed in a bunkhouse and drove twelve-hour shifts. We took on the pea vines from the field to machines that separated the peas. Convicts from the Washington State Penitentiary forked the vines into our truck, and Mexicans pitched them into the viners."

"The machines that separate the peas from the vines."

"Right. The convicts and the Mexicans did the real work. We kids just drove back and forth all day. The drivers maintain a revolving hierarchy from summer to summer. The more summers you had worked, the more perks you had."

"Perks."

"Perquisites. Lower bunk. First into the showers. Best seats at meals. That kind of thing."

"Okay, I see. A microcosm."

"Right. Society in action. One night when I was sleeping in my bunk, I was shaken awake and given instructions to drive one of the vets to a whorehouse. He was horny, but too drunk to drive. I was like a pledge or a plebe. I had to do it. I drove him to the Ritz and parked in an alley. He gave me a ten-dollar bill; he said if I got too horny waiting that I should just go inside and tell the women what I wanted." I looked at Angie and raised my eyebrow.

She grinned. "Come on, now. Tell me what happened."

"He went up some stairs into a second-story door that had a light over it, and I saw a woman welcome him inside. I waited and waited. Soon my gentleman was at attention. Eager for action."

Angie cocked her head. "I bet."

"Wouldn't go down. I had the ten-dollar bill, but it took a while to summon the courage. I went up the stairs and rang the bell at the top. A white woman dressed in what looked like a nightgown or slip answered the door. There was a black woman with huge bazooms there too. The white woman said, 'Yes?' I held up my ten-dollar bill. She said, 'You lookin' to do business here?' I said, 'Yes, ma'am, I am.' "

I fell silent for a moment, savoring the memory of the previous summer.

"Go on," Angie said.

"The black woman said, 'Oh, aren't you a dear?' The white woman, looking me over, said, 'What do you think, Mae?' Mae looked at me with this little smile on her face. 'You don't have much of a butt on you,' she said. 'How much you weigh?' I said, "Ninety-seven pounds.' She looked disappointed. She said, 'Honey, the house rules say all customers have to weigh at least a hundred pounds. That's a fact.' The white woman looked bummed out too. 'And you're probably packing seven pounds of solid action! Oh, we're sorry.' "

Angie giggled. "What happened then?"

"I said, 'Thank you, ma'am,' and bolted down the stairs."

"You were relieved," Angie said.

"Oh hell, yes. Relieved, but proud of myself. I'd tried."

"Nice ladies."

"They were real nice. Back in the alley, I sat in the car and trotted my pony, dreaming of one day having a girlfriend with Brigitte Bardot lips. I've got this magazine with a spread of Brigitte. There's one picture with her bent over looking out a window. She's wearing these horny little see-through underpants." I groaned. "She's got lips just like yours."

She cocked her head. "Which lips are you talking about?"

"I've only seen one pair," I said.

Angie snuggled closer. "If you play your cards right, maybe I'll show you the other."

"Really? Okay! I did my best to get rid of my cherry, but thanks to the ladies at the Ritz, I saved it for you."

"Why, you are a smooth talker, aren't you?" Angie gripped my knee. "Remember the koan about the wild strawberry?"

Yes, I did. In this Zen koan, a man was cutting wood in a forest when suddenly a tiger leaped from the brush, baring its teeth. The man dropped his ax and ran for his life. He came to a cliff. Far below, there was a river. At the last second, he spotted a root sticking out from the cliff. He grabbed the root and hung on just as the tiger arrived and began taking swipes at him with its claws. He looked down at the river. There a hungry crocodile waited. He felt the root coming out. He saw a wild strawberry growing from the side cliff. It was red and ripe.

I said, "It tastes so sweet." Thinking of the extra sensitive, lubricated, reservoir-tipped Trojans in the glove compartment and Angie's warm thigh beside mine—not to mention her comment about the lips—I hit the gravel shoulder of the highway and damn near drove the Wheeled Turd into the Columbia River.

SIXTEEN

THERE WAS NO ESCAPING the fact that girls matured faster than boys. There was a time, in the seventh and eighth grades, when almost all the girls in my class were boobed and butted out, and most of them taller than us boys. God, how those honkers of theirs turned my mouth dry! I wasn't the only late-maturing male; I was just the last in my class to experience the burst. Angie Boudreau told me she was fully developed by the time she was fourteen—at which time I was a towering five feet tall and a hefty ninety pounds—but I had been reading and exploring ideas by myself long before she showed up in Umatilla. When you're a watcher, you have a lot of time to think.

Angie and I were driven together by our hormones. We understood that, but at the same time we had turned everything into an intellectual exercise. We believed that we had free will. Why? we wanted to know. Everything was why for us.

We decided that most of life—church, school, and the admonitions of our parents and, in her case, of her older sister—was a ritual form of training. We had been conditioned, allegedly for our own good, to take certain approved forks to the exclusion of others. The black-and-white box was loaded with stories telling us what to do. This neverending lecturing and browbeating and the establishing of outright silly laws, we felt, were at the heart of the "beating down" against which the Beats were rebelling.

Both of us had read Shirley Jackson's short story "The Lottery," in which, one a year, a person in an enclosed community was selected at random to be stoned. The reason for this barbarous ritual had long been forgotten. It was rarely questioned and never successfully challenged. It just was—a periodic horror to be confronted.

Angie and I imagined ourselves as travelers addressing a series of existential forks—paths that split this way and that in a wilderness of yeas or nays. We all proceed into the unknown. Did this or that trail lead to sunshine or gloom? Was that a meadow or a forest up ahead? Was the sky clearing, or were those rain clouds gathering on the horizon? Should we turn left or hang a right? We were determined to see where the yea branch led. All we could do was take our chances as everybody did. We would experience the high. We would have our splendid moment. We would fly. Later, maybe, we would crash. But later was later. Now was now.

I had no idea whether or not Angie was a virgin, and I didn't care. I certainly wasn't going to ask her. Past forks taken or ignored were irrelevant to the decision before us. We had a private bond between us, an understanding. As far as I was concerned, that was all that mattered.

With a packet of extra sensitive, lubricated, reservoir-tipped rubbers in the glove compartment, we headed for the buttes on a clear, cold night. The stars were out, and there was a circle around the white moon. The heater of the Wheeled Turd was one of those old-fashioned things, a small box on the floorboard with wires that turned orange and a rubber-bladed fan that pushed the air out with a lulling *whump, whump, whump* sound. The Turd had those big, broad bench seats covered with mouse fur that had been popular in the forties, which gave us more than enough room for what we had in mind.

I found a place to park just below some rimrock overlooking the darkness that was the Umatilla River with the distant view of the lights of town.

We had learned to take our time, so we began with some heavy kissing. Our tongues twisted like writhing snakes. I did her ears with my tongue. That drove her wild, and I had to grab a handful of hair to hold her head in place. I then proceeded to her bumpers. She really liked the breast action, especially gentle nipple chewing, so I lingered there, making her squirm.

Slowly, item by item, we stripped, cozy in the warmth of the front seat of the Turd.

I spread her legs and licked and kissed her thighs. Taking my time, I did her button with my tongue until she screamed and twisted from my grasp.

I quickly set about rolling the condom, wishing I hadn't bought one with yucky jell to deal with. Angie sure as hell didn't need lubricating. Although this only took seconds, it seemed like several days. Stupid damned thing.

Then, pushing Angie's legs back with my arms, I entered her, and she was so warm and sweet and good that I could hardly believe it. We were quickly into a delicious rhythm, rocking against each other's warm bodies.

WHAM, WHAM, WHAM, WHAM!

Somebody was banging on the car door, marking the thrust of my butt.

I froze. I twisted and looked up, but the hammering continued, the rhythm unchanged.

WHAM, WHAM, WHAM, WHAM!

I pulled out of Angie, feeling stupid, violated, and enraged. I saw who it was.

Billy Karady retreated into the darkness.

I pulled on my shorts and flipped on the headlights of the Wheeled Turd. I saw Karady running down the road.

I doused the lights.

"Did you see who it was?" Angie said.

"Yes, I did. How about you?"

"I saw him," she said. "How long had he been there?"

I said, "I have no idea. The last twenty minutes I was in a zone."

She sighed heavily. "So was I."

We sat in silence, contemplating the turn of events.

Then, Angie said, "What are we going to do?"

"I don't know. By the way, I've been meaning to ask you something: did Billy Karady try to rape you by the mouth of the Umatilla?"

She hesitated a moment, then said, "Yes, he did. If it hadn't been for your yelling, he would have succeeded."

"Do you think he's the one who killed those girls?"

"In Kennewick and Hermiston. Yes, I do."

I thought about that, saying nothing.

She said, "You saved my life, by the way. That's why I sought you out that first day after school."

"And here I thought it was because I was such a handsome stud."

She grinned. "I wanted to thank you, but I didn't have the courage to tell the whole story."

"There's something big-time wrong with Billy."

"Yes, there is," she said. "I think he's likely crazy."

"The question is, who will believe us?" I said.

"Nobody. Nobody would have believed me if I had gone to the police, and nobody will believe this. He's Billy Karady, and he's going to lead the Umatilla Vikings to the state football championship."

"The question is, who're we?"

"Skeeter Hawkins and a new girl with pierced ears."

"Meaning we're nobodies."

"Nobodies who've been reading books about existentialism and Zen Buddhism." Angie started putting on her clothes.

I said, "I found a pair of underpants in the willow grove that day. My sister's boyfriend says they were made and marketed in Canada."

"The state cop."

"Tom Agnopolous, yes."

She said, "Turn on the dome light, and take a look at these." She handed me her underpants.

I looked at them in the dim light. They were Mystiques. Lime green. A match to the yellow underpants I had found.

She said, "I bought these and the ones you found in a trip to Calgary with some friends."

"Say, you wouldn't mind giving them to me, would you?"

"To compete with your magazines or as a souvenir?" She gave me a lopsided smile.

"I want to show them to Tom Agnopolous and tell him you're the girl we've been looking for."

She thought for a moment, then said, "Sure." She looked disconsolate as she began pulling on her tights. She knew what my next question was going to be.

I said, "Would you talk to him? Maybe you know something that would help."

She didn't answer.

"I know it's hard," I said.

"Only if you talk to him first and tell me what he says. If he's cool about it, okay. If he wants to drag me in front of strangers to grill me about all the gory details, then no. It was an experience I'd just as soon forget."

"Thank you. I'll talk to him tomorrow."

"I want you to be there when he asks me the questions."

"Done," I said.

She took a deep breath and let it out slowly. "Do you suppose you could find another place to park?"

"If I put my mind to it," I said.

"I hate to start something and not finish it. You know what I mean?"

I laughed and grabbed myself by the crotch. "Do I know what you mean? Jesus!" I started dressing too.

Five minutes later, Angie and I set off again to find somewhere to finish what we had started.

I drove across the bridge to Washington—this was located just downstream from McNary Dam—knowing I was locked in an odd duel with a killer. I knew nobody would believe what had happened, with the possible exception of Tom Agnopolous, but strangely, I was not afraid. I was determined to do whatever it took to prevail.

It wasn't until the next day that I discovered that the left front door of the Wheeled Turd was dented from the beating it had taken from Billy Karady's fist.

I was in San Ignacio in southwestern Belize, about ten miles from the Guatemalan border. Every evening I had a supper of beans and rice in Eva's Cafe with a German friend who ferried tourists into isolated Mayan ruins in his four-wheel-drive Mercedes truck. I had developed a routine: after supper I walked down to the Macapal River to take a couple of hits of pot on his walk-around pipe, after which I pushed on to Carlito's, a hangout for Spanish speakers. I spoke Spanish well enough to order Belekin beer and peanuts or chicharones *and catch passing snatches of conversation, but not well enough to communicate on any meaningful level.*

The regulars knew I was a writer, that I was likely stoned, and that I liked to sit by myself and think. They may have even sensed that I was on the run from something, although they had no idea from what. I was in my own little world, so they didn't bother me. By establishing a routine—choosing their watering hole over others—I had become one of them. I was their writer, el Americano *who hung out at Carlito's.*

Being in the tropics, Carlito's had large, folding doors that the management removed every morning so that the nearly thirty feet of the front was open, facing the sidewalk and street outside. Sitting inside one night, I happened to look up as two pretty Creole girls passed by on the sidewalk. As they did, a drunk, undulating his hips in a fucking motion, began slamming his hand on the table, wham, wham, wham, wham, *marking their stride; his companions, eyeing the swaying behinds of the girls, began laughing. Har, har, har.*

The incident jarred me. For years, I had believed that life moved in a linear fashion, proceeding from one decisive fork to the next. Beginning with my interview of Mame Van Doren in Waikiki, I had slowly come to conclude that while the part about the forks was accurate—navigation was difficult—the choices moved in hoops, or loops. Again and again, ever haunted by the visage of Billy Karady, I pushed into what I thought was new territory only to find myself walking down the same path.

SEVENTEEN

THE NEXT DAY THERE was a story in the *Oregonian* saying the Oregon State Police and the Umatilla County Sheriff's Department were operating on the assumption that the killer of the girls in Kennewick and of the girl in Hermiston was the same person, although the police felt the killer most likely resided in Kennewick or the Tri-City area. The Tri-Cities were, Pasco, Kennewick, and Richland. An *Oregonian* source said this conclusion was based on a detail of the crime that continued to be withheld so as not to compromise the investigation.

I wasn't about to remain quiet about what I knew—either about the screaming I had heard at the river or about Billy Karady's obsession with Angie and me. Yes, Carl Sellers had denied having heard the screaming; yes, it was his word against mine. But I was telling the truth, and Tom Agnopolous knew it. Billy Karady had tried to knock my head off after the Brenda Lee concert, and then had banged on the door of the Wheeled Turd in the buttes. I was too scared of what he might do next to hold out on a state cop who was dating my sister. Face it: I needed help.

I called Tom Agnopolous, and he took me on another drive so we could talk. This time, he took me to Pendleton and back as we talked—about a sixty-mile round-trip. As we drove along the old highway along the Umatilla River between Umatilla and

Hermiston, I told him about Billy Karady's following us almost everywhere we went. I told him about the door-banging incident, including enough detail—without getting too specific—for him to get the picture of what Angie and I were doing.

Tom listened and didn't interrupt. He knew what happened when boys and girls got together in the buttes. When I finished, he said, "I take it you had brains enough to use some protection."

"We made a trip to the popcorn wagon," I said.

"The one in Walla Walla," he said. This was a statement, not a question. Everybody knew about the popcorn wagon in Walla Walla. He said, "Good thinking."

"Bought some popcorn too. Can't stop eating that stuff. Tastes like movie popcorn."

We drove in silence for a while, both thinking our separate thoughts.

Finally, I said, "The *Oregonian* says you guys think the killer is from Washington, yet you tell me there's a detail that leads you to believe it could be Billy Karady. Which is it?"

He slowed the car as we entered Hermiston. "Can't do it."

I said, "What if I told you it was Angie Boudreau that Billy tried to rape?"

"What?"

"Angie was the girl screaming in the willows. She says if I hadn't yelled, he would have gotten away with it too."

"When did you find that out?"

"She told me after the door-banging incident last night. She's afraid for her life. Who can blame her?"

Tom fell silent. We were rolling through sagebrush between Hermiston and Stanfield. To our right, we could see the lights at the Union Pacific rail yard at Hinkle that some years earlier had effectively replaced the roundhouse and repair yards at Umatilla.

I knew he was thinking about the detail the cops were keeping secret. I said, "I take it you checked out those underpants I found?"

"Made and marketed in Canada."

"Angie moved here from Sunburst, Montana, which is about a hundred miles south of Calgary. She bought those underpants in Calgary. Here." I pulled Angie's underpants out of my jacket pocket and gave them to Agnopolous, holding up the label for him to see. "Angie gave me these for you to compare with the ones I found in the willows. Mystiques. The same as the others except for the color. Size five. Also the same. Do you think Angie and I are making all this up? Why on earth would we do that?"

Agnopolous perked up. "Is Angie willing to press charges?"

"Not if it's her word against Billy Karady's. She knows how far that will go. The new girl in town versus the star jock. Even Carl Sellers lied to protect Mr. Hundred-Yards-a-Game, remember? Now will you tell me what you're holding out?"

He thought about that a moment, then said, "I'll tell you, but if you tell anybody else, I'll call you a liar. You have to keep it to yourself."

"If the detail suggests Billy Karady, I'll want to tell Angie. She has a right. It's her life that could be on the line."

Agnopolous sighed. "Okay, Angie too, but with the same understanding. You keep it to yourself."

"I agree."

He grimaced. He still didn't want to tell me. "We found a *K*."

"A *K*?"

"In each case, the killer used a nail or something sharp to scratch a *K* on the chest of the dead girls after he murdered them."

"He what?"

"*K* for Kennewick. *K* for Karady. Or maybe we're looking for someone named Kenneth. When a killer leaves a clue like that, it's generally because he secretly wants us to catch him.

It's a matter of time before we do."

"Billy Karady," I said. "You're looking for Billy Karady."

Agnopolous shrugged. We rumbled across some railroad tracks by the Tum-a-Lum Lumber Company and pulled to a stop at Rohrman's Ford on the street that took north-south traffic through Hermiston. He hung a right, drove a short block, and stopped again at Hermiston's main drag.

"Have you talked to him?" I said.

"Based on what? Just because he's an idiot with a last name that begins with a *K* doesn't mean he's a killer. We checked the records of every male high school student in Umatilla and Morrow counties so we wouldn't draw attention to our interest in any one specific student. It was the best we could do. There's nothing in Billy's records to indicate there's anything wrong with him."

I said, "Those girls were raped before they were killed. Right?"

"Right."

He crossed the street, and we headed south past the Snappy Snack Drive-In and around the curve to the left that led over an irrigation canal, past a water tower, and out of town.

"Will Angie talk to us?"

"She'll talk to you."

"Me?"

"If I think you'll be cool, and if you let me be there when you ask the questions. It's not easy for her. You can imagine. At the same time she's convinced that if I hadn't been screening for arrowheads, she'd be dead."

He thought a moment. "The answer is yes, you can be there when she talks to me, and yes, I understand her predicament. I'll be cool. Maybe she'll know something that can help us. I can't find out what she knows unless I talk to her."

He slowed at the top of a hill. Below us lay the sleepy town of Stanfield.

I said, "Everybody sees you hanging around the DQ waiting

for Gracie to get off work. Easy to figure that she'd tell me what happened. Quick leap from me to you. That means it's likely you know that he tried to rape Angie."

We started down the hill. "Those're fair deductions," he said.

I said, "He's likely figured she's afraid to testify against him, but can he count on that forever?"

Watching me, he said, "Each new dead girl adds to the odds that she'll speak up."

"If she were dead, it would be impossible for her to testify, wouldn't it? If he's already killed three girls, what's one more?"

Agnopolous didn't answer. He cruised slowly down Stanfield's main drag, passing the Frontier Room, which imported strip artists every Friday night. At the far end of the town, we rounded a bend to the left, passing some buildings that had housed some German and Italian prisoners during World War II. The prisoners had helped harvest wheat so young Americans could fight the war.

I said, "By the way, how're things going with my sister? You checked out those num-nums, have you? Those things poke right out there. I have to say that even if she is my sister."

He gave me a look of disapproval. "You think I park in the buttes with your sister? Jesus! Give me a break. I'm an Oregan state cop."

"I know. I know. You have an image to uphold. A role model. You're also close to thirty years old, and Gracie was married two years before Len flipped his car. I just bet you money, marbles, or chalk neither one of you is a virgin."

"Hey!"

"Are you trying to tell me you two have been spending all your time playing Monopoly? I don't believe it."

Agnopolous raised an eye. "Monopoly takes more than two players to be any fun."

"Cribbage then."

He pulled to a stop at the highway to Pendleton, then hung

a left. We rode in silence once again.

Finally, he said, "Ray, I want you to let me take care of this. If Billy Karady is a killer, he's dangerous."

"What if this were Gracie who was in trouble, not Angie? What would you do? Sit around picking your nose?"

"If it were me, and I knew a state cop, I'd let him take care of it."

I rolled my eyes. "Horseshit. You yourself admitted you don't have any evidence for any of the murders. You've got the letter *K,* but what does that tell you? You don't know any more than I do. In fact, you might know less. At least I know who the killer is."

"You do? You have circumstantial evidence and no more."

"He tried to rape Angie. His name begins with a *K.* He assaulted me in Pendleton. He's been following us around. He went so far as to bang on our door while we were parked in the buttes."

"None of that means he raped the other girls, much less killed them."

It was my turn to give him a look. "Right."

He clenched his jaw. "By the way, Billy Karady is moving in with Brian Mungo. Did you know that?"

"He what?"

"His family is moving to The Dalles. His dad has a job at the aluminum plant. The state athletic rules say if more than a month has passed since classes began, he's allowed to finish the school year where he started. He just made the cut."

"He's moving in with Coach?"

Tom nodded yes.

"I hope he likes muscle magazines."

"What?"

"Never mind."

"What muscle magazines?"

"Coach lifts weights," I said. "The magazines advertise protein supplements, carrot juice, and that kind of thing. Barbells and stuff."

"Plus pictures of guys with muscles."

"That too," I said.

Agnopolous didn't say anything, but he was obviously wondering about something.

EIGHTEEN

THE NEXT MORNING, THE day of the Vikings football game at Fossil, Angie Boudreau and I had our talk with Tom Agnopolous in Plymouth, across the Columbia River from Umatilla. To call Plymouth a town was a stretch. It was an unincorporated hamlet of maybe a dozen houses. What I liked to call the central business district was comprised of a Phillips 66 gas station, the Plymouth General Store—which didn't sell a whole lot outside of cold beer, pop, Van Camp's pork and beans, Campbell's Soup, potato chips, and Twinkies—plus the Horse Heaven Tavern and Selma's Desert Cafe. It had always been a puzzle to me what people in Plymouth did for a living. There was nothing in the Horse Heavens. Zero. Nada.

I was a regular at Selma's. For the last couple of years, I had been screening tiny blue, green, yellow, and red trade beads from the sand a couple of hundred yards to the east. This was my secret place. I had discovered it by accident. I was walking around one day, staring at the ground, when I spotted the entrance to an ant colony that included several colorful beads— hardly larger than the head of a pin—mixed in with the tiny stones the ants had collected. Selma's was a good spot for a cold Squirt at the end of the day. Outside of me, few people in Umatilla had ever been inside Selma's or the Plymouth General Store. Although Plymouth was just across the river, it was in

Washington State, which had a sales tax, rendering it as hospitable as Mars to Oregonians.

Tom took us to Selma's and sprung for cheeseburgers and French fries, which we ate as we talked. We sat in a booth by the window overlooking sagebrush and the distant cliffs above McNary Dam.

Tom dipped a French fry into a puddle of ketchup at the edge of his plate. "You want to tell me what happened, Angie? Tell it in your own way."

"Well, I took the bus from Montana to Umatilla, where I was going to live with my sister. I was tired of waiting around to begin my new life, so I had taken an earlier bus than I was supposed to. I had been riding almost fourteen hours when I got to Umatilla. That was when I met Ray. A Friday."

"The day before the mouse stomp," I said. "I was cleaning the toilets and mopping up at Baker's."

"When I got to Umatilla, I phoned my sister," Angie said. "Nobody was home. I decided to go for a walk. I asked Ray to go with me, but he had to finish his chores."

"Face it: I was a dumb shit," I said. I bit into my cheeseburger, but it was tasteless. I still felt like a dolt for not taking her up on her offer that first night. If I hadn't been the chickenshit Watcher Hawkins, none of what followed would have happened.

Tom, eyeing Angie, shook his head with disbelief. "A girl like Angie invites you to go for a walk, and you say no. What on earth were you thinking of?"

I shrugged. "Like I said, 'dumb shit.' "

Angie smiled at me. "He was still in his Skeeter mode."

"I guess," Tom said.

"I had only gone a block or two when it started to rain, and the wind kicked up. Then it started thundering, and lightning began to flash. I found shelter under an awning in front of the Koffee Kup Cafe." She stopped for a drink of Coke. "That's when this kid pulled up in his fancy black car. He obviously thought he was hot stuff. He wanted to know if he could give me a lift. I said no thanks. He sat there, glaring. 'What do you mean, no? It's raining,' he said. I told him no shouldn't be too hard to understand; it wouldn't rain forever. He was furious and took off with his tires squealing." She stopped, thinking.

Tom took a sip of coffee.

Angie said, "When it stopped raining, I went back to Baker's Drugstore to call my sister again. Ray was gone, but my sister was home. She and my brother-in-law came to pick me up, and when we were putting my bags in the trunk, I saw the obnoxious kid in the car across the street, watching. I got in the car, and my brother-in-law drove me home. I forgot all about the jerk. The next day was a Saturday. I decided to explore the town. I walked along the river toward the bridge into town, then decided to go all the way to the Columbia. I walked under the train bridge and was almost to the willows when I heard a car behind me."

"Billy Karady," Tom said.

"Yes. I was amazed. He'd apparently been following me, which scared me. I hurried into the willows to get rid of him. When I heard his car door slam, I knew I was in trouble. It . . . I . . ." She stopped. "I'd never had anything happen to me like this. But I knew something was wrong with him. I was in danger."

"No hurry. Take your time," Tom said.

Angie glanced at me. She bit that sexy oversized lower lip of hers. "I haven't even told Ray about this part."

"Ray's on your side. We both are," Tom said.

"He . . . he just burst out of nowhere and grabbed me and threw me to the ground. I started screaming as loud as I could. He started ripping my clothes off. I kept screaming." Angie gave my knee a secret squeeze. "That's when I heard someone yelling, 'Hey! Hey! Hey!'—a young man, I could tell from his voice. Billy stopped for a moment, which was all I needed. I twisted out of his grip and ran."

"He didn't follow you?"

"No. Whoever was yelling 'hey, hey!' was getting closer. He ran back to his car, but it wouldn't start. I could hear the engine going *RRRRR, RRRRR, RRRRR*." Angie took a deep breath.

"What did you do?" Tom asked.

"While he was trying to start his car, I raced back and grabbed what was left of my clothes. Then I hid in the brush by the edge of the river. I didn't want to move around for fear he would see me. Eventually, he left. After a while, I heard another vehicle."

"Did you see that vehicle?" Tom said.

She shook her head no. "I stayed hidden. I didn't want anybody to see me."

"That was Coach Mungo's pickup," I said.

Tom said, "Then what happened?"

"I heard voices in the willows, and I peered in and saw Ray and another man talking. I was amazed at the person whose yelling had interrupted the rape. It was the boy I had met in the bus station the night before. Then the two of them disappeared. A few minutes later, I heard Billy's car start up again and leave."

"After Sellers and I talked to him," I said.

Angie said, "Boy rescues girl. Girl falls in love with boy. Isn't that how it happens in the movies?" She squeezed my hand.

"I was a regular John Wayne," I said.

Tom said, "John Wayne. Right."

Angie licked her lips. "Did Ray tell you what happened after the Brenda Lee concert?"

"And about what happened in the buttes the night before last. Yes, he did."

"Do you think Billy murdered those girls, Mr. Agnopolous?"

It was obvious that Tom thought Billy had, but he said, "Hard to say."

"He follows me everywhere. He won't leave me alone. He's crazy."

"Not good, I agree," Tom said. "When did you get back home?"

"About an hour later. I was dressed in rags and didn't want anybody to see me, so I stayed along the riverbank, looking for fishermen."

"Did your sister or brother-in-law see you when you got back?"

She shook her head no. "They've got a key hidden outside. I used that to get in."

"Did you tell your sister what happened?"

She shook her head again. "Only Ray. And now you. Ray tells me the other man denied hearing any screaming."

"Carl Sellers," I said.

Tom didn't answer.

I said, "Any other details you haven't told us?"

He thought for a moment. "No."

I said, "Tell us this. Do you have any other suspects?"

He shrugged.

"Nobody?"

"We're watching a couple of people."

"Really? You think either one of them did it?"

"We don't have any evidence."

"That's not my question."

He grimaced. "Do I think either one of them did it? No. Probably not."

"Then that leaves Billy Karady, doesn't it?"

"Billy Karady is a possibility, yes."

"What can we do?"

Tom said, "For one thing, you have to be extra careful, Angie. Don't go anywhere alone, ever, until we get this sorted out. He won't break into your house. That's not his style."

"Chickenshit is his style," I said.

He glared at me. "We keep our wits about us. All of us."

Angie's chin began to bob. She was about ready to cry. She was no liar. Billy Karady had tried to rape her. She knew what he was. She was a witness. Now he was stalking her.

"We keep our wits, right," I said.

I had returned from my self-imposed exile for a short visit to the United States. Being gone all that time didn't do a whole bunch for my career, but I was more comfortable well outside the territory of the evil Billy. My publisher set me up for an interview with a woman talk show host in Philadelphia, a long-time fan of my novels, who asked me a familiar question. Why had I chosen to write crime fiction? Why not science fiction? Or why not mainstream fiction, whatever that was?

I said I wrote suspense fiction. Entertainments.

The interviewer said, "Aw, come on now. Don't dodge the question."

I rested my feet on the coffee table in my hotel room. "I wanted to be a professional. I wanted to live off book royalties. I didn't want to be a professor who wrote fiction on the side. I thought suspense fiction was more commercial."

"You're still dodging my question. I want to know why."

I said, "Mysteries have to do with life-and-death issues— with living and dying."

"Who lives and who dies."

"That's right," I said. "They're about violence and justice and revenge—about lions and lambs and predators and victims. Look around you. It's about turf and territory, about eating and being eaten."

"And motive too?"

"Certainly motive. Sex and greed and ambition. They're stories of the human condition and of rules of civilization put to the test."

"Ahh," she said. "Now we're getting somewhere."

"Ultimately, the attraction is people and passion. What more do you want?"

"Love?" she asked.

I paused. "Yes, they're about love. And hate. And revenge. The whole complicated ration."

NINETEEN

THIS WAS ONE OF our rare night games. Ahead of us, the sun was a sliver of orange, setting. Below us and to our right, the Columbia River was a darkening gloom. The Umatilla school bus was a big yellow clunk that made an awful noise as the driver, a jowly man named Ben Filchen—combination janitor, mechanic, and driver—pushed it for all it was worth; that wasn't a whole lot, maybe fifty miles an hour at best.

We passed Arlington at dusk. It was going to be a cold night for a football game. From the front of the bus, Coach Mungo called my name. "Ray, would you come up here? We need to talk."

Coach wanted to talk to me? I could hardly imagine why. This was to be another game of sitting on the pines for Watcher Hawkins. Nevertheless, I made my way past Billy Karady and his admiring pals to the front of the bus where Coach Mungo was engaged in a serious conversation with his assistant, Rocky Holmes.

Coach looked at me with that long, sad face of his and ran his hand over his crewcut. "Looks like you'll be our quarterback tonight, Ray."

I blinked. Quarterback? Me?

He said, "You know that Doug's got a pulled muscle in his groin. Doc Ford says he needs to rest it a week."

I turned around. "What about Jimmy?" This was a reference to the backup quarterback, Jim Tate.

"His mom says he's come down with the mumps."

We rode in silence for a full ten seconds. "I don't know the
plays."

"You were the backup last year, weren't you?"

"Well, yes . . ." I was dumbfounded.

Coach said, "Tonight you'll start. We'll put tape on your
arms and diagram the plays. It'll all come back. It's either that
or forfeit. We can't do that."

"You're going to tape the plays to my arms?"

"No other choice. We have to do the best we can."

Brian Mungo's abilities as a coach depended on his team's
record. Never mind that he'd lost his only two quarterbacks
and only had twenty-three total players. He had Billy Karady
in his senior year as tailback, and everybody in Umatilla expected big things. He was not about to throw in the towel and
forfeit the game, so somebody had to play quarterback, even if
it was me, the forever watcher. I had sat on the bench as the
reserve quarterback the previous year; he had no other choice.
He said, "What this takes is intelligence and presence of mind,
son."

"Better take off your shirt so we can get to work," Rocky
said.

I did as I was told. I held out my arms. Coach and Rocky
began laying strips of white tape up my forearms and biceps.

Mungo set about diagramming the plays with an ink pen,
using tiny Xs and Os. Watching his pen, I said. "Who's going
to call the plays?"

Coach said, "You are."

"Me?"

"You're the quarterback. A quarterback is in charge of the
offense. He calls the plays."

I felt a rush of anxiety, but said nothing.

He said, "You find what works and stick with it until it

doesn't. Just watch the sticks, and pay attention to their defense. If you see a weakness, take advantage of it. It doesn't have to be pretty or clever. In the end, the only thing that matters is who has the most points on the board."

"Do what it takes to win," I said.

"That's right. Don't be intimidated. Don't let other players try to tell you what to do. You're the quarterback. You're in charge. You call the shots. It's entirely up to you."

"Better stay in the box," I said. "That way I won't have to take snaps and hand off. Safer that way."

He looked pleased at what I'd had said. "That makes sense." He watched me, then said, "You can do it. Just relax, and pretend you're Johnny Unitas."

I said, "Johnny Unitas, right."

He grinned. "You have to think positive. You can do it if you think you can. If you convince yourself it's impossible, you're beat before you start."

I said, "The final score. That's what matters."

"That's the only thing that matters. We win. If we can get past this one, we'll get Doug and Jimmy back, and we'll be okay."

When I got back to my seat, my arms white with tape covered with tiny Xs and Os, my teammates, to their credit, left me alone. They knew this turn of events was a shocker for me, and they assumed, correctly, that I needed time to think. But I didn't think about football. I thought about the existentialist philosophy that Angie and I had been discussing in long rides in the Wheeled Turd.

The existentialists believed that a person did not experience life—that is, he did not exist or live—unless he risked life, put it on the line. To risk death was to affirm life, to feel alive. It's what the Stranger had done when he killed the Arab on the beach. He had felt estranged. Given an opportunity, he had decided to act. An unforeseen and unpredictable combination of events, a pulled groin and the mumps, had put me in an unusual position with respect to my nemesis, Billy Karady.

That night, I decided, I would put the philosophy to the test.

I would live.

When I was forty-two years old, I found myself physically in Camus territory, or close to it. The Stranger had been set in Algeria. I was on the coast of Morocco in the amiable company of a Scot and a German; we had come together on the boat from Algecira on the coast of Spain to Tangier. We had made our way to the town of Lareche, built alongside the ruins of an ancient Moorish fortress at the mouth of a river.

Near dusk we had made our way along the coast, past a shepherd with his goats; at sunset, we stopped on some jagged rocks overlooking the Atlantic and lit up our hash pipes. The rocks looked like lava that had spilled into the water and shattered. Above the overlook was a large, crumbling stone wall that had been built to protect an orchard of some kind, although we had no idea what the neatly planted rows of trees produced. Stoned on hashish, we watched the orange orb of the sun turn slowly red and slip under the horizon—warmth for the new world that lay beyond.

On the way back, the German wanted to circle to the right around an outcropping of rock and a bramble so as not to disturb the shepherd and his goats. He wanted to see new territory. The Scot disagreed. He said there was a settlement of some kind to the right. It was now dark, and this was unknown territory; he wanted to avoid it. I agreed with the German.

We circled right and at length came to the only way back to the coast, and then Lareche. It was down a narrow lane that ran straight through the center of a Berber encampment—a distance of about 150 yards.

The Scot balked. He said it was not too late to do the sensible thing; we should retrace our steps, circle around the briars and the rocks, pass the shepherd, and return to safety. The German, giddy at the prospect of testing the danger of the path ahead, insisted we proceed down the lane. Again, I agreed.

We smoked some more hashish, and thus stoned, walked down the lane three abreast with veiled Berber women screaming and fleeing on either side.

"Look straight ahead," the German said.

No sooner than we had entered the beginning of the lane than three sullen Berber men fell in less than a yard behind us, matching us stride for stride. The Berbers were furious at this violation of their space.

I knew the Scot was right. It was stupid to invade the Berbers' privacy in the darkness. We were at the mercy of the Berbers, who were famous for using knives on their enemies. I understood immediately what had happened. We had come to a fork where we could have gone left or right. We veered right. This had been the wrong decision. But our choice was irreversible. We were stuck.

When at last we reached the safety of the trail along the coast, we burst out laughing. We could not stop laughing. It felt so wonderful to be alive! We smoked some more hashish and walked back into Lareche, where we bought some overpriced red wine and spent the night laughing, recounting in amazing detail almost every step of our harrowing walk down the narrow lane.

As we celebrated the joys of life, I remembered the decision that I had made in a yellow school bus on my way to a football game in Fossil, Oregon. That game was the beginning of a path without end. After that memorable night, I was to be condemned forever by a choice I made.

TWENTY

THE FOOTBALL FIELD AT Fossil—a rodeo grounds with white stripes laid out neatly on the dirt—was not exactly the Los Angeles Memorial Coliseum, but then we weren't the sissy Rams. We were Vikings, and we were ready to play anywhere. The students and folks from Fossil and the students and visitors from Umatilla both sat in the bleachers opposite the chutes where the bulls and bucking broncos were released.

The home team got the bench in front of the bleachers; we got a bench in front of the chutes, where the dirt smelled like fermented piss. But that wasn't the biggie problem, we being Vikings and all. Owing either to bad wiring or burned-out bulbs, not all of the overhead banks of lights worked; one end of the field—from the thirty-yard line to the chutes where the horses and animals were released for calf roping and steer wrestling—had been plunged into darkness. Better not to throw passes at that end. The running game wouldn't do much better, inasmuch as an oval wallow of mud ran from the fifteen-yard line to the chutes. This wasn't just so-so mud, it was borderline soupy, and what caused it was as uncertain and unexplained as the lights that didn't work. Was it a broken underground pipe? Had a prankster soaked it down with a hose? We didn't know and were never told.

We Vikings got to warm up in the dark, swampy end of

the field, presumably so we could accustom ourselves to the conditions. Playing on dirt instead of grass was bad enough, but the swamp in front of the end zone was flat crazy, and we were all joking and singing *doo-de-doo-de-doo-de-doo* "Twilight Zone" music.

Nevertheless, as the designated quarterback of the night, I stepped up behind the center, my arms white with tape, and sailed passes into the darkness at our ends and backs, who plopped through the mud like padded ducks. I acted like I knew what I was doing. Not that I would be calling any pass plays, but the team from Fossil needed to think we could pass if we wanted, never mind the telltale tape on my arms. Ordinarily, I couldn't throw a spiral to save my life, but on this occasion, for reasons that were beyond me, I was putting a neat, tight spin on the ball. I felt like Norm Van Brocklin or Y. A. Tittle. I was getting plenty of support, what with everybody calling, "Atta boy, Skeeter," "Do it, Skeets," and so on.

One reason that I wouldn't be calling any pass plays was that Coach Mungo did not believe in passing except under desperate circumstances. The idea of an interception drove him nuts, and what good was an incomplete pass: zero yards! Whenever we put the ball in the air, which was rare, he stared at his feet and clenched his teeth. The way he saw it, better to keep the ball on the ground and eat up the clock so the other team couldn't score. He did not believe in speed or deception either. He wasn't a flying wedge man, but close. He liked a straightforward kind of smash-mouth football; his strategy was to get as many bodies in front of the ball carrier as possible and horse the football up the field, eating up the clock in the process.

It was obvious that he would have preferred to remain entirely in his beloved single wing, the Notre Dame box, but the T-formation was the latest rage; if he lost without at least some tip of the hat to fashion, it would have been his job pronto. His solution was to devise a shift from the newfangled T-formation into the Notre Dame box. How he managed to do this was incomprehensible as far as I was concerned. It went like this:

The Vikings lined up in a straight T-formation with the fullback flanked by two halfbacks lined up directly behind the quarterback. The quarterback started the count, "Seven, nine . . ."

Then came the shift; the quarterback counted, "Three, four, five," as the backfield went into a little dance. The left halfback stepped to his right, directly behind the center, becoming the tailback. The fullback took one step forward and to his right, becoming a single-wing fullback. The right halfback, taking three giant strides forward and to his right, became a wing back. And the quarterback, moving three steps to his right, became the blocking back. It was this latter switch that puzzled me. Since the tailback ordinarily did the passing in the single wing, it would have made far better use of skills, if a confusing switching of bodies, to turn the quarterback into the tailback.

The quarterback, his transformation into the blocking back complete, finished the count, "Six, seven."

So there it was: if the ball was hiked on the opening seven or nine, the Vikings ran from the T-formation; if the Vikings shifted to the Notre Dame box, the ball was hiked on the second seven. I was to remain under the center for two counts as a quarterback, then switch to blocking back, where it would be my job to precede Billy Karady into the hole and go one-on-one with the Fossil linebacker.

Finally, it was time for the game to start. Our captain, Buddy Inskeep, went out for the flip of the coin, and we won.

I was not to play on defense or on the receiving team. I waited on the sideline as Billy Karady received the ball on the ten and ran it back to the forty-yard line. A good start.

Coach gave me a pat on the rump and said, "It's all yours, Skeets."

I felt a surge of confidence as I trotted out onto the field, and looked up at the two rows of faces watching me, waiting for the call. I said, "Shift right thirty-two." This was Billy Karady's number.

I went up to the line and checked out the Fossil defense. The middle linebacker was looking past me at Billy. I started our count. "Seven, nine."

We went into our shift. "Three, four, five." The shift was complete. "Six, seven." The ball was hiked to Billy.

I did my best to block for him, but he was met nearly head-on by the linebacker and gained only a couple of yards.

I went back to the huddle. I checked the yard marker, then the tape on my arm. I said, "Shift right thirty-one." This was a play for Buddy Inskeep, fullback up the gut.

With me in front of him doing my best, Buddy gained seven. I went back into the huddle and called on Buddy again, and he delivered for the first down and then some.

We went back into the huddle with a first down past mid-field. I looked up at the two rows of faces. Billy Karady had his thing going with hundred-yard games. He wanted the football real, real bad, but hey, hadn't the coach told me to find out what works and stay with it? Watch their defense. Look for weaknesses. Besides, Buddy was my good friend. Billy was a raging prick.

I called Buddy Inskeep's number all the way to the end zone.

The linebacker across from me, number fifty-five, a freckle-faced kid with a bony face and a shock of dirty blond hair over his eyes, was just as frustrated as Billy Karady. He was the most aggressive player on the Fossil defense, and his coach had obviously told him to key on Billy every play. But Billy wasn't getting the ball. Buddy was. That wasn't the way it was supposed to be.

I went one-on-one with this linebacker almost every play. Fifty-five was bigger and faster and more aggressive than me, face it. It didn't take long for me to understand that because he had his eye on Billy, I was able to get a better angle on him when Buddy carried the ball. He roamed back and forth along the line of scrimmage like a hungry coyote, eyeing Billy, trying to figure where he was going next.

In the huddles, Buddy was grinning like a shit-eating dog at this turn of events. Billy was downright sour. He had his hot-damn record of one-hundred-yard games on the line, and here I was, an upstart selecting the plays from tape on my arms, and calling Buddy Inskeep's number almost every down.

To keep the linebacker guessing, I let Billy carry the ball once in a while, but it wasn't what he was used to, that's for sure. He was the tailback, the main man of the Viking offense, not Buddy Inskeep. Buddy was a fullback. Fullbacks blocked.

The amazing thing about Buddy was that the more he got the ball, the more confident he became. He started ripping off yards in great chunks, which made it easier for me to keep giving him the ball. He was having fun. He had a huge grin on his face. With each down, Billy looked more and more sour.

Finally, Billy could take it no longer. In the huddle, he snarled, "How about giving me the goddamn ball once in a while, you little fucker?"

I looked Billy straight in the eye. I said, "Wham! Wham! Wham! Wham!" I called another play for Buddy, leaving it for the team to figure out the wham, wham business.

I knew my fun would likely end at halftime. We had a better team than they did—except for the roaming linebacker—and if we were ahead, Coach would make me call Billy's number whether I liked it or not.

Number fifty-five went flat nuts the second half. That's because I hit on an unusual tactic. I would catch the Linebacker's eye, mouth "Karady" and glance at the hole Billy was coming through. On Coach Mungo's instructions, I called Billy Karady's number just about every play, and each time there was

Fifty-five to meet him head-on at the line of scrimmage. Fifty-five loved to hit and teed off on Billy with glee and then some. The Vikings were ahead twenty to zip, so I couldn't very well argue for returning to Buddy Inskeep.

On the side, Rocky Holmes was carefully marking Billy's yardage total with each play, and, judging from the expressions on his and Coach's faces, whether or not Billy was going to maintain his record was questionable. He was taking a horrible beating, and was obviously slowing with each play.

Each play number fifty-five, enjoying my treachery, watched my eyes for his cue.

With less than a minute left, we were fourth and four at the edge the mud wallow. This was our own eighteen-yard line, which ordinarily would have called for a sensible punt, but Coach Mungo called our last time-out and motioned me to the sidelines.

I trotted to the sidelines and looked up at him. To put it mildly, he was concerned.

"Is Billy going to make it?" I said—as if I gave a flying fuck.

Holmes, looking over Mungo's shoulder, said, "He's two yards short."

Coach Mungo clenched his jaw.

I said, "I've been doing my best, Coach, but Fifty-five is everywhere."

He looked out at the mud wallow and grimaced. The football was sitting in the slop, but Fifty-five would get to fire off from dry ground. I knew what Coach was thinking. We had been running out of the single wing the entire game; now was the logical time to cross Fifty-five up with a quick opener out of the T-formation, but I hadn't been practicing taking snaps; Coach didn't trust me to give Billy a good handoff. It was foolish to try to go wide in that muck. The only alternative was to bull our way forward as we had been doing.

Coach said, "We'll run right over the son-of-a-bitch." He

called a spinner, in which the ball was hiked to Buddy, who spun and gave it to Billy off-tackle. The idea was to fake fifty-five into thinking Buddy was going up the gut as he had been doing in the first half.

"Got it, Coach," I said and went back out to the field.

I looked up at the two rows of faces waiting for the play. They all knew Billy's record was on the line. I called the play. "Let's do it," I said.

In the dim light, I trotted up to the center. As I had been doing the entire second half, I caught Fifty-five's eyes. Once again, I mouthed "Karady" and glanced at the hole in which Billy would be coming. Fifty-five grinned. He had no idea why I hated Billy, but he was having the game of his life. He obviously relished slamming the fabled Karady to the ground play after play.

I knew there would be no keeping my treachery secret. Somehow, word would get out. I didn't care.

I hoped Fifty-five wasn't tiring on this critical down. I counted, "Seven, nine, three, four, five."

Fifty-five moved down the line of scrimmage as we shifted into the single wing. He got low and dug his cleats into the dirt for a better start. His body tensed. He looked lean and mean and hungry. I remembered the line from Shakespeare in one of Miss Davis's English classes: *Yon Cassius has a lean and hungry look. Such men are dangerous.*

I counted, "Six, seven."

The ball was hiked.

TWENTY-ONE

BILLY KARADY WAS BILLY Karady. He had his admiring circle of suck-butts, but beyond that there weren't a whole lot of Vikings who were going to lose any sleep over the fact that his string of hundred-yard games had been broken. The Fossil linebacker had knocked the wind out of him on that fourth down in the mud wallow, separating him from both the ball and his helmet, but he had recovered, and now sat quietly in his seat as Ben Filcher fired up the bus for the ride back home.

We rode along a winding highway flanked by wheat stubble and summer fallow. We had won the game with a quarterback calling the plays from tape on his arms, and the players were all whoop-de-do and hot damn! Amid the celebratory din, Coach Mungo called me to the front of the bus.

His eyes looked concerned and his face was grave. He said, "I'd like a word with you, Ray."

I said, "Sure." My stomach twisted. I could tell by his manner what was up. He had somehow figured out what had happened. Just how, I had no idea.

He said, "I talked to the Fossil coach after the game. He congratulated us on our win, but he told me something he felt I should know."

"Oh?"

"Something I found hard to believe." His eyes looked grave

and puzzled and resigned all at once.

"What's that?" I said.

"He said that you were tipping off that linebacker of theirs the entire second half."

I furrowed my eyebrows. I was a terrible liar. "How would I do that?"

"By mouthing Billy's name and looking at the hole he was coming through. No damn wonder Billy couldn't run the ball."

I licked my lips. Caught. I said, softly, "Yes, I did that."

He looked at me, amazed. "You took something from Billy that can never be replaced. This is his fourth year as a starter. He has gained a hundred yards or more a game for three straight years. That's a remarkable record and a possible ticket to an athletic scholarship at a good school. You stole it from him. It's lost. Gone. I would never have believed you were capable of doing that kind of thing."

I shrugged. "I did it."

"Why? There's just got to be a reason for you to do something like that, but I can't imagine what it is. Are you jealous of him? What is it? I want you to tell me why."

"Billy knows why. Ask him."

He glanced down at the aisle at Karady, who was staring out of the window, obviously crestfallen that his record was gone.

Coach shook his head. "That won't do. You're the one who did it. I have a right to know. You tell me. You tell me now. Right here. You owe me that. You owe Billy too."

I said, "Billy tried to rape Angie Boudreau and would have if he hadn't been interrupted."

Coach looked astonished.

"It happened in the willows at the mouth of the Umatilla. Billy had problems with his car. You remember the day."

Coach looked out into the darkness. His face was an impenetrable mask.

I said, "He's been following us around ever since. He got

drunk and punched me in the face after the Brenda Lee concert in Pendleton, and then one night he started banging on the door when Angie and I were parked up in the buttes. I don't have to tell you what we were doing. Use your imagination."

He cleared his throat. "He did what?"

"That was the topper, as far as I was concerned. There comes a time when he has to know that we won't take it anymore. That we will strike back. We have an elementary right to defend ourselves. It's basic."

He switched his gaze back down the bus. The celebrating continued, but on a subdued level. Everybody was obviously wondering what Coach and I were talking about with such earnestness. Billy Karady, who had been looking out at the darkness, now turned his attention our way. He knew what we were talking about.

I said, "You say I took something from Billy that can't be replaced. That's correct. I did that. I did it deliberately. I ambushed him. Maximum chickenshit, if you don't know the whole story. The truth is he had it coming. He deserved it. You should ask him yourself what he did. Listen to what he says. Compare his story to mine, and decide for yourself which one of us is lying."

"I . . ." He closed his mouth.

"Three girls have been raped and murdered—two in Kennewick, one outside Hermiston. You want to think about that?"

He cocked his head, watching me. "Have you and Angie talked to the police about this?"

"Yes, we did. We told them the truth."

Coach Mungo took a deep breath and let the air out slowly. He looked tormented. He said, "What did they have to say?"

"That Angie shouldn't go anywhere alone."

"Do they think Billy murdered those girls?"

I shrugged. "You'll have to ask them. He tried to rape Angie. No telling what else he might have done."

Coach knew I was telling him the truth. He said, "I would

appreciate it if you kept this conversation between us."

"I'll have to tell Angie and the police officer we talked to. I can't hold out on them."

"But nobody else."

"Nobody else," I said. "No reason."

Coach's entire body slumped.

"This is serious business. I have to think about Angie's safety."

"You can go back to your seat now, Ray." His voice was tired. Coach was not a bad person. He knew I wasn't either. He knew that I would have never pulled a horseshit stunt like that if I hadn't been pushed in the extreme.

As I drew alongside Billy Karady in the aisle, he looked up at me with raw hatred in his eyes. A prick with ears, he was. He knew what I had done to him in the second half. Either Coach Mungo had told him, or he had figured it out for himself. Either way, he knew.

It was true what Coach had said. I had taken from Billy something that couldn't be replaced. In a manner of speaking, I had raped him. As I walked past, I said, quietly, "Tit for tat. How does it feel?"

Behind me, he murmured, "You fucked over the wrong guy, pal."

I didn't say anything. I sat down. It was just possible, as my mother would have said, that I had bitten off more than I could chew.

My conversation with Coach Mungo was over. The horsing around picked up, with my teammates calling me Johnny Unitas and everything, but I was frightened to the bone. Billy Karady would have his revenge; there was no doubting that.

That night in The Coop, I turned on the electric heater and lay in bed thinking. I couldn't sleep. I turned on my right side, then my left, then on my back and over onto my stomach. I had committed legal theft in Fossil. I had stolen something from Billy Karady that was akin to Don Larsen's perfect game in the World Series. A four-year run of hundred-yard games couldn't be topped. It could be tied maybe, but never topped.

I flipped onto my back.

What if somebody had done that to me, screwed me out of a record like that? What would I do?

You fucked over the wrong guy, pal.

I had acted on impulse. I had been given an unusual opportunity, and I had acted without considering the consequences. I had been filled with too much nonsense about existentialism. Philosophy was great to talk about and everything, but this was entirely different. Existentialism had a dangerous edge to it. I remembered the little saying that was a favorite of my cousin Eddie: *If you ever get hit by a bucket of shit, be sure to close your eyes.* Right.

Now I had earned the lasting hatred of a possible murderer. I tried to put myself in his position. What would he do next?

I turned over on my stomach. Tom Agnopolous said the police had no physical evidence in the murders of the girls. I wondered how many murderers actually got caught and convicted. How many murderers just disappeared? There had to be means, motive, and opportunity. And there had to be a body, proof that a murder actually occurred. Juries didn't convict people without proof. If he wanted, Billy Karady could just throw open the door of The Coop and slit my throat and disappear and likely get away with it. Maybe he would be questioned, after what I had done to him. But would there be any proof?

How many murders went unsolved? What were the statistics? Was this some awful, appalling number that never got reported because both cops and journalists saw no point in scaring the daylights out of the public? What was the truth?

I saw the linebacker looking at me before the start of each play, an eager accomplice in my treachery.

You fucked over the wrong guy, pal.

I tried my left side. I was cold. I turned up the heat. I had made an awful, screwed decision from which there was no turning back. It was one thing to defend myself against Billy Karady and avoid him. It was another to steal from him the pride of his existence. I had taken a step into lethal danger.

I flipped onto my left back again. I checked the clock on the floor by my bed. Four o'clock. There would be no sleeping that night, I knew. How much better my life would have been had none of this happened. If I had not been there that night cleaning the toilets at Baker's? If Angie hadn't arrived on that particular bus? If I hadn't been screening for arrowheads the next morning? If I hadn't caught Billy Karady soda popping?

If, if, if, if, if. . . .

Leading deeper and deeper into the thicket of the unknown. My stomach turned.

I thought about the look on Coach Mungo's face when I told him why I had screwed Billy out of his record. I liked Coach. I didn't hold it against him that he never put me into any kind of game. I had been small, but slow. I was now average, but still not especially aggressive or coordinated. An athlete didn't think; he just acted. I thought too much. There was something about Coach's reaction that had gone beyond mere shock. His pain had been deep and powerful—something that went beyond his concern for one of his players. I didn't understand it, but I knew it was there.

Albert Camus would have said that by taking a risk, by challenging a murderer, I was feeling life. Stupid fucking Frenchman. Such bullshit!

I couldn't sleep. What could I do besides wait? Nothing.

You fucked over the wrong guy, pal.

I heard geese outside, rising off the Columbia. Winter was coming on, and they were heading south. Up there, the cold wind was howling. Inside The Coop, there was a terrible stillness.

• • •

Everybody else had a pistol or an assault rifle—an Uzi, a Hechler and Koch, or an M-16. I had an automatic shotgun with no plug so I could get off five uninterrupted rounds if necessary. Just point and shoot. We were driving down a narrow road through tall sugarcane near Mt. Canlaon on the island of Negros in the Philippines. This was territory disputed by the New People's Army.

Owing to the sugarcane, there was no wind at all here—a form of sweltering, suffocating doldrums.

Suddenly, the road in front of us was blocked by a vehicle loaded with men brandishing assault rifles. One of them appeared to be fixing a flat tire. Were these soldiers of the Philippine army, or were they NPA? The Philippine army did not have the resources to issue uniforms to all its troops, so there was no telling for sure.

In my vehicle, a Toyota Landcruiser, the safeties went off. Click, click, click, click. *I readied my shotgun.*

The driver put the Toyota in reverse, but did not move. The engine idled. My host's personal bodyguard warily got out to see who the armed men were. There was nothing to do but wait. Would the moment explode into a carnage of blood and bullets, or would it provide entertaining stories for marienda, *our daily session of beer drinking and bullshit?*

The men with the flat tire turned out to be soldiers.

Later, as we drove out of the cane field, laughing, I remembered my walk down the lane in the Berber village; I was struck by similarity of the aftermath—jubilation, exuberance, a feeling of intense existence.

That afternoon, in addition to our usual San Miguel, my Filipino friends and I had a special treat for marienda . . . *celebrate our successful passage through the cane field, we had* putay baboy, *pork pussies artfully skewered on bamboo sticks and cooked over charcoal. But the encounter in the cane field had been a quick burst of danger, then it was over. Better that, I thought, than the lingering, corrosive fear of Billy Karady that kept me in permanent exile.*

TWENTY·TWO

TOM AGNOPOLOUS WAS NOW a regular item with Gracie, and when he came to the Hawkins's residence to pick her up the next night, he was all full of congratulations about the Vikings' victory in Fossil. There had been a small item in the *Oregonian* telling how the Umatilla Viking quarterback, Ray Hawkins, had played the game with the plays taped to his arm. It also told how Billy Karady's string of hundred-yard games had been stopped at thirty-three straight, thanks to a bone-jarring tackle in the final minute of the game.

I took Tom to The Coop, ostensibly to show him some arrowheads that I had found, and told him what I had done to Billy.

He listened, pretending at first to be interested in my collection of detective and crime novels. He didn't say much when I told him about the first half—giving the ball to Buddy Inskeep, but when I got to the second half and my unspoken agreement with the Fossil linebacker, his mouth dropped. "You did what?"

I felt the old flutter in my guts. "The opportunity presented itself, so I did it."

He looked at me in disbelief. "Jesus, Ray. You kick a guy in the balls like that, he's going to figure a way to kick back. You ever think of that?"

"He should have thought about that before he tried to rape

Angie. You try to rape somebody, you have to expect they'll try to rape back."

"That's different," he said.

"Is it? Whether Angie gets her revenge directly or I help her out, what difference does it make? Or what about banging on the door of the Wheeled Turd? You see somebody parked in the buttes, you leave them alone. That's elementary."

He suppressed a smile. "Except if it's me."

"You're a state bull doing your job. That's different."

"I'm paid to be an asshole."

"Right," I said. "But I bet you've never banged on anybody's door. What do you do, flip your lights off and on a couple of times to give them a little warning?"

He grinned.

"See, you're an asshole cop, but an okay asshole cop, or I wouldn't have encouraged you to date Gracie. Unfortunately, my linebacker pal told the Fossil coach what we had done, and he told Coach Mungo. On the way home, Coach called me to the front of the bus and asked me why I did it."

"What did you say?"

"I told him the truth."

"Including talking to me?"

I nodded yes. "I told him everything. You should have seen the look on his face. It was like I'd whacked him on the head with a Louisville slugger."

Tom sighed. "Well, he had to find out sooner or later, I guess."

"He told me not to tell anybody. Except for you and Angie. I agreed, and I'll keep my word. What happens now?"

"We keep an eye on Billy. We don't have any evidence linking him to the murdered girls. Not much else we can do."

"You could talk to him," I said.

"True. But it wouldn't do any good. It's impossible to catch anybody in a contradiction unless you have something concrete. We don't have any evidence. Not a shred. If we had one teensy-tiny little secret, we could maybe build on that. We don't have anything."

"So you're telling me all you can do is watch him and hope he doesn't do it again."

"That's about it, Ray. That's why I don't like hearing that you went out of your way to poke a stick in his eye. Better to let sleeping dogs lie."

"So now if he murders Angie, we can all say it was my fault."

He looked annoyed. "I didn't say that."

"That's what it comes down to, isn't it? We're supposed to spend all our time figuring out how to stay out of his way and not offend His Majesty. He's the cocksucker, not us. We haven't done anything but mind our own business."

"Until you screwed him out of his record. That's gone forever."

"Well, there's that," I said. "That was probably a mistake, I agree."

He picked up another paperback from my collection. "James M. Cain. Who is this guy?" He flipped through a copy of *Double Indemnity*.

"Judging from his books, a writer who's had his problems with women," I said.

"Didn't they make a movie out of that with Barbara Stanwyck or somebody?"

"Barbara Stanwyck and Fred MacMurray," I said.

"Is he any good?"

"Cain?"

"The *Double Indemnity* guy."

I said, "I'm no literary critic or anything like that, but I think he's very good. He likes to write these stories about people who fall in love and get themselves into a jam."

"How do they turn out, good or bad?"

I grimaced. "Almost always bad."

• • •

Billy Karady did not cruise by Angie Boudreau's house that day or the next. This was unsettling in the extreme. Better to see him prowling, sharklike, in his wonderful Cunt Wagon, than for him to simply withdraw. A shark would have been predictable to some extent. There were do's and don'ts in shark-infested water. But Billy Karady was traveling one brick shy of a full load. Angie was a link between Billy and the murdered girls, and I had deliberately robbed him of his dream football record. He wasn't about to let those facts rest. Attempted rape. Casual assault. Pounding on our door in the buttes. Who knew what he was capable of doing next?

If he had continued stalking Angie, we would have had grist for a complaint to the Oregon State Police, but maybe somebody, most likely Coach Mungo, had had a serious talk with him.

It wasn't that Billy was ignoring us completely. He was likely incapable of doing that. He wanted to be careful, yet he wanted us to know that he was still there. He hadn't quit or retreated from our lives. He wouldn't do that. Or possibly couldn't. He just didn't want to do anything that could be witnessed and used as evidence against him. If we happened to drive down Main Street past the parked Cunt Wagon with him staring at us with his lethal lizard eyes, we couldn't very well charge that he was harassing us. If we found him staring down the hall in our direction at school, who was to say he wasn't looking at something beyond us?

The Snappy Snack in Hermiston was the favorite of the west end of Umatilla County, and that's where the girls were to be found. That was also Billy Karady's favorite. He was always there, showing off his Cunt Wagon and impressing the assembled beavers, as he called them. To shoot a beaver was to sneak a quick look up a girl's legs; that was where the fur was, the much-sought-after pelt that gripped his imagination. Mine too.

Beavers from several high schools ordinarily gathered at the Snappy Snack, bedecked in their sweaters, Dickies, long skirts, white bucks, and rolled socks. A new hirsute fashion was in the news, the bouffant, in which females piled their hair high on their heads like huge beehives; both Angie and I knew what that meant. In a few months all the girls in Umatilla would be walking around with their heads looking like huge beehives.

We also knew that Billy Karady, sitting back in his Cunt Wagon with his practiced James Dean look—Mr. Rebel—didn't give a damn what was on top of a beaver's head—much less what was inside it. He was only interested in the quality of the pelt down below, and he had demonstrated interest in Angie's.

Two days after I had scuttled his record at Fossil, Billy Karady showed up at the Dairy Queen in Umatilla and ordered a cheeseburger. No big deal in the course of human events, but for cool Billy, it was a major break. It was hard to believe he was that hungry: there were precious few beavers at the DQ to admire his Cunt Wagon or to speculate on the wonders of his mighty wad. But the following night he was back. Within a week he was a regular. But he didn't go there any old time. Only when Gracie was working the window. That was disconcerting in the extreme.

I was traveling solo on an Indonesian vessel between Manado, on the northern tip of the Minahassa Peninsula of the island of Sulawesi, to the town of Balikpapan on the southeast coast of Borneo. This was the southern edge of the Celebes Sea. The decks of the vessel were covered with folding canvas cots—so many there was little or no room for the second-class passengers to stand on the deck. The interior was packed as well, including my cramped first-class cabin, which I shared with seven prosperous Indonesians.

The cabin was sweltering, but there was nowhere to escape. The first night out, I was having trouble sleeping because the interior light remained on to frustrate thievery if not outright murder. I had always found it hard to sleep with light in my eyes.

Suddenly the shuddering engines of the vessel stopped. Lying there in the bunk that was too short for me, awash with sweat, annoyed by the light, I waited for the engine to restart. I waited and waited. Nothing. I checked my watch. The vessel had been drifting for more than an hour.

Taking my notebook computer and day pack with me, I went outside to find a bit of space in the cool night air. As I did, the decks began to pitch. A tropical storm was brewing. Within minutes, the vessel began to wallow in growing troughs. Still the engines did not start. It was obvious that the captain needed to pilot his ship into the wind, but no, we drifted.

A large wave crashed over the rail, drenching the second-class passengers sleeping on their cots. Soon they were all awake and alarmed and jabbering in their many languages.

Still the ship drifted, engines silent. There was nothing the other passengers or I could do. Were we to be capsized or driven aground by the storm, or would the crew get the engines running so they could regain their course? Nobody told us what had gone wrong with the engines or how long it would take to fix them. We were at the mercy of events beyond our control. All we could do was wait, and ponder our fate.

A broken engine. An incompetent crew. A storm.

Was this to be it, then?

I had seen stories like this before on CNN. But it happened to other people, not me. I'd had a chance to assess the dangers before walking through the Berber village, so the responsibility for the screwup had been mine. In my encounter with the NPA, I'd had a shotgun in my lap—the ability to defend myself.

Now, surrounded by people talking a language I did not understand, I was trapped by circumstances. I had no options. I could only wait and hope. I waited with a dry mouth to see who would win the mortal contest—the gathering wind or the

Indonesian mechanics working feverishly on the stalled engine.

It struck me that this was roughly my situation with respect to Billy Karady. I was drifting in dangerous exile. Living with such vague angst for decades on end was wearing. I began thinking about ending my exile. If I returned to the United States and he was out there yet stalking me, I would at last confront him and bring our struggle to its final conclusion.

TWENTY·THREE

TWO DAYS LATER, I was at the window of the DQ ordering hamburgers from Gracie for Angie and me when Billy Karady rumbled up in his Cunt Wagon. Eyeing him and handing my order through the window, Gracie said, "Here's your wonderful friend in his cool black car."

I glanced at Billy. "Some friend."

"He gives me the creeps."

"He should," I said.

"He just sits there in his car and stares at me. Spooky."

I raised an eyebrow. "Come on, Gracie, don't give me that. I bet a lot of people stare at you. Bumpers like those." I teased her, but I didn't like the idea of Billy Karady taking an interest in her. Not good.

"Oh, stop it."

"Have you told Tom about him?"

"Tom says he has a right to come here if he wants, as long as he behaves himself. The best thing to do is to ignore him, Tom says."

"Right," I said.

Apparently taking that as his cue, Billy got out of the Wagon and sauntered to the window. "Evening, Skeets. I see where you got your name in the *Oregonian*. Hotshot quarterback with the plays taped on his arms. Real hero. Large Coke,

Gracie." He eyed the top of her white uniform. "You're looking real fine tonight, I have to say."

Billy knew I didn't like him leering at her like that. My sister and my girlfriend were my turf. I felt like I should do something to back him down, but what? Challenge him to a fight? He was bigger and stronger and faster than I was; he would have kicked the shit out of me.

Gracie, wanting to get rid of him, gave him his Coke immediately. Having succeeded in embarrassing Gracie and humiliating me, Billy took his Coke and sauntered leisurely back to the Wagon. He took a slurp of Coke, fired up the engine, and rumbled off.

Watching him, Gracie said, " 'Ignore him,' Tom says." She bunched her face in frustration. "How am I supposed to ignore somebody like that?"

"Good point," I said.

She said, "Tom's a cop. You'd think a cop could do something to make him leave me alone."

I rejoined Angie on the front seat. What could I do? What could anybody do to somebody with an ego like that? What he wanted, Billy Karady took—screw anybody who might be in his way. His obsession with Angie was bad enough; I sure as hell didn't like him adding Gracie to his list.

Later, Angie and I were on our way to Hermiston on the road flanking the Umatilla River when a set of headlights appeared behind me. The driver flipped them on high beam, nearly blinding me.

Squinting, I checked out the lights through my rearview mirror. "Dim 'em, asshole," I said.

The lights drew swiftly closer. It was a pickup.

WHUMP! The pickup banged into my bumper.

I speeded up.

The pickup drew closer.

WHUMP!

"Jesus," I said.

Angie, holding on, turned in the seat, staring back into the high beams. "Is it him, do you think?"

"Could be," I said.

Coming up was a notorious stretch of highway directly above the river. Here was where Gracie's husband had run off the road and drowned, and he wasn't the first. There were metal guardrails here, yes, but the highway also curved a couple of times, and if a vehicle hit the rails at the right angle, it would just sail over the top.

I put the accelerator to the floorboard. "Hold on," I said.

The dangerous stretch was coming up.

I rounded the first curve, going far too fast.

The pickup stayed right behind me.

I negotiated the second curve, still going too fast.

The river was below us and to our right a dark gloom in the night. This was October, and the river was low, but there was still plenty of water down there.

The pickup started to pass.

As it did, I slammed on the brakes.

The driver yanked the steering wheel, swerving in my direction.

WHACK!

The pickup missed a broadside hit, which was the driver's intention, but its left rear bumper clipped the Turd's right front bumper. The blow knocked the Turd 180 degrees, and I found myself sliding backwards facing Umatilla. In my mirror, I could see the pickup skid onto the gravel shoulder and bounce off the metal guardrail above the river.

I came to a stop. The Turd's engine was stalled. I tromped on the floorboard starter. *Rrrrrr. Rrrrrr. Rrrrrr.* The damn thing didn't want to start.

"He's turning around. He's coming back," Angie said.

Rrrrr. Rrrrr. Rrrrr.

"Hurry."

The Wheeled Turd fired up. Shifting gears for all I was worth, I headed back toward Umatilla pretending to be Juan Fangio or Bill Vukovich.

As we entered the city limits, the pickup, a light green Ford, zoomed around us. We could clearly see the driver, grinning malevolently at us as he passed:

Billy Karady.

When we got back to Umatilla, I parked the Wheeled Turd at the side of Baker's Drugstore, which was across the street from Coach Mungo's apartment. Billy Karady's Cunt Wagon was parked outside the front door. I got out to inspect The Turd and found it was missing its front bumper, and there was a fresh scrape on my left fender.

Angie and I went inside Baker's. I called the Oregon State Police and asked for Tom Agnopolous. He was out, I was told. I gave the lady the number of the phone booth. "It's important," I said.

Angie and I ordered cups of coffee. Five minutes later, Tom called. I told him what happened and where we were.

He said Gracie had called him earlier complaining about Billy Karady hanging out at the DQ. He was maximum pissed. "Sit tight. I'll be right over," he said.

"What are you going to do?"

"Have a talk with Coach Mungo and Billy if I can find him. You stay put now. I'm on my way."

Forty-five minutes later, Tom Agnopolous came into Baker's. He did not look happy. He looked downright sour, in fact. He joined us at the counter and ordered a cup of coffee himself.

"What happened?" I said.

"I spotted the pickup parked in front of the Silver Dollar. There's brown paint on the right rear bumper." The Silver Dollar was just around the corner from Coach Mungo's apartment.

"You check the Turd?"

"Yes, I did."

"See there. Turd scrapings. What did I tell you."

"The pickup belongs to Harold Darnell, who works over at Pendleton Grain Growers."

I knew Harold Darnell. He was the guy who loaded gunnysacks of oats into the trunk of my car. "You know Harold Darnell. And you know damn well he's not the kind of guy who is running around trying to force people off the road," I said. "Did you talk to him?"

"Yes, I did. He's been shooting pool with his friends for the last two hours. He left his keys in his pickup. He's as pissed as you."

"There you go. Got that hot-damn Billy Karady. Easy bust."

Tom grimaced. "Coach Mungo and Billy were eating popcorn and drinking RC colas when I showed up. Mungo says Billy has been home all evening. Says they've been watching television."

"What?" I could hardly believe he said that. This was Coach Mungo. Coach. How could he say something like that?

"They're lying, both of them," Angie said.

"She's right. That's a goddamn lie. Watching what? 'The Twilight Zone'?" I said.

"You've got reason to be sore," Tom said.

"It was him," I said. "He tried to push us into the Umatilla River. That's not a little funsies joke. That's the stretch where Len drowned."

"I believe you, but it's your word against theirs," he said. "Brian Mungo survived the Bataan Death March and is a highly respected coach. With Billy Karady at tailback, he's also got a shot the state football championship."

"What do we do now?" Angie said.

"We wait."

"Right," I said.

"We wait. Sooner or later Billy Karady will make a mistake. When he does, he's ours."

"He tried to run us off the road. He did it deliberately. If I hadn't slammed on my brakes in time, the Turd would likely have been knocked into the river. Who knows what would have happened then?"

"I know. I know."

I mocked him. "You know. You know." Tom was a state cop and all, but he was still my sister's boyfriend and therefore mockable. "The question is, when are you going to do something about him? Angie and I are obviously on his list. Maybe now he's added Gracie. Teach all of us a thing or two, you included. You ever stop to think of that?"

Agnopolous had a distant look in his eye. "Yes, Ray, I've thought of that."

"I saw him at the DQ tonight, staring at Gracie like she was standing there naked. She's scared," I said.

"Yes, she is."

"Jesus Christ, isn't there anything we can do about this ass-hole? He tried to rape Angie. He poked me in the face in Pendleton. That was entirely without provocation, unless you count my having had the temerity to ask Brenda Lee to dance. He banged on our door in the buttes. He tried to bump us into the Umatilla River with a stolen pickup, for Christ's sake. His last name is begins with a *K*, same as the letter scratched on the chests of the dead girls. How much more does it take? How much? We have a right to ask that question."

Tom frowned. "Yes, you do, that's a fact."

"What are we supposed to do, just wait around until he takes us under?"

"I told Billy there'll be no more hanging out at the DQ or bothering you two or we'll get a legal restraining order. I also told him he's on our list of suspects for the rapes and murders. If he's smart, maybe he'll lay low for a while. That will give us the time we need to come up with some physical evidence. In the meantime, I'll buy you a new bumper," he said. "You can't drive around without a bumper."

"A new bumper. Great."

"You don't want it?"

"I'll take it. I'll take it," I said quickly. I couldn't stay sore at Tom Agnopolous. None of this was his fault. He was in love with Gracie. He didn't want her sucked into Billy Karady's obsession any more than I did. God knows what inner turmoil he was going through. But he was a state cop. He had sworn to uphold the rules of state cophood. He had to behave like a state cop.

TWENTY-FOUR

ANGIE BOUDREAU AND I had committed no crimes that we were aware of, unless my robbing Billy Karady of his football record was a form of grand larceny. Angie had objected to being raped and so had screamed, which was presumably her right. Would any preacher at any pulpit in the land or any politician on the stump have suggested she remain silent and accept her fate? I had responded to an obvious cry for help and had interrupted Billy Karady before he got his unwelcome end in. I assumed no priest, preacher, or politician would have advised me to remain silent in those circumstances.

For those sins, Billy had made our lives miserable, and he seemed to be pushing the stakes higher and higher.

One attempted rape did not prove Billy had succeeded in raping and then murdering three other girls, but in a population as small and isolated as that of northeastern Oregon and southeast Washington in 1957, he had to be a suspect. One thing was obvious. He hated us with a murderous obsession. If he was the murderer, he was capable of killing us as well, and it was possible that he had added Gracie to his list.

What could we do to defend ourselves?

The next night, Angie and I were on our way to Hermiston to pick up some oats and milk filters from Pendleton Grain Growers. As we passed the spot where Billy had tried to run us off the road, Angie said, "Maybe we should kill him."

I had been thinking the same thing myself; only I didn't have the hair to be the first to mention the subject. "Murder him?"

She cocked her head and said, mildly, "Self-defense isn't murder, is it? We have a right to defend ourselves. What good are moral lectures and laws prohibiting murder when you're being stalked by a killer? Are we supposed to take our chances and hope Tom Agnopolous finds some evidence before Billy gets to us?"

We rode in silence for a minute, both of us lost in our private thoughts. Angie and I had an advantage over the great vast herd of believing cretins who were forced not only to trust in the cops, but to revere them like they were distant gods in blue uniforms. At least, I knew one of them personally. Tom Agnopolous's ambition was to be my brother-in-law one day. He was not so stupid as to deny the logical connection between Billy Karady's hatred of me and his sudden interest in the DQ in Umatilla. Gracie was now threatened.

Be careful, Tom had said. Right. Like the cops were going to have people following us around day and night to make sure nothing happened to us.

Angie said, "If the state police can't protect us, who will? Are we to be good little lambs and wait for enough evidence to convince a sports-loving prosecutor? Or are we supposed to pray along with Oral Roberts and hope for divine intervention?"

I grinned. "Maybe our prayers would come true, and Jack Webb would show up flashing badge 714. 'Morning, Mr. Karady. We're police officers. We'd like to ask you a few routine questions.' "

Angie laughed. "And Billy, knees knocking, thinking, *Oh no, Jack Webb, the jig is up,* will bolt and run. Guilty, guilty, guilty!"

But we were not in the city and county of Los Angeles. We were in Umatilla, Oregon, surrounded by sagebrush, cacti, and sand. I said, "You're saying, 'Why shouldn't we act in self-defense?'"

"Correct. What good are laws that require us to await our fate like little Goodie Two-Shoes and her pal Skeeter, or go hide in California or somewhere. We don't know anybody in California."

"Good point," I said.

"Why should we allow our lives to be uprooted by a whim of somebody else's obsession? Why?"

I didn't say a thing. I couldn't answer her question. We didn't say anything more about the subject until the way back home from Hermiston, when I blurted out, "There should be no body. Billy Karady should simply disappear. If there's no body, there's no proof a crime has been committed."

Angie put her finger to her chin, thinking. "He's eighteen years old and living with his coach. His parents have moved to California. Who is to say what might happen to a kid like that or what he might do? Maybe he just took off. Who's to know?"

I said, "Owing to our past run-ins with Billy, the two of us will have to have an alibi of some sort. And there should be no evidence linking us with the murder."

"I agree. The perfect crime," she said.

Did we have a logical choice to do anything other than enter into this discussion? We were not Leopold and Loeb planning the murder of Bobby Franks just to prove we could get away with it. We had no choice. It was defend ourselves or risk dying.

At first talking about murdering Billy Karady had a strange, almost surreal quality about it, but that had suddenly disappeared. Now it was as though we were discussing a new recipe for spaghetti. How much garlic we should use. How many tomatoes.

"I agree," I said. "The perfect crime or something close to it."

"Something simple, rather than complicated. What can go wrong, will."

I said, "Everybody knows that. For example, we shouldn't dump the body in the river. Bodies, or parts of bodies, have an awful habit of washing up later on. Better to bury him in the desert somewhere."

"It would have to be deep enough to prevent him from being dug up by animals. The next question is how we can do that without leaving a trail. We have to answer all the questions."

What could go wrong and why? What were the odds of this or that unforeseen circumstance? Our discussion of murder inevitably turned into an intellectual game.

"Hey, look there!" Angie said.

Billy Karady was sailing along the top of the railroad tracks on top of his Cunt Wagon.

Billy gave us a wave. He seemed in a cheerful mood.

Not long after the incident of the ferry, I lived for three months in Chung King Manor on the Kowloon Peninsula of Hong Kong colony. Chung King, on Nathan Road, was famous for its cheapie accommodations—diminutive, Spartan rooms favored by student and hippie travelers. The lower floors were a hive of shops and Indian and Pakistani eateries. Getting to the rooms on the upper floors required impossible waits for tiny, packed elevators or taking the stairs that led through kitchens down dank, filthy, cluttered hallways.

My room was off-white in color and hardly larger than a coffin, and had contained no furniture other than a single pee- and come-stained mattress on the floor. Following the crazed trail of stairs to the ground level had taken twenty minutes. Later, I told an Irishman in Bangkok about the experience, and the Irishman, an old Asia hand who knew all about Chung King Manor, burst out laughing. He thought I was crazy for living there.

In Chung King, I fell into the habit of eating supper at a

Nepalese cafe. I sat at a small table each night and ate my spicy vegetables with companionable Gurkha soldiers, mercenaries for the British army; after supper, we all watched Indian movies. These romances and adventure stories were usually in the Hindi language, but I didn't care; I found the English-speaking Gurkhas more amiable and interesting company than American suits. In fact, I found suits to be more lethal because most of them either had no idea who they were or routinely lied to themselves. The Gurkhas were unapologetic killers. They had hired themselves out to the Brits and were proud of it.

I had a long-standing obsession of rereading, page by page, The Elements of Style, *a slender little book on writing by William Strunk, Jr., formerly a professor at Cornell University, with additions by his onetime student E. B. White. It wasn't that I felt that I would become as good a writer as White; it was fun to reread the book. Each time through it, I learned. And learning, for me, had been a lifelong form of pleasure. Strunk and White were like a couple of writing coaches I could tuck into my hip pocket. Between books or turns on the laptop, I checked Strunk and White on matters of form.*

One night sitting there with the Gurkha lovers of romance and adventure, I was well into Part II, "Principles of Composition," when I came, once again, upon reminder sixteen: use definite, specific, concrete language:

"Prefer the specific to the general, the definite to the vague, the concrete to the abstract."

As usual Strunk and White gave examples of good and bad sentences: the poor on the left; the better on the right.

A period of unfavorable weather set in.	It rained everyday for a week.
He showed satisfaction as he took possession of his well-earned reward.	He grinned as he pocketed the coin.

Sitting there with the companionable Gurkhas in Chung King Manor, I understood that committing a satisfactory murder was in many ways analogous to composing a sentence; it should be straightforward, vigorous, and to the point. No clutter.

Strunk and White said the emphasis of the sentence should come at the end, not at the beginning. There should be no ambiguity. The meaning should be clear. I tried to follow that form in the murders I imagined in my fiction. But all that came later, after Billy Karady.

In riding on the top of his car, Billy Karady was upping the ante in what had become the latest sport at Umatilla. Somebody had discovered that the wheel base of cars made just after World II exactly matched the rails. We assumed this had something to do with national defense; if the Japanese bombed the roads, our troops could still drive cars and light trucks on rails or whatever. All a person had to do to drive on the rails was to find an intersection, get the tires aligned with the steel, then proceed slowly. The pressure of the rails made a natural groove in the tires; letting some air out was an advantage, but not necessary.

The trick was not to go too fast or to attempt to steer, although a car could be driven off the rails and out of the way of an oncoming train. Trying to steer was the easiest way to get a car to slip off the rails. Once off, a derailed car was impossible to get back on the steel again; it had to be driven to the next intersection on top of the ties, a bone-jarring exercise that was hard on the tires and suspension, not to mention the driver's nerves.

At first, the competition for driving on rails was always at night. Who had the courage to do it even once? After virtually everybody had lost his cherry, the challenge was escalated to separate wusses from those with real hair. Who had the balls to cross the railroad bridge over the Umatilla River?

By now, almost everybody had done that, including me.

Who had the courage to take on the greatest stretch of tracks between crossings? That was the current challenge.

In those years, cars had both chokes and throttles. It was possible to get a car rolling on the rails, adjust its speed with the throttle, and climb on top of the roof, as Billy was doing. If the Cunt Wagon slipped off the rails, he'd have to climb back through the window with the tires whacking and banging along on the ties at a fixed speed. On top of that, he was driving a three-mile stretch in daylight. No question that this was major hair.

Watching fearless Billy glide by in the opposite direction, I said, "What if we killed him with a blow to the head? We put him in the front seat of his Cunt Wagon. We put the car on the rail and get it started. We throttle it for a steady ten miles an hour, or whatever is safe. We jump and go somewhere to establish an alibi. The Cunt Wagon continues, in the middle of the night, until it smashes square into the front of a west-bound freight train. *Ka-bam*!"

Angie turned, watching Billy disappear around a curve. "What happens if they change the train schedule, and we don't know about it?"

"There's that," I said.

"Also, why on earth wouldn't he just drive his car off the tracks when he saw the oncoming train. No problem doing that."

"Picky. Picky."

She said, "The basic idea is interesting, I'll admit. Creative."

We rode for a minute in silence, then she said, "Here's a variation of the theme. One of our problems was finding a place to bury his body, right?"

"Right."

"Well, under ordinary circumstances that covers just about any place that can be reached by car."

I said, "Lot of territory around here."

"Ahh," she said, "but the risk of its being found always remains. Better to bury it in a place that can only be reached by foot or . . . you see what I'm driving at?

"Or by rail."

"We kill him. We drive him down the rail to an isolated spot where cars don't go, and we bury him there. We drive off, leaving no trail. Who's going to look out there?"

Angie grinned.

"There you go. Not bad."

"A possibility, do you think?"

"Not bad, not half-bad."

That's how we addressed each plan. First the basic idea. Then a list of things that could go wrong. We were enthusiasts. We talked through every detail, but we really didn't expect anything would go wrong. Not if we were careful and smart enough. And we didn't believe there was a big hurry. We had time enough to do everything right. After he had tried to run us off the road and Coach Mungo had been forced to lie to an Oregon state cop to save his ass, even Billy Karady would have brains enough to lay low for awhile.

Tom Agnopolous had made it clear Billy's name was at the top of the list of K murder suspects.

Until now the phrases *law of the jungle* and *state of nature* were abstractions. But when you were threatened by a flesh-and-blood foe who meant to rape or kill you, they became real.

Angie and I had no idea how much of a reprieve we would have from Billy's obsession. Weeks seemed likely. Perhaps even months. But we weren't thinking first strike. We would prepare ourselves. If he kept his distance, fine. Good riddance. But if he returned with his obsession intact, Angie and I had no choice but to somehow defend ourselves. To do nothing was to gamble with our lives.

We decided that next time Billy Karady stepped over the line and threatened us in any way, we would launch a preemptive strike big, big time.

TWENTY·FIVE

OUR FIRST CHORE WAS to dig the grave. No matter how we chose to give Billy Karady the deep six, we knew the grave had to be prepared and waiting. It couldn't be a last-minute chore, subject to errors in judgment and unforeseen circumstances. The question was where to bury the worm food.

It was easy enough for Angie and me to get a schedule of passenger trains without being obvious, but the freight trains, which provided the bulk of traffic to and from Portland, presented another problem entirely. In the end, we decided, the only way to learn the schedule of freight trains was to watch the tracks that passed through Hinkle.

We decided we would dig the grave between 11 P.M. and midnight on a Saturday, which was the day of our usual late-night date. We parked in a different spot just west of Hinkle four Saturday nights in a row, watching the tracks. No traffic. Unless we encountered an unscheduled special train, we were clear. Even if we did spot a train while we were digging, I would have time to climb into the Wheeled Turd and drive it off the rails. To make sure, I practiced this six times while Angie timed me with the second hand of her wristwatch. I was able to jump into the Turd, start the engine, and get it out of the way of an oncoming train with an elapsed time of under thirty seconds.

On the last Friday in November, we drove to Pasco, Washington, to buy a tire pump. We chose Pasco because we didn't want anybody in Umatilla or Hermiston to remember we had bought one. Pasco was just twenty-five miles north of Umatilla, but it was in Washington State; nobody knew us there, and certainly nobody would remember that we had bought a tire pump. People bought tire pumps all the time.

That afternoon we loaded the trunk of the Wheeled Turd with coconut-sized river rocks. We had considered cement blocks, but realized that if the wind blew the sand from cement blocks, a passing train engineer might get curious.

Late the following night, we drove to an intersection just west of Hinkle. We knew from practice runs that the Turd would stay on the rails with fully inflated tires, but slightly deflated tires were more stable, so I released a little air from each one. That done, I could drive faster without risk of coming off the rails, and an inadvertent bump of the steering wheel would be less disastrous.

Angie got out to help me align the Turd with the tracks. I eased onto the steel. Angie climbed onto the seat beside me, and we were off thigh by thigh, hand in hand. Her beauty never ceased to amaze me, and when I glanced at her beside me, off to dig a grave, I swelled with pride.

Driving on rails was always an experience that amazed me. On macadam or concrete, there was always a slight rumble, a background noise that was always there. It made no difference if you drove an insulated Cadillac or Lincoln or Buick, the sound was always present. Always. Not so with driving on rails. The steel was perfectly smooth, and driving on it gave the impression of being in a sailboat; on a road or highway, a car was a forever motorboat.

It was as though Angie and I were on a flying carpet riding the wind. The Wheeled Turd, a clunker with bad suspension, suddenly had wings. It was a calming, relaxing ride. Tranquil. Dreamlike. Another zone.

Since I didn't have to steer, Angie and I necked as we glided west. We slid silently past the Umatilla Ordnance Depot and stopped at an isolated stretch of desert just shy of the Boardman Bombing Range. It took a couple of minutes for my hard-on to subside. Then we got two shovels out of the trunk of the Turd and, just off the right-of-way, we proceeded to dig a shallow grave for Billy Karady.

Angie had brought her transistor radio with her, and the disk jockey at KORD played Buddy Holly for us while we dug.

> *All of my love,*
> *All of my kisses,*
> *You don't know what you've been missing.*
> *Oh boy! Oh boy!*

I knew we were likely going to fuck on the way back, so I dug like a man possessed.

When we finished, we retrieved the river rocks from the trunk of the Turd and put them in the grave. We covered the rocks with a piece of canvas and piled a thin layer of dirt over that. Our plan was simple enough: when the time came to bury Billy Karady, we would pull the canvas, remove the rocks, put the corpse on the bottom, and cover it with the rocks and then the dirt. The rocks would prevent larger animals from digging the body up. The bugs and bacteria could pig out. We didn't care. The dirt would soon be covered by desert grass and sagebrush, and there the murderous, obsessive Billy Karady would slowly decompose. If it so pleased him, this stalwart hero of the herd could rape and torment worms. Let him impress bugs and bacteria.

Our chore completed, we climbed into the Wheeled Turd and continued west, gliding soundlessly on the rails. I was suddenly, unaccountably horny. I glanced at Angie and could see that she was too. This was more than just a need to give my nuts some relief from our necking on the way out. This was a basic urge to fuck. Not just to neck. To fuck.

I looked at those great brown eyes of hers and those lips. "On the backseat, do you think, so we don't risk bumping the steering wheel? What do you say?"

She gave a crooked grin. She was a lusty one.

I said, "I can set the throttle. No problem."

She ran her tongue over her remarkable lips. This alone was nearly enough to make me pop my cookies. "Sure, on the backseat," she said.

"If there's any unscheduled train, we'll be creamed," I said.

She grinned. "That's what makes it sexy. Let's do it." She climbed over the top.

I throttled the Turd to a steady thirty miles an hour and joined her on the backseat. She was already naked. She gave her nipples a quick little twist with her fingers, a gesture she knew turned me on.

There was plenty of room on the wide bench seat. I started to get a rubber out of my wallet. This was always a fumbling, frantic moment that I hated.

Angie said, "To hell with that thing. Not tonight. I want to feel you."

"Good thinking," I said.

"Hard," she said. "I want it hard."

I entered her, banging her head against the door with a hard thrust.

"Harder," she said.

I did, and she cried out, both from pain and pleasure.

I had never put it to her as hard, and she had never responded with such urgent insistence. I whacked with a fury against her pubis. I did this deliberately with strokes that were as long and savage as I could manage. Each blow of pelvis against moist vulva stitched our compact. She came first, twisting in a long, shuddering spasm.

When we were finished, we lay back on the seat, enjoying the warmth of our bodies and the wonderful smells. We were aware that the longer we lay there, the more dangerous it became. For one thing, we risked passing our crossing. For another, our zone of safety was closing fast. Who knew what trains passed after midnight?

We waited.

The tension mounted.

The Wheeled Turd glided along on ribbons of steel.

We kissed.

Time passed.

We started necking.

I got another hard-on, a big-time boner.

The Turd rolled on.

We started licking and chewing and sucking.

The longer we stayed there naked, hands and tongues and mouths moving over one another's bodies, the more time was somehow stretched. Seconds were as days. Minutes were as weeks.

It was as though, sliding silently, eerily along the rails, we had somehow compressed time.

Then seconds were as months. Minutes were as years.

We couldn't maintain the challenge forever. This was a main line of the Union Pacific Railroad. The freight traffic was heavy. If we continued to ignore it, something truly awful would happen.

Yet, we both ignored the danger. We did this deliberately. Risk everything now, or face it later.

Angie grabbed my balls.

I spread her legs, getting ready to enter her again.

Suddenly, I couldn't take it anymore. I had an awful premonition. Call me chickenshit. Call it a natural instinct for self-preservation. Whatever. We had already pushed our luck far, far too much. To start fucking again under these circumstances was insanity. I said, "Maybe I should take a little peek first. Check it out."

She grinned. I had cracked first. "What happened to your nerve?"

I licked my lips. My mouth was dry. "There's a difference between nerve and being crazy."

"Well, if you really think you have to," she said, but I knew she was relieved.

"Help us relax," I said.

She gave me a nudge with her pelvis. "Don't be too long, big boy."

I sat up and took a quick peek over the top of the seat.

JESUS MOTHERFUCKING CHRIST!

A LIGHT!

COMING RIGHT AT US!

I scrambled over the seat. I didn't have time to slip behind the steering wheel and get my foot on the accelerator. I pulled down on the steering wheel with my left hand and simultaneously yanked the throttle with my right.

For a lethal heartbeat the rear wheels slipped on the polished steel. Then the Wheeled Turd shot forward, bouncing heavily. The spinning wheels hurtled the rails and WHUMP, the Turd settled on the gravel. We were off the tracks.

VVVVVVVOOOOOOOOOMMMMMMMMMMM!

The diesel whipped by, rocking the Turd with a rush of air.

The freight cars thundered by a couple of feet from the Turd's rear bumper.

CL-CLACK, CL-CLACK, CL-CLACK, CL-CLACK.

Staring up at the freight train thundering past, I turned off the engine of the Turd. My heart was hammering, and my blood raced. I said, "Chickenshit, I know, but it was probably a good thing I checked."

She was staring up at the passing train, her eyes wide and mouth open. She looked at me and grinned. "I guess we did cut it a little close."

I broke out laughing and climbed over the seat to join her in back. Nothing to do now except let the train pass. Life was to enjoy.

CL-CLACK, CL-CLACK, CL-CLACK, CL-CLACK.

"Where were we?" I said. I took her in my arms. The din of the passing train was amazing. The Wheeled Turd rocked with the passing of each car.

She squeezed me tightly. "Mr. Cool."

CL-CLACK, CL-CLACK, CL-CLACK, CL-CLACK.

Looking up at the freight cars zipping past, she grabbed my cock and squeezed it tightly.

CL-CLACK, CL-CLACK, CL-CLACK, CL-CLACK.

"You know, I just hate being interrupted like that," she said.

"Me too," I said. "Breaks the concentration."

"Just plain uncivilized." We kissed, and she slipped her tongue inside my mouth. She grabbed my balls. Amazingly, amid the clanging and banging of the freight train, my cock responded instantly to her touch. Within seconds, I was up and ready.

"Well, look at you! Up and at 'em, Ray." Angie turned and spread her thighs.

"I love you," she whispered.

"And I love you," I murmured.

I eased into her. We began a gentle rhythm and within seconds were into a private zone, as if the freight train of our destruction had never existed. It was maybe three feet away, but might as well have been clattering and banging its way across Siberia or Texas or Argentina. It had nothing at all to do with us. We were in a special place, outside schedules and timetables.

Whereas our first round had been violent and crazed, this turn was long and leisurely—a union of grateful lovers. We both knew it was likely to be the most memorable sex of our lives. We made it last as long as we could, savoring each measured stroke and pause, knowing the sharing would eventually end as all things do. It was so very, very sweet.

After the last freight car had passed—its rattle and banging receding in the east—we enjoyed the warmth of union in the quiet of the night, thankful to be alive for one more dawn.

Later, still spent, we lay there, joined, exhausted from the sex. If nothing else that night, we learned the importance of train schedules.

TWENTY·SIX

WE HAD BILLY KARADY'S grave waiting for him for him like a made bed, but we still weren't sure we wanted to go through with putting him to sleep and tucking him in. Murdering him sounded good in theory, but we both knew actually doing it was something else again. Did we really have the nerve? When push came to shove, could we actually do it? But short of taking him out, what recourse did we have? That question plagued us. In a community like Umatilla, we were at the mercy of our word against his. In that tribunal of small-town opinion, he won every time.

Our problem was, there seemed to be no halfway measures. We thought of pouring sugar in the gas tank of the Cunt Wagon as a way of temporarily grounding him. But we knew he would immediately figure out who had done that, and if he wasn't already in a murderous mood, he quickly would be after having to buy a new block for his engine. Besides, the wonderful town dads, eager to have a happy Billy lead the Vikings onward and upward to glory for Umatilla, would see to it that he got his engine fixed.

We went through the logic again and again. Each time we came to the same fork. When we considered the alternatives, our conclusion remained the same. We were trapped merely for being who we were: the mosquito and the new girl in town. We didn't have to be geniuses to see our story played all around us on all kinds of levels. The herd thundered blindly on, guided by the yipping and yelping of the cowboys who understood and fed its needs. If you were strays like we were, you got out of the way or got trampled. It was almost as simple as that.

Nevertheless, we nursed the hope that Billy had given up whatever it was that possessed him to follow us around tormenting us. If the visit of Tom Agnopolous to Coach Mungo's apartment had somehow convinced him he should lay off, we would be spared having to act. If it hadn't? Not choosing was a form of choice, Sartre had written. To do nothing was to accept our own destruction.

We decided we needed to establish some sort of predictable routine, so that if Billy began following us again, we could lure him to a nice private place to put him under. The question was where. Not the buttes. That was too popular for parking. Not the circle by the Willows. That was too close to town. We began cruising country roads every night after I had finished football practice and my chores at home.

Early one night, we drove over the irrigation canal above Angie's house and took Power Line Road south. This was the road to the mouse-stomping grounds. A couple of miles from the canal we hung a right over a road that was little more than two barely perceptible parallel tracks in the ground. This road, if it can be described as that, meandered west, through stomping territory, and was apparently used by the rancher who had cattle out on the desert. This was poor range that couldn't support many animals, but strays did have to be found, and fences had to be fixed. The road stayed within a hundred yards of the fence. South of the tightly strung barbed-wire fence there was more desert and—for a stretch—earth-covered ammunition igloos of the Umatilla Army Ordnance Depot.

Aside from that there was nothing except for the railroad right-of-way where Angie and I had prepared Billy's grave. In several places the road looped north in large circles. In the win-

ter, the rancher must have used these loops to deliver bales of
hay to hungry animals. We counted three loops in all, leading
to winter feeding drop-offs for the eastern, central, and western
sections of the desert range. The third loop was the end of the
line.

We drove almost four miles east to the central loop, which
we decided was the perfect spot for necking. It was isolated.
There was no traffic. The loop prevented us from being effectively trapped. Even if he blocked the way with his Merc, it was
possible to drive off the road and back on again if we avoided
stretches of pure sand. He couldn't follow us off the road because the Merc rode too low to the ground.

Out there we could waylay him and not risk accidental encounters with passersby. This was a good necking spot. There
would be no state cops rousting us this far from civilization.
And it was romantic in its way; nobody out there but us and
the moon and stars and the vistas of our dreams.

On our way back, we found Billy waiting for us at the
entrance to Power Line Road. We could see him grin as we
hung a left to return to Umatilla. Did that mean he was back
for good?

The next night we returned to the same place. On our way
out, we were shocked to find the Cunt Wagon parked on the
makeshift road about a quarter of a mile away. We hadn't seen
him, but he'd been out there, watching us—perhaps even peer-
ing in on us as he had been doing the night he banged on the
door. We circled the Cunt Wagon and continued on our way.

Still we didn't act. We weren't murderers. We were just two
teenagers who wanted to be left alone. We tried everything to
justify doing nothing. We decided that encounters didn't mean
he was going to torment us every night of the week. Maybe he
would remember Tom's visit and come to his senses.

On the third night, Billy Karady dashed that hope. Angie
and I went back to our chosen spot. The moon was out, and it
was an unaccountably warm night, with a gentle breeze. This

was a nice respite from the cold November nights, and we decided to go for a romantic walk. We were strolling along in the moonlight, holding hands, when suddenly a bit of sand flipped up by my feet.

We heard a loud snapping sound in the distance.

Sand exploded by Angie's foot, followed by another loud snap.

Billy Karady was having himself a little fun with a .22 automatic, firing right at our feet.

We sprinted for the safety of the Wheeled Turd with .22 slugs ripping into the ground dangerously close to our feet. It was night, and he couldn't see very well. A miss of a few inches one way or the other could have caught one of us in the foot or leg. We could hear the sound of Billy's laughter carried by the wind. Great sport. Send skeeter and the sexpot running. It was like a bad guy using his six-shooter to scatter people in a bad western. Ha, ha, ha!

We slipped onto the front seat of the Turd and ducked our heads. As we did, one, two, three .22 slugs glanced off the windshield in front of me, chipping divots in the glass. Angie's window was partly rolled down, and we heard more laughter. Ha, ha, ha! We sat there for a minute, frozen, not knowing what to do. We were at Billy's mercy. Were we to be ambushed on our way back to Power Line Road?

We sat there for more than an hour, scared stiff. Finally, I fired up the Turd and drove warily back the way we had come. There was no kidding ourselves now. Billy Karady was back, big-time. This time Billy had been content to scare the manure out of us. Who was to guarantee he wouldn't raise his sights next time out? If he had already raped and murdered three young women, what was to prevent him from taking us under too? What did a couple more bodies mean after he had already experienced whatever thrill he got from committing murder?

We decided there was no sense putting it off. If we waited, we risked him striking us first. It was him or us. After the incident of the .22, our decision was easier. By such increments of incident and mounting logic, we took one more step down that spooky path that we both knew would likely change our lives forever.

TWENTY-SEVEN

WE DECIDED TO DO what we had to do on a Saturday night, an obvious necking night, and because we knew Billy Karady would follow us out into the desert. He had established a pattern of varying the nature of his torments, so we felt it was unlikely he would bring his .22 again. Unlikely, but there were no guarantees. This was a risk we had to take. The radio said there was a storm front moving in from the north. We decided that was good, not bad. A storm would add to the mystery of his disappearance.

As a weapon. I decided on my baseball bat, a thirty-two-inch bat with a thick handle. This kind of bat, also called a bottle bat, was used by Nellie Fox, second baseman of the Chicago White Sox. I couldn't hit a baseball worth squat, but I figured I could make contact with a target of Billy Karady's skull. I threw the bat onto the rear seat, and we were off, facing the most important fork of our lives.

On the way out to our parking spot in the stomping grounds, we talked through every conceivable detail of our plan. Question: where should I deliver the first blow? Low or high? Not high, we decided, because people have a natural instinct to defend themselves with their forearms. Billy Karady might well block the blow and proceed to kick the living shit out of me. No, better to go for his shins as hard as I could, break them if possible. The kneecaps would be best, but if I missed and hit his thigh, I wouldn't do a whole lot of damage. Karady was an athlete, determined and durable or he wouldn't have been as good as he was. His advantage was speed. Eliminate his speed. That was my first objective.

I slowed the Turd a couple of hundred yards short of our agreed-upon spot, and pitched my Nellie Fox special through the open window, aiming for the base of a large sagebrush.

When we got to our spot, I parked the Wheeled Turd, and we waited. We knew he was out there. We couldn't see him, but we could feel his evil presence. Finally, after an hour had passed, it was time. I pretended to start the car, but didn't really tromp on the starter. The engine struggled then stopped. It struggled then stopped. Finally, I got out and opened the hood and pretended to look under the engine.

Then I went around to the window on Angie's side and said, "Here goes."

"We do it," she said.

"Together."

"Both of us."

"I love you," I said.

"I love you."

"Forever," I said.

"Forever. Until we die." She gave me another soft kiss to seal our bargain.

I started walking in the direction of Power Line Road. Already my pulse was racing. I felt certain Billy Karady was watching me. I didn't have to walk as far as wherever he had parked the Cunt Wagon to know he was there. When I got to the large clump of sagebrush, I grabbed the baseball bat and circled back toward the Wheeled Turd.

When I spotted the Turd, I saw Billy immediately. He was standing outside the car jawing loudly at Angie, who had the windows rolled up and the doors locked. I didn't see any rifle or weapon, but it didn't take Sherlock Holmes to figure out

Billy was up to no good. I felt a stirring of wind from the north as I eased up behind him. This was the leading edge of the storm that they were talking about on the radio. Closer, I got. Closer still. Soon, I could hear him talking.

"As soon as Skeeter spots my Wagon, he'll be back, thinking he's John Wayne. Gonna protect his sweetheart. Little pecker ain't got at a whole lot going for him that I can figure. He's small but slow. Dumb as hell too, considering what he did to me at Fossil."

Was small, I thought. Not so dumb as to take your horseshit without fighting back.

"He can't shoot a basketball worth fuck. Can't field a ground ball. Can't hit. No damn wonder he spends his life riding the pines. He's a skeeter, easy to swat. What you could possibly see in him beats hell out of me."

Angie stood her ground, saying nothing.

"Come on, roll down that damn window. Least you can do is be civilized. I'm not going to hurt you." He laughed loudly. He knew he had Angie scared half to death. Great sport.

He had tried to rape her once. Now she was supposed to roll down the window and invite him to yank her out of the car. Right. I felt another blast of wind. It was cold as hell. Pretty soon the storm would be full upon us. The wind made it easier for me to get close. I got to within ten feet, then six. I was in the danger zone. If he turned around now, I was in trouble. I drew closer still. I thought, *Don't look my way, Angie. Don't warn him.*

Her eyes were on him. If she saw me, she gave no hint of it.

I yelled, "Hey!"

He turned, surprised.

As he did, I stepped to one side and swung the bat as hard as I could, aiming for his shins.

POW!

He was right. I couldn't hit shit. I landed high, catching him square on the left kneecap with the sweet spot in the fat of the bat. It was a full, dead-on, jarring blow.

He yowled and pitched forward, clutching his knee. I had crushed the kneecap. He stared in disbelief at the spreading blood on the leg of his pants. He looked up at me, his eyes glazed with pain. He said, "What the fuck?"

I stood for a moment, watching him. "Triple off the right kneecap. Not bad for a skeeter."

Angie opened the door and jumped out of the Turd.

Billy was stunned by the blow. He blinked. He tried to get up, but pitched sideways. "Jesus Christ!"

"Easier to hit than a baseball," I said.

"Do it," Angie said.

He was suddenly on his feet.

Instinctively, I stepped back and took the other kneecap with a full swing. This wasn't as cleanly delivered as the first, but it did the job. Ground-rule double, minimum.

He said, "Shit!" and went down again.

"God, I bet that smarts," I said.

"Finish him," Angie said.

I swung from the hips as hard as I could and landed a terrible blow on the side of his head. Just teed fucking off like Mickey Mantle. KLOCK!

He pitched forward onto the sand, bleeding from one ear and his mouth. He spit a mouthful of teeth and blood onto the ground.

I started to kneel to take a closer look.

He made an odd, burbling noise in his throat. Did he honest to God think he could go around banging on the door of people having sex without pissing someone off? When you see dogs doing it, you have the grace to leave them alone, for Christ's sake. He had tried to rape Angie. He had slugged me at Pendleton. He had tried to knock us into the Umatilla River. He had fired his .22 automatic at our feet. Har, har, har! Now the horseshit was boomeranging. He was getting his and then some. He deserved every bit of it.

"Not too close," Angie said.

She was right to be careful. I circled him, bat at the ready. He was burbling, so he was dangerous. He put his hand to his mouth, then took it away. He spit some more teeth onto the ground. He tried to say something, but it was hopeless. For one thing, his jaw stuck out at an odd angle.

"You fractured his skull."

"I think so," I said. "His jaw too."

"You have to give him another shot. We can't leave him like this."

Yes. Once committed, it was all the way. Had to be. I felt the stirring of a cold wind, coming from the north. I prodded Billy with the bat. Suddenly, he was on his feet, charging me like a raging bull. Before I could think, he grabbed me around the throat and was choking me. I struggled with him, shocked at the feel of his warm blood. He had hold of the goddamn bat. I grabbed his left knee and gave it a yank. He screamed and dropped the bat.

Angie picked it up and WHACK, damned near removed his head from his shoulders. God, but she slugged him. Hit him with the fat of the bat as hard as she could swing. Pulped him. A regular Ralph Kiner she was.

Billy slumped over on top of me. Smothered by a corpse. Yuch. I pushed him off of me and stood. My mouth was dry. My pulse raced. My stomach twisted. Now he was dead for sure. I pushed him off me. I was soaked with blood. The wind suddenly began picking up. It was going to be a murderous night in more ways than one.

Angie Boudreau and I had just murdered Billy Karady. I stood there, blood soaked, with the gathering storm beating against me. I had defended my turf against a challenger. I felt a surge of pride. Triumph.

The corpse grabbed me by the ankle.

"Yeowwwwww!" I jumped like I had stepped on a rattler, yanking my leg from his grip. Now I was pissed. "Give me the goddamn bat," I said.

Angie gave it to me.

Billy Karady's left eye was popping out, and the other was nearly swollen shut, so he couldn't possibly see anything. He groped about making his strange burbling sounds. I could see teeth on the ground, mixed in with the blood and the sand. His mouth was cut clear through, and what was left of his upper lip flapped gently as he struggled to breathe. His jaw sat at a cockeyed angle.

He looked up at me. His broken face was a sheen of blood.

I was rocked by a gust of wind. I hunkered my shoulders. "Gonna be a cold mother, don't you think?"

He burbled in reply.

"You think you can do any damn thing you want and get away with it? An untouchable? The heroic Billy Karady? You think I won't defend myself, is that it? That I'll just put up with it because I'm just a little skeeter. An annoyance. Do you think that?"

The heroic Billy Karady, I had said. Hero of what? What was it that made me so furious?

"Do it. Finish him," Angie said.

Hero of the herd. That's why I hated him so much. He was the hero of the herd. They adored him for reasons that were inexplicable. I hated his confidence. His self-assurance. His conviction that things were going his way, no matter what.

I clenched my teeth. "*Was* a little skeeter. You play a hard game, you pay. Measure for measure, asshole."

I gave him one last shot, like Mickey Mantle golfing a low fastball over the wall. This was the final, ultimate, crushing blow, delivered with as much strength as I could muster. WHOCK!

That was it. Billy Karady's head was a featureless, bloody pulp. I had removed what was left of his teeth and broken his jaw in another place. Still wary, I kneeled and grasped him by the wrist. No pulse that I could feel. Jesus, but his shattered head was a mess. There was blood coming out of his mouth, his nose, both of his ears, and his left eye. His right eye was swollen shut.

My hand was shaking. I looked at it and willed it to stop.

Angie had a wild look in her eye. I knew that she too was pumped on adrenaline.

I squatted by the corpse and patted the pocket of Billy's jeans. I found the keys to the Cunt Wagon.

"Well, I suppose we should get on with it."

"We've got a lot of work to do," she said.

Billy Karady wasn't going anyplace. We walked together to get the Cunt Wagon.

The tires of the Wheeled Turd and the Cunt Wagon were the same distance apart. Our idea was to wrap Billy's corpse in black plastic that I had lifted from a construction sight. We would put the corpse in the Cunt Wagon. If we made a mistake and got his blood on the inside, no big deal. Then we would drive both cars to a railroad intersection on Power Line Road and put them on the tracks, Cunt Wagon first. I would drive the Merc to the grave site, followed by Angie in the Chev. We would bury Billy, pile the rocks on him, and cover the rocks with sand so it could sod over, then pull the throttle of the Cunt Wagon and send it on its way toward Portland. We would follow the Cunt Wagon in the Wheeled Turd, exit the rails at the first crossing, and go back home.

One of two things would happen to Billy Karady's Mercury. It would collide head-on with a train going east or be overtaken by a train going west. There wasn't much else in the way of tweenies. The police would examine the demolished Mercury, looking for its driver and find nothing. Their conclusion would be what? That the driver had jumped out of the car before the collision. They would trace the registration and learn the car belonged to Billy Karady.

Where was Billy Karady?

The police would issue all kinds of bulletins trying to find him, but he would never be found. Then they would suspect foul play, perhaps going so far as to interview Angie and me. They would look for a body but find nothing. There were no roads within miles of the grave, and the only way to get there would require cutting through barbed-wire fence. The fences on both sides of the tracks were tightly strung and intact. Nobody, but nobody could carry a corpse that far. No body. No crime.

What happened to Billy Karady? That would be the mystery of the year in Umatilla County, Oregon. That and the murdered girl in Hermiston. Was Billy Karady the *K* killer? Was that why he had taken off after having screwed up on the railroad tracks? Let the police and the public speculate all they wanted.

As we walked to the Cunt Wagon, the cold north wind descended on us with a force. I took a blast of sand in the face. I spit it out. It was going to be a cold, cold night, there was no doubt of that. As we walked, the sand whipped against our backs, and raced along the ground, zipping through sagebrush and cacti. Come morning, the landscape would be rearranged. As the years and the winds passed, the landscape would be altered again and again. There would be countless winter winds to come. The warming Chinooks would melt the snow in late February or early March. The gusting heralds of summer thunderstorm would blow in from the west. Through all of these, the sand would blow and drift and blow and drift until Angie and I and the missing Billy Karady were long forgotten.

I don't know what I expected to feel, but as I walked hand in hand with Angie Boudreau, I felt more alive than I had ever felt before. I had risked everything. I had taken my struggle with Billy Karady down to the nitty-gritty of survival. He was dead, and I was alive. All Angie and I had to do was bury him in the grave by the railroad tracks and send his car on its way toward Portland. When that was done, we would have completed the perfect murder. We would be forever free of Billy Karady's obsession.

While living in the torpid, lethargic tropics, I became interested in the way weather influenced culture. Most atlases described the world's climate by modifications of what was called the Kopper system. The southeastern United States, southern Brazil, and southeastern China were all Caf systems, meaning they were subtropical and humid. The Amazon basin, Equatorial Africa, and Borneo were all Af—tropical rain forest. Parts of Brazil, central Africa, India, Thailand, and northern Australia were Aw—tropical savanna.

I was especially interested in BSk or middle-latitude steppe, the climate of Ulan Bator in Mongolia, Tselinograd in Kazakhistan, Ankara in central Turkey, and Umatilla, Oregon. I had ridden the trans-Siberian Express across the Soviet Union, but the train passed just north of Mongolia and what was then called Kazakhskaya, and so I had not seen the similarities in climate firsthand.

Were there terrible windstorms in Mongolia, Kazakistan, and Turkey? Yes, of course there were, just as there were people and passion and blood and murder. The world pulsed and swirled with both physical and emotional currents.

TWENTY-EIGHT

ANGIE AND I FOUND the Cunt Wagon and drove it back to the Wheeled Turd where Billy Karady's body lay. So far, so good. No, not so good.

Billy Karady was gone.

Gone! Yes! I had slugged him in the head with every ounce of strength that I could muster, and so had Angie. The blood coming out of his ear was a clear-cut a sign of a skull fracture. He had smashed kneecaps and a jaw that was broken in two places, and he could hardly breathe for the blood in his mouth and nose. Each step had to be painful in the extreme. It was impossible to believe that he had somehow gotten up and walked off.

And yet . . . gone. He was gone. Hamburger Head was gone.

Angie looked stunned. "Where is he?"

That struck me as one of your basic dumb questions. "How do I know?"

"He's gone."

I felt like saying, "No shit, Red Ryder," but I restrained myself. This was no time for flippancy. "Yeah," I said. I took a quick look at the Wheeled Turd, but saw no blood on the door handle or seats. If he'd tried to start the Turd, there would have been blood somewhere. He'd been covered with blood.

"What do we do now?"

"We've got a flashlight. We find him. He has two smashed kneecaps, so he can't have gone too damn far. They'll be swelling on him. One eye was popped out of its socket, and the other one was closed, so he can't see. He's probably got a fifty-aspirin headache. That's not to mention this wind."

Angie held herself with her arms to keep warm. "It shouldn't be hard to follow him in this sand. Besides, he's probably leaving a trail of blood."

I got my flashlight out of the Turd's glove compartment, and we started following Billy Karady's trail. That was easier said than done. For one thing the night was completely black. The blowing sand now obscured all starlight and moonlight. And the sand was rapidly covering everything, so there was no trail of blood or footprints that we could find.

It was spooky following him in the storm. He was as close as humanly possible to being a walking corpse. We had the keys to his Cunt Wagon. The odds of him making it out of the desert alive weren't just poor, they were borderline impossible. It was hard to imagine him making ten yards in the condition he was in. Who could get far with that kind of pain? And the wind. Jesus, the wind!

Angie and I took our time. I remembered him grabbing my elbow, and his pulped face looking up at me as he waited for the final blow. I say pulped face instead of Billy Karady because the face had a bizarre, otherworldly look about it—like it belonged to an alien or some beast, not a human being with a name and a mother somewhere who presumably loved him.

We followed what we thought were his footprints for about twenty yards. The tracks led to a patch of small, but thick, sagebrush. I held the blood-stained bat at the ready. It was hard to look for footprints while fearing that he might rise up from the sagebrush like a demented Frankenstein monster and grab one of us by the throat. His only chance was in surprising us, so he would most likely lie in ambush. We proceeded with extreme caution, careful to make sure there were no mysterious dark forms on the ground in front of us.

We circled all large sagebrush warily and with bat cocked. This time we would really put him under.

Was he attempting to go straight ahead, or was he circling?

After about ten minutes of searching, it was obvious that whatever faint trail Billy was leaving was itself being covered by blown sand. Angie said, "He's circling. Has to be."

"How could we lose him?" I said. "How?"

"He has to be around here someplace. We'll find him. We have to be patient, and we can't panic."

We retreated to the Cunt Wagon and Wheeled Turd, not knowing for sure what to do next. Then we tried it again. We retraced our steps, our shoulders turned against the wind, hoping to find the spot where we lost what we had thought was his trail. But now it was even dimmer, and, as before, we lost him in the sagebrush.

It was then that we became aware of another problem. Time. Not only was the blowing sand covering our footprints as well as his, but the longer we searched, the likelier it was that if we were seen on the way home, our vehicle would be remembered. This was not the kind of night where lovers decide on an extra hour of necking.

With each passing minute our margin of safety was growing slimmer, and we both knew it.

Finally, I said, "We need to go through the logical possibilities. The longer we stay out here, the more dangerous it is. A car on the road on a night like this is remembered if a murder has been committed."

"I agree," she said.

"The first question is, where the hell is he?"

"Out there dead, most likely. But he could be hiding. He knows we're trying to kill him. His only hope is to survive until morning and hope somebody finds him."

"In this wind?" I said. "It's below freezing already. Has to be."

"If he doesn't bleed to death, he'll freeze, I agree. We're isolated enough that the animals will likely eat his corpse, but the possibility of his being discovered remains. If we come back to bury him, we risk walking into the arms of waiting police."

If Billy somehow made it out alive, we were facing charges of attempted murder. We could deny it, but we faced the same problem as when he had tried to rape Angie and later when he had tried to run us off the road. It was our word against his. Billy Karady, heroic jock, against Skeeter and new girl Angie.

But he wouldn't survive. How on earth could he? He was blind. He was bleeding. He could hardly breathe. The night was as cold as a well digger's ass. And the wind, which made the cold even worse. Christ, the wind.

"I say we finish our plan as best we can and go home," Angie said.

"If he survives, we deny everything."

"That's the only thing we can do. Let him prove it."

We drove both vehicles to the railroad crossing according to our plan. Billy's Mercury had a nearly full tank of gas, which was good. Bundled in a heavy coat to protect me when I hit the ground, I eased the car onto the rails, headed west. With the door open, I eased out the throttle, and when I had it going about ten to fifteen miles an hour, I leaped out and rolled onto the rocky rail bed, slamming the door shut behind me.

Angie joined me as I scrambled to my feet, and we stood there hand in hand in the buffeting wind, watching the fabled Cunt Wagon disappear into the night. Then we turned, not saying anything, and walked back to the Wheeled Turd. Still in silence, I turned around and headed north on Power Line Road.

We had murdered Billy Karady. Or had we? Maybe we had bungled it. Where had Billy gone? Would he survive? Would his corpse be found? We knew intuitively those were the questions we would face each morning until we knew his fate. And if his corpse was found, what would happen then? Would we be suspected of having killed him? Even if we escaped for lack of evidence, we would not be free. People would know. Coach Mungo would know. Tom Agnopolous would know.

Even then, I knew why people sought refuge in daily routine. In routine lies the comfort of the predictable, of knowing what happens next. Routines are little stretches of death, but we long for them, me included. To kill time. Isn't that the expression? To kill a little time. The possibility that Billy was still alive meant that he could yet rise up, in the manner of an evil, possessed Lazarus, and take us under. We would be eroded by anxiety, a form of lingering, debilitating emotional acid. Not knowing was the horror. Until we knew what had happened to our tormentor, we would be deprived of comforting certainty.

TWENTY-NINE

THE WIND HAMMERED AND shook The Coop that night more violently then ever before as far as I could remember. I had a small electric heater on the floor, its fan pushed air past wires that were orange with heat. The Coop was no more than ten feet long and maybe five feet wide. The fan usually kept this space warm enough, but I was bone cold and then some. Ordinarily the tiny Coop didn't make me feel claustrophobic, but it did that night. I felt like I was lying in a coffin being buffeted by the cold wind that blew hard out of Canada and down across eastern Washington. There were gusts that I swear lifted the northern edge of The Coop off the ground.

The wind was presumably piling sand against Billy Karady's corpse lying out there in the sand. Given enough time, it might even bury him.

I say presumably. What if Billy were still alive? He was an athlete, after all. He had been strong and vigorous before Angie and I had taken our licks with the baseball bat. There were all kinds of amazing stories about the will to survive. Supposing he had made it back like one of those determined, never-quit characters in Jack London's fiction. What if, inch by painful inch—with crushed kneecaps and a broken jaw, bleeding from his nose, mouth, and ears, and with one eye popping out and the other swollen shut—he had managed to drag himself across the desert? Was that impossible?

Lying there, feeling the wind shake The Coop, I twisted and turned in my cocoon of warmth under the covers. I imagined Billy Karady, a huge, bloody worm in the wee hours of the morning, depositing himself in front of an oncoming car on Power Line Road.

I pictured the driver of the car, perhaps a man returning from the graveyard shift at Hinkle, stopping to pick him up.

The driver pulled the bloody worm out of the frigid, blowing wind onto the backseat of the car and headed for the hospital in Hermiston. As he sped off, the worm lay there, making his weird burbling sounds, and kept alive only by his hatred and his desire for vengeance.

What if?

Couldn't be, I told myself. Just couldn't. Not even Billy Karady could pull that off. He was strong, yes. A royal asshole. But even royal assholes have their limitations.

Still, the possibility remained. Even if he had died, his corpse, with the skull bashed in by a Louisville slugger, would lay exposed, waiting for discovery. If that happened, Tom Agnopolous would be forced to come calling with some specific questions for Angie and me. If Billy was dead, our only hope lay with the wind. The wind was our ally. The wind could stop him, frozen, or it could bury him.

I couldn't sleep. I twisted. I turned. The wind shook The Coop.

Blow wind, I thought. *Blow hard. Don't stop. Blow, blow, blow!*

I lay there, twisting with anxiety, listening to the wind.

Then I was aware that it was light outside. Dawn.

I flipped on my radio and tuned quickly to the news. The Cunt Wagon had made it twenty miles west of Boardman before it ran head-on into a freight train. The 1950 Mercury coup registered to William Earl Karady of Umatilla, Oregon, was totally destroyed. There was no sign of the driver; the Oregon

State Police were looking for Karady.

I was exhausted from a night of no sleep. So, the Mercury had crashed, but Billy Karady was still missing. Time to get ready for school. If Billy had somehow survived or if his body had been found I would soon be learning my fate.

Although its initial fury was spent, the wind was still blowing as I drove to Angie Boudreau's house to pick her up for school. The sky was a curious yellowish gray from the morning sun, an orange orb trying to shine through the blowing sand. From horizon to horizon it was as though the sun were saturated with dust and blowing sand. The cold wind ruffled whitecaps up on the Columbia River, which reflected the yellowish muddle of the sky.

The buffeting wind rocked the Wheeled Turd as I drove toward Umatilla.

I knew from the moment Angie slipped onto the front seat of the Turd that our relationship had changed. This was not necessarily for the worst, but it was different. In one way, we seemed more intimate than before. This was, I supposed, because of the shared knowledge of what we had done. I wasn't sure.

"The Mercury crashed into a freight train just west of Boardman," I said.

"I heard it on the radio," she said.

I gave her a kiss on those large, soft lips of hers. "Did you sleep?" I asked. Before, we hadn't thought about trains and train schedules. Now we knew.

She shook her head. "No. You?"

"Not a bit," I said. I slowed the Wheeled Turd for a turn. "He couldn't have made it out of there. Couldn't. Nobody could do that. Nobody. Not with those knees and not being able to see. One of his eyes was completely gone, and the other was completely shut."

"He knew the wind was coming from the north. That's all he needed to know to keep from going in circles. Wind in his face, north. Wind at his back, south. Wind at his left, east. Wind at his right, west. Simple as that."

I hadn't thought of that. "Nothing to the east except for the Umatilla River. If he went in any other direction and stayed the course, he'd eventually run into a barbed-wire fence. What then?"

"He'd crawl over it."

"With that knee?" I said.

"If he made it that far, he wouldn't care about the pain, would he? It all comes down to survival. The will to live. Look how far we went to make sure he went down, not us. How far can hate take him?"

I said, "If he survived, we'd already know by now, wouldn't we? He'd have told somebody in the hospital. The people in the hospital would have called the police. The police would have picked us up. We'd know. He's dead."

We rode in silence, both thinking that if he was dead, then there was a body out there somewhere waiting to be found. Until we knew for sure what had happened to him, we weren't off the hook.

I said, "If he's dead, how can they possibly prove it was us? The wind would have covered our tire prints."

She said, "They might suspect us, but they can never prove it."

"Exactly," I said. We both knew all this was talk. When I stopped at the sign for the turn over the bridge, I said, "So what do we do? Just wait?"

She took a deep breath and let it out slowly. "Nothing else we can do."

"His corpse will freeze in this weather."

Looking across the river toward Umatilla, she said, "Should we try to find him, do you think? If we found him, we could still bury him."

I checked for traffic to my left and turned onto the bridge. "I don't think we should be seen anywhere near there. What if somebody else finds his body? They'll start asking questions about who has been driving out that way. No telling who has seen us coming and going in the last few days. We don't want our names to come up."

"Maybe . . ." She started to say something more, then stopped. "Maybe we shouldn't have . . ."

"We didn't have any choice. It was him or us," I said. "We have a natural right to defend ourselves."

She gripped my knee. This was a gesture of togetherness, and yet, in an odd way, I felt this was the beginning of the end of our special relationship. Things would never be the same between us. It was not that we had just lost our honeymoon. We had lost more than that. We hadn't considered all the consequences of murdering Billy Karady. Where once we had been in love and carefree, we now depended on each other for our very survival.

I said, "We remain calm. We stick with our plan. We'll be okay."

She said, "This morning I woke up thinking about us and the train the other night."

I grinned. "You too?" That was big talk. We both knew we would never again have sex like that night on the rails. Never. It was a once-in-a-lifetime thing.

THIRTY

WE WERE FACING THE state quarterfinals in Joseph, Oregon, but Coach Mungo canceled practice that night—both because of the storm that had the area in its terrible grip and because Billy Karady had failed to show for practice. The missed practice wasn't crucial. But Billy was. Without him, we'd get our butts kicked, and everybody knew it.

As everybody was leaving the locker room, Coach was in his locker room. He motioned to me with his hand. "Ray, would you come here for a minute? I want to talk to you."

My heart thumped. This didn't have anything to do with football or the upcoming game, I knew. I stepped inside his office. Everything was neat and in its place. Coach was that kind of guy, meticulous, a detail man, but not obsessed. Was this a prelude to the arrival of the police? Was he preparing me for the shock of consequence—my life destroyed by bad judgment and screwed luck? Face it, trying to take care of Billy Karady by ourselves was just plain stupid.

Watching me carefully, he said, "Ray, have you seen Billy?"

"The Oregon State Police can't find him, and you're asking me if I've seen him?" I tried to sound disbelieving. I felt his eyes boring right through me.

He said, "When was the last time you saw him?"

I figured what the hell, if I was to go under, I might as well go with flags flying. Let the world know I had reason to do what I had done. "Well, I saw him when he tried to run Angie and me off the road to Hermiston. He tried to kill us. Hard to forget that."

"I asked you about the last time."

I thought for a moment. "At the game Friday afternoon. I sure as hell wasn't with him last night when he was out there driving his Cunt Wagon on the rails."

Coach winced at the term Cunt Wagon. He didn't like that one damn bit. "His Mercury had a throttle. We both know anybody could have put it on the tracks and sent it on its way. You didn't see him after Friday?"

I shook my head no.

He clenched his jaw.

I said nothing, then, "You told Tom Agnopolous you had been watching television with him. That wasn't true, Coach. He was out driving around in a stolen pickup."

He ignored that. "You haven't seen him since Friday?"

"I told you no." I suspected he knew I was lying. I could see it in his face. There was nothing I could do but push forward. "Listen, Coach. Really. I haven't seen him. It's not like Billy and I are old pals or anything like that. Let's be honest. The less I see of him, the happier I'll be. You think something happened to him? Hey, he likely just jumped off when he saw the train coming. That's what they're saying on the radio."

"What they're saying on the radio is speculation. Why didn't Billy just drive his Mercury off the tracks? He told me that was no problem. He loved that car. Why wouldn't he make some effort to save it?"

I shrugged. "Beats me. I wasn't there."

He chewed on his lower lip. "Your little girlfriend told the Oregon State Police he tried to rape her. Agnopolous said the police suspect Billy might be the K killer."

"I don't have any idea what the police think."

"Tom Agnopolous is going with your sister, isn't he?"

"Yes, he is, but he doesn't share police business with me. By the way, Billy did try to rape her, and he would have gotten away with it if I hadn't heard her screaming. You were there that day. I bet you knew something was up. If Billy denies it, why don't you ask her? Get both sides of the story. She's real, real scared, and a person can hardly blame her. What if he *is* the K killer?"

He watched me, saying nothing.

I knew his calling me into his office had nothing to do with the arrival of the police. Nobody yet knew what had happened to Billy, if anything. I said, "Listen, Coach, if you're going to cancel practice, I want to go home."

"Billy never killed anybody."

"I didn't say he did. I said, 'What if?' There's a difference."

"But you think he is the K killer?"

I looked him directly in the eyes. "Coach, what I think doesn't matter a whole lot, does it? Billy will show up. When he does, we'll go back to our practices, and we'll beat Joseph, no problem."

Coach took a deep breath. "Well, one thing is for sure. Billy never raped that girl they found over at Hermiston. I can prove that for a fact." He said that with conviction.

"Do it then," I said. "Clear his name. Be my guest." Having said that, my stomach churned. It was like I expected Billy Karady to walk through the door with his knee swollen as big as a watermelon and with one eye swollen shut and the other popped out a weird angle. "When you do find him, would you do him and me and Angie a favor and tell him to leave us the hell alone? We have a right to go about our business without him following us around in his stupid car. He slugged me in the face at Pendleton. He tried to drive us off the road. He also shot at us with his .22. Did he tell you that? Maybe he wasn't trying to hit us, just scare the crap out of us, but it wasn't very damn funny to us." With that said, which was too damn much, I left.

Behind me Coach sat in his office wondering what he would have done if he were in my place. I was Skeeter Hawkins, bench warmer and forever spectator in the little world of Umatilla High School. I milked cows in the morning and night and spent my spare time pawing through dirt looking for arrowheads. Would I go so far as to do Billy Karady bodily harm? Hard for him to imagine, I knew that. Even harder for the Oregon State Police.

Russ Storm was suffering from a bad cold, so I helped him milk the cows that evening. Russ didn't like the idea of me helping; he had his pride and didn't want to be thought of as an old man who couldn't do a simple thing like milking three cows. I wasn't especially anxious to help, I admit, but my mother insisted. I didn't want to be accused of taking advantage of Russ, who was always good to me, so I trudged down to the barn with him in the cold, with our breath coming in frosty puffs and him grumbling to himself all the way. He was sore at my mother, not me. To understand what followed, it's necessary to understand the barn, the chore of milking, and the disposal of manure—more importantly the nature of the tool, a kind of pitchfork, used to shovel dried cow shit.

To be honest, the Hawkins place, as my parents' small farm was called, didn't have much of a barn. It wasn't one of those big, picturesque red barns with a high-pitched roof like you see in romantic landscapes of farm scenes. The crude Hawkins barn, originally built by my father during the Depression, was fashioned of unpainted, rough boards; it was maybe eighty feet long and twenty feet wide with a dirt floor and a flat roof of rusting corrugated tin that sloped from the front to the back. It looked like it might be a pigsty, maybe, but not a barn. A wide door swung open at one end to admit the cows come milking time; bales of dried alfalfa, needed to feed the cows in the winter when the ground was covered with snow, were stored at the opposite end. One of Faulkner's families might have called it a barn—the Bundrens or the Joads, maybe—but no farmer with any respect. It did the job for us, though.

The barn had six stanchions for the cows—a stanchion being a place where a cow's head was locked into place while she was getting milked. It wasn't like cows avoided the stanchion like it was a form of torture or something. On the contrary, getting milked also meant they got grain, usually oats, which they just loved, together with relief from the milk that had built up in their bags. If they went too long without getting milked, the milk just leaked out onto the ground. My parents claimed an unmilked bag was painful to the cow, although this assertion was hardly scientific. How did they know? The truth was, they wanted to make me feel guilty if I didn't get the job done on time; those poor, suffering cows, walking around with milk draining from their tits!

We stored the oats in a fifty-five-gallon drum with a rusting exterior and a piece of plywood for a lid. Each cow got a ration of a half gallon of oats, scooped out of the barrel with a large can. The cows knew what that tin can meant. Oats! To a cow, apparently, oats were the most delicious thing on the planet. They'd chow the oats down like there was no tomorrow, then stand there drooling and chewing on their stupid cuds while they were milked. All I had to do was go behind the barn come milking time and yell, *"Yoooooooiiiiiiieeeeee! Yoooooooiiiiiiieeeeee!"* They'd come running with their bags swinging like Jayne Mansfield's sweater.

It always struck me that getting milked was a bovine equivalent of getting a relaxing massage. I was a farm boy, not a city kid. Milking wasn't foreplay. I didn't pull tits. I yanked them. And I yanked them hard, believe me. I don't think the cows minded this at all; it was hard for me to believe my fingers were any rougher than a calf's teeth. When I started out on a cow, each squirt of milk hit the bottom of the metal bucket with a rhythmic *pow, pow, pow!* When the milk began to collect, with foam billowing, the squirts made a soft *foof, foof, foof* sound. I was taught to milk the tits on the corners, left front and right rear, or right front and left rear, but not simultaneously on the front, rear, or sides. Whether this was for reasons that were somehow biological and scientific or whether it was cockeyed farm wisdom—something recommended in the *Farmer's Almanoa*—I never knew. We usually had a barn cat hanging around, and I'd give it a few loops of milk that it'd catch in its mouth. This was its reward for keeping the mouse population under control, and I'd done it long enough that I was pretty damn accurate with a squirt of milk.

You'd think the cows would be halfway friendly to me for giving them oats and relief from having to lug all that milk around, but no; the damn things were always trying to piss on me or shit on me. The fresh shit collected in a six-inch-deep trough; this trough, the exact width of a square-bladed shovel, was situated directly below the poop chutes of the cows lined up at the stanchion. When I finished milking, it was my job to scoop up the plop and shovel it through the goo window—a four-by-six-foot open space that was closed by a kind of shutter or door that hooked onto a roof beam. We lowered the shutter in the winter to help keep the barn warm and left it open in the summer to air out the smell, but there were times in July and August when the stench inside was enough to knock a dog off a gut wagon. The lip of this window, and the wall below it, were always encrusted by brown crud that accumulated like cooling lava.

The pile of dried manure outside grew over the fall and winter until it was five or six feet high come spring. Then it was my chore to break it with a special fork that had flat broad tines with rounded ends rather than the round, sharp-pointed tines of a regular hay fork. I spaded this high-octane fertilizer into my mom's garden so it could be recirculated as vegetables.

So there I was, sitting on a milking stool, *foof, foof, foof*ing milk into a nearly full bucket and with a wholesome ration of fresh plop steaming away in the trough. I was milking my mother's favorite, Madame Queen, a Jersey who was a good cow; that is, she delivered three gallons or more with each milking. I had shackled Madame Queen's rear legs to keep her from kicking, but after she had insisted on taking a dump, I had neglected to pin her sodden tail into the shackles. It was easy enough to use a stick to poke the gooey tail into the shackle, but I had been too lazy. After you milk cows long enough, you know from the way a cow moves that her tail is on its way. A tranquil scene this was, when Madame Queen, chewing her cud lazily, turned her head. She looked both bored and annoyed. I felt a presence behind me.

"Ray?"

I turned.

It was Coach Mungo.

Madame Queen—perhaps unnerved by Mungo's unannounced arrival—switched her tail, the end of which was a ball of wet grunt. Sensing the wad was on its way, I leapt nimbly off my stool, taking my bucket with me.

The tail missed me, but caught Coach Mungo *splat!* on the calf of his khaki trousers.

Yuch!

"Jesus!" Coach jumped back in shock. He looked down at his leg, which was plastered with steaming, greenish-brown cow shit.

"Sorry, Coach," I said. I stopped and picked up a stick from the barn floor. I gave it to him. "The only thing you can do is scrape it off. You'll just have to put up with the smell until you can change your pants."

Looking annoyed, Coach Mungo set about removing the disgusting goo from his leg. He staggered momentarily, grabbing the edge of the grain barrel for support. The barrel was almost empty and nearly turned over, but Coach regained his balance. I caught a whiff of booze. He was drunk. I didn't even know he drank, and here he was obviously bombed. I didn't have to be told the reason for his visit. Russ was milking the end cow, and I could hear him mumbling away to himself.

I said, "They find Billy yet?"

He straightened and pulled his wet trousers from his skin. "That's why I'm here, Ray."

I got butterflies in my stomach. Had they found his body?

He said, "I want to know where he is." He glared at me with reddened eyes. This behavior was very unlike Coach Mungo, who ordinarily was a kind, thoughtful guy.

"I already told you, Coach. I haven't seen him since Friday."

"Bullshit."

"Really," I said.

"Bullshit. No way Billy abandoned his car on those railroad tracks."

"Well, like I say, I don't have any idea where he is."

"I want to know where you and your little girlfriend have been parking lately. You tell me."

I didn't especially like the way he said "little girlfriend." I wondered if I should return to my milking as we talked but thought better of it. "I'm not sure that's anybody's business," I said mildly.

"After the cop paid his little visit, I asked Billy if it was true that he was following you around."

Now we were getting somewhere. "What did he say?"

Coach scowled. "He denied it." Coach didn't believe Billy. Why else would he ask me where Angie and I parked? He said, "Tell me, where is it you kids go when you stomp mice?"

I didn't answer.

"In the desert up behind the irrigation canal, am I right? Over towards the army depot."

"You seem to have all the answers." Had Billy told him where we'd been parking? I should have lied. I should have said no, we parked off a road near Irrigon or somewhere. Too late. I had blurted out a nonanswer and was stuck with it.

Coach grabbed my shirt around the throat and jerked me off my feet, sending my bucket of milk flying. "Now listen, you lying little bastard, I want you to tell me what you've done to Billy. You and your half-breed girlfriend did something to him up there, didn't you? I want you tell to tell me now." He had a crazed look in his eye.

I heard a mumbling.

Coach Mungo's eyes widened. The tines of a shit fork were aimed at his throat.

Russ Storm, who had a crazed look of his own, said, "I believe you better put that boy down. You better put him down right now."

Coach Mungo put me down and lurched from the barn. I knew he would be scouring the stomping grounds come dawn.

THIRTY·ONE

AFTER SUPPER THAT NIGHT, I retreated to the privacy of The Coop to think things over. I turned on my little heater. The wires turned orange. The rubber blades began going *whump, whump, whump.* I settled in under my blankets. Coach Mungo was in no mood to give up on finding Billy; that was obvious. It also seemed a fact that Billy had said something to him about where we had been parking. In just what context was hard to figure, but there wasn't much doubt that Coach Mungo knew.

Billy Karady must surely be dead, I thought. If he had survived the night of the windstorm, the temperature was now diving again. The weatherman had predicted temperatures in the midtwenties. Even if Billy had survived the first night in the desert, it was unlikely he could make it through another. How in the hell could he?

What would happen if Coach Mungo went prowling around up there and found Billy's corpse? What if this? What if that? What if? What if? What if? I went over and over the territory again. Each time I arrived at the same conclusion. There was nothing to do but wait. I couldn't very well go up there in the morning and try to beat Coach to the evidence of the crime.

I decided to whip my wire. Maybe that would help relieve the tension so I could sleep. I closed my eyes and tried to think of Angie's warm body, but that inevitably led me back to Billy Karady and the never-ending what ifs. I turned to my magazines. Diane Webber didn't do it for me. Mame van Doren didn't work either. I tried my Mickey Spillane mysteries. No action there. I turned to the good spots in *Lady Chatterley's Lover*. No go. Finally, I gave up, resigned to another night of no sleeping. I yanked the string dangling from the switch of the lightbulb on the ceiling.

Someone thumped on my door. "Ray?"

It was Tom Agnopolous. I switched the light back on and opened the door. "Hey, come on in."

He said, "Kind of early for bed, isn't it? A young buck like you."

"I didn't get much sleep last night, what with that wind and all. Damn near blew my little coop over."

"Ah, yeah. I can see that." He sat on the end of the bed, obviously still wondering why I had tried to go to sleep at nine o'clock. "I take it you've been listening to the stories about Billy Karady's disappearance."

I got up and slipped on my pants. "Who hasn't? It's on every radio station. Kind of stupid to leave his car on the tracks like that. You find him yet?"

Tom looked around the interior of The Coop, pretending to be interested in the newspapers tacked onto the walls for insulation. He sighed. "No, we haven't. That's what I want to talk to you about."

"Me?"

"Ray, I want to know the last time you saw Billy."

"At the game against Stanfield on Friday. Coach Mungo asked me that same question. I gave him the same answer, which is the truth."

Tom bunched his face. "Coach is convinced you and Angie had something to do with Billy's disappearance."

"Coach is full of shit too. In addition to having it all over his leg."

"All over his leg?"

"He came by the barn tonight when Russ and I were milking. He was loaded and mad as hell. Madame Queen got him with a sloppy tail. That was before he picked me off the ground with a handful of my shirt wanting to know what I had done to Billy."

"He what?"

"He went crazy. If Russ hadn't threatened him with a manure fork, no telling what he might have done."

"He came by to see us this afternoon too. He said he wanted to get some facts cleared up. He said there was no way Billy Karady raped and killed that girl in Hermiston."

"Oh, how's that?"

"Coach Mungo is a homosexual," Tom said. "He says he and Billy had sex twice during the hour preceding the time we say the girl was raped and murdered. He says Billy would have had less than fifteen minutes to leave his apartment, drive to Hermiston, find the girl, then rape and kill her. That's in addition to getting it up again. Impossible, he says. Billy is not the *K* killer."

I was dumbfounded. Billy Karady and Coach Mungo having sex? What the hell was that? "What are you talking about?"

"Sex, Ray. They were having sex."

I still didn't get it.

"I shouldn't have to draw you a picture," Tom said.

I sat there on the bed. Sex between Coach Mungo and Billy Karady? It didn't calculate.

"Coach Mungo is in love with Billy. That's why he went to you this afternoon—to defend his lover."

"In love? Lover? I don't understand. We're talking Coach Mungo and Billy Karady."

"You're in love with Angie. I'm in love with Gracie. We both know what that means."

I blinked. "Yes, I guess we do. Angie and Gracie are female, for Christ's sake. These are two males."

"Whatever the sex of the lovers, the emotion is the same. You wanted to protect Angie from Billy. You know how much Billy pissed you off. Well, Coach wants to protect Billy from you."

"Angie and I didn't do anything to Billy. We may have wanted to, but we didn't."

Watching me, Tom ran his hand down his jaw. He sighed. "We both know what will happen when this all gets back to the school board."

"Coach is out of here in ten minutes," I said.

"Out of here and with no recommendation for another job. He's finished as a coach. This is one strike and you're out in almost all school districts."

Jesus, no wonder Coach had been loaded when he'd showed up in the barn. He loved coaching; that was obvious. Now he'd given it up to protect Billy. "I don't get it," I said. "Billy really did try to rape Angie. Angie didn't lie about that. No way. And he's been following us around ever since. He tried to drive us off the road. He shot at us with a .22 automatic."

"He shot at you?"

"That's his latest. I haven't had a chance to tell you. I figured, what's the use?"

Tom stared at the floor of The Coop a full minute without saying anything. "Well, Billy's just eighteen years old. Maybe he's trying to get the sex business sorted out in his mind. It can't be easy on him, being a high school hero and everything."

Then I understood something. "The muscle magazines," I said.

"Muscle magazines?"

"I told you Coach has a huge pile of muscle magazines in his apartment. I always wondered what that was all about. I know he lifts weight and everything, but I couldn't imagine why anybody would want to look at pictures of men all slathered down with oil." I paused, still blown away by this revelation.

"I like Coach Mungo. He's a good guy and a good coach. He really is. We all like him. I didn't hold it against him because I never got to play. Until this year, I've always been small, but slow. Now I'm just slow."

"No reason not to like him because he's homosexual. No reason he can't be a good coach either. The world's a complicated place, Ray."

"Jesus, that's a fact."

"Which brings us back to Billy Karady. Where the hell is Billy?"

"I told you, Tom. I have no idea."

Tom thought a moment. He didn't believe me entirely. I knew that. He said, "Well, he'll turn up someplace. Bound to."

Bound to. That was my problem.

Despite an all-points bulletin issued by the state police, and an intensive search of Umatilla County and the surrounding areas, Billy Karady was not found. There was one interesting bit of news that made the radio the next morning. A train engineer, asked by the police to look for anything suspicious along the right-of-way, was moving a short string of empty boxcars from The Dalles to Hinkle when he noticed what looked like a shallow grave beside the tracks. His schedule and rail traffic allowed him to stop for a few minutes to investigate. He found that the grave-sized hole was filled with large rocks, and he spotted a piece of canvas wrapped around the base of a large sagebrush about fifty yards south of the tracks.

State police officers later investigated and said the hole was freshly dug—by whom, they had no idea. They speculated that the canvas had been placed on top of the rocks, then covered with a layer of sand that had been blown away by the storm. There were no roads near the site, and nothing to indicate that the grave, if that's what it was, had anything to do with Billy Karady.

Not only was Billy gone, but Coach Mungo had disappeared too. He was seen leaving his apartment in the morning. He did not return. Police later searched his apartment, finding his barbells, muscle magazines, clothes, and all the rest of his belongings. That night, in an emergency meeting, the Umatilla school board named Mungo's assistant Rocky Holmes as the interim head coach.

The next day, Coach's pickup was found abandoned in the desert four miles southeast of Irrigon. This was about two miles west of the spot where Angie and I had taken Billy Karady down with a baseball bat. The police had no explanation or even theory of why Coach Mungo had parked there. His disappearance remained a mystery.

Angie and I both had a good idea why Coach had parked his pickup in the stomping grounds, but we were as mystified as the police as to where he had gone. The spotting of his pickup sparked a worrisome search of the desert, but nothing was found—not Billy, not Coach.

By the end of the week, the entire town was abuzz with queer jokes, and at school anybody who had ever been to Coach's apartment was the subject of suggestive razzing. It was hard for me not to feel sorry for Coach. He had never done anything out of the way with me or my friend Buddy Inskeep, and I don't believe with anybody else either—except for Billy Karady. And nobody knew for sure how his relationship with his star athlete got started. It remained difficult for me to adjust to the concept of males being in love, but if Coach felt about Billy the way I felt about Angie, I understood why he had lied to Tom Agnopolous. Anyway, both Billy Karady and Coach Brian Mungo were gone. Nobody had any idea where they were.

THIRTY·TWO

THE LOVE OF MY young life had begun on a hot August night with the arrival in Umatilla of a Greyhound bus from Spokane and with a thunderstorm brewing in the west. I remember standing with Angie at the door when Billy Karady rumbled down the street in his sleek black Cunt Wagon. It ended almost four months later, ten days after Angie Boudreau and I had taken Billy Karady under, this time with arctic blasts of frigid wind rushing south out of Canada.

The awful news came with a simple phone call in which Angie said her brother-in-law had been offered a job as the assistant manager of a hardware store in Tucson, Arizona, by a former catcher for the Walla Walla Bears who had been Paul's battery mate. She had to go with her sister. She had no choice. She had nowhere else to go. It was not like she was a star athlete with the whole town eager to find her a place to stay. And she could hardly stay at our tiny house, which just didn't have enough room as it was.

Hearing this, I had a sudden urge to vomit. "When?" I said. When she had first mentioned having to move, I was thinking of some civilized time in the future, the next month maybe, or springtime. Some decent warning.

"The truck is here now. They're packing our stuff."

"Doing what?" I could hardly believe it.

"We're on our way to Arizona in the morning."

"That's crazy. Why the rush?"

"Paul won't say. He just said he'd been offered the job, and he couldn't turn it down. He has a family to raise. This is a chance for him to have an inside job for a change. Get in out of the cold."

"Tomorrow morning!"

"Come pick me up, Ray. We need to go for a ride."

"Yes, we do. I'm on my way," I said. I hung up, stunned. Paul Remillard had never mentioned he was dissatisfied with his current job, and here he was, moving his family to Tucson, Arizona. I still didn't understand the reason for such a quick move.

I filled the Wheeled Turd with gas and picked Angie up straightaway. We first drove to Walla Walla, where I had bought the condoms at the popcorn stand. The popcorn stand was gone, but so were the migrant farmworkers whose unprotected dicks worried the city fathers. We then drove to Pendleton past the Round-Up grounds and the National Guard Armory, where I had danced with Brenda Lee. We had a passionate session in the buttes. We parked for a while in the turnaround by the stand of willows at the mouth of the Umatilla River while Elvis Presley sang "Heartbreak Hotel."

Finally, in the early hours of the morning, with my eager gentleman plumb tuckered from all the action, and with the snow beginning to accumulate on the ground, we took the road into the stomping grounds. We found the spot where we had smashed Billy Karady's head in. I don't know what we expected to find, but it wasn't Billy Karady—or Coach Mungo for that matter.

The sun was coming up when I took Angie home. I gave her a final embrace and a soft, sweet kiss, and we separated without looking back. I drove home feeling empty. I crawled into bed in The Coop. I felt numb. A part of my life had ended, summarily snuffed by an obscenely quick decision of an adult.

• • •

I loved Angie Boudreau so much it's impossible to describe the emotion. Night after night I lay on my bed in The Coop with pictures of her spread out on the floor. My heart ached when I went to bed at night. When I got up, thinking of her, my stomach bunched in great knots of anguish. God, how I missed her! It was impossible to imagine that I'd ever meet anybody like her again. I would get on with my life, I knew. There would be other girls. But this would be the great, passionate love of my life. There would never be anything to approach it.

Angie and I wrote to each other almost daily for a while. Then, predictably, I suppose, the letters began to slow. First just three or four a week, then one or two. I was busy with school and basketball practice, and, as time passed, there seemed less and less to say; an assertion of love was insufficient. Never mind famous correspondence between literary lovers; a warm body was essential to maintain the real thing. And the business of our having smashed Billy Karady's head in didn't help matters. We didn't talk about it in our letters, but the knowledge of what we had done—and of Billy's amazing disappearance—was always there.

With the passing of time, the possibility grew that we would never again be together. We never mentioned this awful prospect, but we both knew it. Our four magnificent, passionate, unforgettable months were gone. She now lived in Tucson. I lived in Umatilla. I heard a comedian on the "Ed Sullivan Show" say that the greatest distance in the world was the gap between two single beds. I thought, *Try Arizona and Oregon, pal.*

Then one day in late March, Angie sent me a clipping from the newspaper in Tucson. Someone had raped and murdered a young woman, after which he had scratched the letter *K* on her chest. The Tucson police said the MO was the same as in earlier rapes and murders in Kennewick, Washington, and Hermiston,

Oregon. They had no idea whether the *K* killer had moved to Tucson from Kennewick or Hermiston or whether this was a copycat crime, with the MO gleaned from reading newspapers. The police in Arizona were looking for Billy Karady, a missing Oregon teenager who was a suspect in the earlier murders.

That's all she sent me. A single newspaper clipping and nothing else. No accompanying note. No comment. Nothing. The *K* killer was in Tucson. Billy Karady? Was it Billy?

Startled, I showed the clipping to Tom Agnopolous, who was by then engaged to marry my sister, Gracie.

Tom said yes, the *K* rapist had apparently reappeared in Tucson, and yes, the police there were looking for Billy Karady. There had been reports that he had been spotted, but these were unconfirmed.

After a sleepless week of no mail from Angie, I received one of my letters back with a post office stamp saying the addressee had moved and had left no forwarding address. I called her immediately. The operator said the number had been disconnected.

Again, I asked Tom about the appearance of the *K* killer in Tucson. He said the rapes had stopped, but the killer had not been caught.

I thought about asking Tom to call the Tucson police to see if anything had happened to Angie Boudreau, but I decided not to. If Billy Karady had murdered Angie, she was dead. Full stop. If I didn't know she was dead, then the possibility remained that she was still alive. By not knowing of her death, I could keep her alive always in my memory.

I lived through the remaining year and a half of high school wondering when, or if, Billy would show up on my doorstep looking for his final measure of revenge.

I never heard from Angie Boudreau again. After she sent the newspaper clipping, all communication ceased.

The day after school got out the next June, telling no one, I left Umatilla forever. I couldn't stand wondering when, or if,

Billy would show up on my doorstep looking for his final measure of revenge.

I went to college in Hawaii, served in the army, and became a prolific and respected, if commercially marginal author of suspense fiction. As the decades passed, my life was physically adventurous—I traveled all over the world—but it was emotionally a form of doldrums. I never forgot Angie Boudreau. I always wondered what had happened to her. I never forgot Billy Karady either. Hard to do that. In my imagination he was omnipresent; he lurked around the next corner, or up the next alley, or through the next door. He never made an appearance, but he was there still, a haunting presence brandishing a phantom baseball bat. It was for that reason that I wrote my novels under the pseudonym Nicholas van Pelt.

Chief Lapu Lapu killed Ferdinand Magellan on Mactan Island in the Philippines, which was joined by a bridge to Cebu, a larger island north of Mindanao and west of Leyte. On his second attempt to circumnavigate the globe, the great Portuguese explorer had figured out the truth: that to get to the mysterious east, he had to sail west.

If a hurricane of strength equal to that of Typhoon Betty had hit South Carolina or Florida's Gold Coast, it would have been constantly on the tube—on CNN, The Weather Channel, and all the broadcast networks—with Americans all over the country presumably transfixed by the sight of breathless reporters in raincoats passing on the latest prediction of high winds and wild seas. Asians had a different view of things. Not only did Filipinos not have a sky sprinkled with expensive weather satellites, but a typhoon in the Visayas—in the middle of the archipelago—was not a source of great concern in Manila. Sure, there might be a light rain and a restless wind in the capital city, but Manila was on the island of Luzon; nobody there wanted to interrupt Inday Badiday's afternoon interviews with show business celebrities to worry about people in Cebu.

When Betty struck, I was in Fritz's Place, an expat bar on Mactan run by an alcoholic former German ship's captain. Three Germans, two Australians, two Filipinos, an Irishman, a Swede, and I had formed a barkada—*a small circle of friends— that met every afternoon in Fritz's. I had been a member of that* barkada *for close to a year when Typhoon Chris hit on a Saturday night. I soaked up San Miguel that night, eating peanuts that had been cooked in garlic oil, and eyeing the sexy Filipinas who had gathered to troll for long-noses who might take them to North America or Europe.*

The first winds struck late in the afternoon, buffeting the nipa *huts and ripping slabs of corrugated tin from roofs. By nine o'clock—well after the six o'clock bewitching hour when it got dark every day in Mactan—Betty was ripping across the island with 130-mile-an-hour winds. Of course Fritz's was plunged into darkness.*

Despite the typhoon, it was still sweltering inside Fritz's. My companionable band of drinkers and I, resigned to spending most of the night in the bar, began consuming San Miguel in earnest, watching the storm with sweaty faces highlighted by the flickering yellow of candles. The typhoon, a great whorl of violence, moved counterclockwise, blowing sheets of tin, boards, and palm fronds from right to left; the palm trees leaned nearly parallel to the ground.

At about eleven o'clock, the eye of the typhoon arrived, and my barkada, *by then soaked with San Miguel, walked outside and stood in a street cluttered with boards, boxes, parts of roofs, and palm fronds to enjoy the eerie respite. We grinned broadly as we walked around. We hadn't been blown away! Okay! Such a deal. Yet we knew that the storm was not yet finished; the backside of the destructive whorl was every bit as violent as the front. The tranquil eye was an odd and anxious*

*calm; the air was unusually fresh and smelled clean and good,
but that, we knew, was deceptive.*

*A half hour later, the backside of Betty was upon us, and
we retreated inside to drink more beer. We watched in awe,
laughing nervously as the amazing wind—giving the mistaken
impression of having reversed directions—straightened the
palms, then pushed them on their sides left to right. Suddenly,
the thatched roof over Fritz's courtyard lifted and sailed off into
the night, scattering tables and chairs in all directions. We celebrants, grabbing squealing Filipinas, sought refuge behind the
bar where they snatched bottles of Tanduay and Anejo rum
from the shelves. We huddled together, grateful that it was
Fritz's thatched roof, not us, that had been treated so discour-
teously.*

*I huddled with my arm around a slender Filipina, a friend
of the cashier. She did not drink or smoke, which meant she
wasn't a hooker. As the wind ripped the island apart, it occurred to me that my copper-skinned companion, of the Malay
race of southeast Asia, looked quite like Angie Boudreau, who
had disappeared from my life all those years ago. There was no
mystery to this; if the anthropologists had it right, the ancestors
of the Sioux had emigrated to North America over a land bridge
across the Bering Strait tens of thousands of years ago. This
was yet one more circle for me to consider.*

*That night I fell in love with the Filipina, whom I would
eventually marry. That night also, I decided to return to the
United States and take my chances with the backside of my
personal typhoon: Billy Karady.*

II.

AFTER THE PASSING OF THE EYE

ONE

I'VE RETURNED TO THE United States after nearly five years in Asia. I met my Filipina wife in a typhoon, but she is no stormy woman; I can say with great joy and without embarrassment that I lucked out. I love her dearly. She's good-looking, uncomplicated, and caring, and when she beats me in chess, she cheerfully puts up with my frustrated scowling and claims that she lucked out. For forty years, I have allowed myself to be pursued by a ghost, going so far as to spend most of my time abroad. But now, having found a form of peace in my personal life, I've given up exile. Yes, Billy Karady might yet be alive. Yes, he might yet be bent on revenge. I have no idea what I'll do if he shows up. One thing I now decline: no more will I allow my life to be defined by fear of the unknown.

I'm at a New Orleans convention of the American Booksellers Association, standing behind a table piled high with copies of my latest novel. All these years I've published under the pseudonym of Nicholas van Pelt, a name that I picked with a random poke in a San Francisco telephone directory. But now I have decided to reclaim my life. Now, under what is turning out to be a new direction for me—a commercial novel much hyped by my publisher—I am Ray Hawkins. This publisher went just hog-wild, buying large ads for my novel in the trade magazine *Publisher's Weekly* as well as in the *New York Times*

Book Review. Also for the first time I have allowed my photograph on the dust jacket. A photographer friend caught me looking rakish and adventurous in a Panama hat with a colorful band, and my publisher decided to plaster it over the entire back of the book.

All this, I know, means just one thing: if Billy Karady is still alive, he will surely find me; that is, if he pays any attention to books, and given the public fascination with computers, television, and electronic gadgetry, that's a questionable assumption. Nobody in Umatilla High School ever mistook him for a budding scholar. If I luck out and make the top of the list or sell to the movies, that's another story. If he is dead, I have surely made it past the long memory of the law. What evidence could possibly exist that would hold up in court?

This is a huge room at the convention center where publishers, encamped in what amounts to a city of tables and promotional islands, are hyping the titles on their current lists. Up and down the streets, lands, and avenues between the tables of hopeful touters of new titles, roam buyers for both the chains and independent bookstores, editors, publishers, writers, and the curious. Despite television, the Internet, and the rest of it, people still do read. How they select what to read out of all these books is a story in itself.

Since this is my first title under my real name, the pile of books in front of me seems overly ambitious. Nevertheless, I'm there with a smile on my face if not a shine on my shoes, a literary Willie Loman. This of course is not how authors make the bestseller lists. They usually make the lists because a cowboy publisher decides to put them there, manipulating the herd with a financial cattle prod, although every once in a while that old writer's dream, word of mouth, produces a miracle. I've always been known as a midlist writer, a professional who, for one reason or another, never scored a big pop. There is no reason for me to feel like the Lone Ranger. There are lots of good writers out there, like me who, for one reason or another, never scored a big pop. As Ray Hawkins, I'm hopeful my time has come.

My table is surrounded by a six or eight middle-aged women. Women, bless their imaginative, page-turning hearts, are the main readers of fiction. If it weren't for them, most of us writers would go out of business. For the most part, men regard authors as oddities. It's the women who respect us. Prick the skin of nine out of ten women in a gathering like this, and you'll find a wannabe writer.

I take a sip of coffee from a white plastic cup and glance out across the hall. I see a couple my age coming toward my table. I recognize the woman. I'm astonished. It's her. Angie Boudreau. After all these years, there she is, like Lazarus risen from the dead. I'm momentarily taken aback. I try not to appear shocked, but it isn't easy.

She's thicker, yes, but not at all bad for her age. She still has fabulous eyes, that's for sure. After all these years, those large brown cat eyes are still the same. And while her lower lip has lost some of its Brigitte Bardot pout, there is no mistaking her sensual mouth. Her companion, who, judging by their easily familiarity, is most likely her husband, has every right to be proud of his lady.

They walk straight to my table. Her stride has lost that sensual shifting from to hip to hip, but it's unmistakably her, sexy Angie, love of my life.

I take another sip of coffee—a nervous gesture. Hard to believe, after all these years. She is as an apparition welled up from my memory. Once she was a burning coal, now she is a warming sight. "Well, well, well!" I say. "Still alive and kicking, eh?"

"Still here," she says. She looks at me straight on. Her eyes are those I first saw when she got off the Greyhound bus all those years ago. Obviously explanations will have to wait, but I know they'll come in time, or she wouldn't be here.

"You're looking good. Real fine, as a matter of fact."

"Thank you," she says. She glances at the placard on my table. "You know I once read a novel by Nicholas van Pelt. There was something familiar about the narrator that I couldn't put my finger on. I had no idea it was you. You'd have thought . . ." Her voice trails off, then she laughs. Same good laugh. The ice, as they say, has been broken. "This is my husband, David Feuer."

Feuer extends his hand and we shake. "We celebrate our thirty-eighth wedding anniversary next month."

He got the girl, but those things happen. He seems like an okay guy. Too many years have passed for me to feel competitive or anything like that. I instinctively like him. I just want to know what the hell Angie's story is. I say, "You've got good taste in women, I'll give you that."

Angie says, "I've often wondered about your sister. Did she marry Tom Agnopolous?"

"Oh, yes," I say. "And she cloned more Agnopolouses, two boys and a girl."

"David and I have a son who is the city editor of the *Denver Post*. And you?"

"Probably the only people who've seen as much of the world as me are people with inherited wealth and other writers. I've slowed down, if not settled down. I now have a Filipina wife and a two-year-old daughter, a little beauty. My wife is visiting her sister in Canada." I retrieve my wallet and dig out a picture.

Angie looks at the picture, and her faces changes. I know why. In fact my wife looks just like Angie did when she was younger. Angie is half–Native American, and the Asian in her shows. She says, "David is a former police detective in Tucson. Retired."

"Ahh," I say.

"He was in charge of the investigation of the *K* killer in Tucson. He was also in charge of the case when Paul attacked me."

Feuer says, "A young cop. Full of myself."

I blinked. "Paul attacked you? Paul who?"

"Paul Remillard, my brother-in-law. Attack isn't the right word. He raped me. Needless to say, it was a traumatic experience."

"Couldn't get her off my mind," Feuer says. "I went back and asked her out. I was twelve years older than she was, but I thought to hell with that age crap. She was a real find."

"You don't have to tell me that. I knew her in Umatilla." Having said that, I'm momentarily nonplused. First the clip saying the *K* killer had struck in Tucson. Then nothing. I had assumed Angie was likely dead. Now, forty years later, this. Rape. A cop husband. "I have to admit, I thought you were dead," I say. "All these years. I thought he got to you."

Feuer is suddenly alert. "By 'he' you mean?"

"I mean the *K* killer. Billy Karady."

Angie says, "I should tell you David's writing a book about unsolved crimes. The *K* killings is one of the cases."

I say, "How many girls did he kill in Tucson?"

"Just the one," Feuer says.

"And you never caught him?"

Feuer shakes his head. "Never did. Say, would you like to have supper with us tonight? You can talk over old times with Angie, and there are some new developments in the case that you might find interesting. I'd like to hear what you think."

"New developments? With regard to the *K* killer?"

"Having to do with Billy Karady."

"Karady. I see."

"It's been in the newspapers—a small item, so you might not have read it."

A new development having to do with Billy Karady? A flutter of anxiety races through my stomach, although I try not to look like I have *guilty* tattooed on my forehead. "Supper? Sure, why not?" I say.

An attractive thirtyish woman steps up to my pile of books.

She picks up one, looking at the cover.

I say, "Lady, if you read that book, you'll never go back to those stupid old brand-namers, guaranteed. I've got you locked onto my books for life." I know what the deal is. Ordinarily, she would give me a try, but she wants to read the same books as her friends. This is the logic of the herd. I've given up resenting it in any way. It just is. Wonderful that there are still people left who read any kind of books.

I do my best to give her a charming smile, but my mind is on Billy Karady. I had assumed my problem was Karady lying in wait, intent on knocking my block off. It had never occurred to me in my wildest dreams that Angie Boudreau would show up married to a retired cop with a passion for unsolved crimes. Talk about your basic, unpredictable existential turn of events. The path turns left. The path turns right. The path circles back. There is sunshine. There is gloom. There's no way of planning or controlling it.

TWO

WE'RE AT A TABLE in the cocktail lounge of a Cajun restaurant in the French Quarter, having drinks before we eat. I say, "Was the Tucson K-man the same killer as in Kennewick and Hermiston, do you think, or a copycat?"

David Feuer takes a sip of Scotch. "Hard to say for sure. We were never able to find out. Billy Karady was the chief suspect of the police in Washington and Oregon, but he just vanished. It's hard to believe an eighteen-year-old kid from that part of the country could build a new identity and elude the police all those years, but it's always possible. And why would he go to Tucson?"

I think: *To follow Angie, you dumb shit; he was obsessed by her, the sicko son of a bitch.*

Feuer retrieves a newspaper clip from his jacket pocket. He gives it to me. "Two days ago some young men were out stomping mice. They had been drinking in a kind of ritual. An end-of-the-summer kind of thing. Here, read this."

I read the clip. Students at Umatilla High School had been stomping mice when a mouse, closely followed by the foot of sixteen-year-old Jeremy Inskeep, sought refuge in a human skull. Inskeep flattened the skull, forcing the forensics examiners to go through the laborious task of putting it back together piece by piece. Early indications were that the deceased was killed by a crushing blow to the skull. The laboratories of the Oregon State Police determined the badly decomposed skeleton was that of a white male, eighteen to thirty-eight years old. The remains, apparently buried by windblown sand, had been there approximately forty years.

Feuer watches me as I read.

Where in the hell were they? I wonder. Then I find it. The skull was stomped some five miles west of the spot where Angie and I had taken our licks at Billy Karady's head. The ritual of the stomp had survived, it had just been pushed farther west by the long march of French fries. Billy apparently hadn't been thinking clearly enough to use the wind to reckon direction. The bones were found close to the spot where they found Coach Mungo's abandoned pickup. No Billy. No Coach. Which one was the skeleton, if either? "They were on a Great Stomp," I say.

"Oh?"

"A mouse stomp. We called them kangaroo rats, but they're mice. They bound, like miniature 'roos. Good to read there were no females involved. Still a male thing. No harm in leaving us with a little territory. Pajama parties, girls. Mouse stomps, boys. What the hell?"

"You've stomped mice, have you?"

I grin. "The Inskeep kid is the son of an old friend of mine, Buddy Inskeep, a onetime fullback." I glance at Angie.

He says, "A suggestive report, do you think?"

I shrug. "Nostalgic for me. You think the skull was Billy Karady's?"

"Happened about the same time he disappeared."

"Or Coach Mungo's. Isn't that near where they found his car?"

"Could be his. That too," Feuer says.

"Coach Mungo was a prisoner of the Japanese during World War II. The army probably checked him out in a hospital after he was freed. Maybe they can help. Dental records or something."

"A request is working its way through the Department of Defense as we speak."

I catch Angie's eyes, couldn't help it. I remember the night we had dug Billy's grave. The crazed fucking. The time we spent on the backseat wallowing in the smell of sex. Then the train, coming right at us. The leisurely fucking after it had passed. We had dodged it then, but we knew it remained on the tracks, hurtling our way.

Is Angie thinking about that night too? She is. Has to be.

Feuer says, "I read the investigative reports of the Oregon State Police. Sergeant Tom Agnopolous noted in a report that he had talked to a high school girl who claimed Karady had tried to rape her, but she refused to testify because it would be her word against his, and he was a star athlete at Umatilla High School."

Tom had kept his word. Good for him. "I can believe that. That's the way things worked in places like Umatilla in 1957. By the way, that's Tom Agnopolous, my brother-in-law. I was a junior then when Billy Karady disappeared. He was a senior." I stop. How much should I tell him? He isn't stupid, and he has read the report. The problem was I haven't. I have no idea what is in it. Feuer has spent some time thinking about this crime; that's obvious. I say, "Billy Karady was a raging asshole, evil to the core of his being."

Feuer watches me, waiting. He's a professional cop. I assume that a good cop, like a good reporter, knows when to keep his mouth shut. When he knows I'm not going to volunteer anything more, he says, "There was one detail covered in the investigative reports that wasn't included in the newspaper reports. There was a loaded .22 automatic rifle in the trunk of Karady's Mercury. A Marlin."

"Where's the surprise there?" I say.

"He disappeared the first week of December. Would he have been hunting then?"

I say, "Good question. We used to shoot jackrabbits with

.22s but that was usually in the summertime. Did Tom's report say it was me who interrupted the attempted rape at the mouth of the Umatilla?"

"Yes, it did."

"It happened in a grove of willows. I was screening for arrowheads about 150 yards to the west when I heard the girl screaming. Was that in the report?"

"Yes, it was."

"But no mention of the girl's name?"

Feuer glances at Angie. He obviously knows Angie was the girl who had screamed. How much more does he know? "No. Agnopolous said he talked to the girl, who declined to press charges on the grounds that it would be her word against his. She also said Billy Karady was stalking her."

Was David Feuer the engineer on the oncoming train, arrived at last after all these years?

Feuer said, "After Billy disappeared, Coach Mungo talked to Agnopolous. He told him the Hermiston rape attributed to the *K* killer was impossible. He said Billy had had two orgasms within an hour of the rape. The suggestion in the report was clear: Mungo and Karady were homosexual lovers. No mystery why Mungo would take off. The school district in a small town like that would never let him keep his job. The question is why he would abandon his pickup in the desert. Where did he go? Did he murder Billy Karady and put his car on the railroad tracks? The questions and possible answers go in circles."

"Don't they?" I say. I take another sip of rum. "You smoke pot?"

"I'm a retired cop."

I smile. "That wasn't my question, but it was a good answer. If you'll excuse me, I have to go the john." Without another word, I get up and thread my way through the tables to the men's john. I find a stall, lock the door, load a one-hit pipe with some sticky green, and light up. Holding the smoke in my lungs, I reload. When I'm finished, I leave the john stall smelling like cannabis and return to the table.

I sit down, feeling mellow and in that odd, drifty zone of being stoned; the world is at once wonderful, absurd, and slightly askew. "Good bud," I say. "Sticky green." I pause, grinning. "You're not going to call the fuzz or anything like that."

Feuer laughs. "Angie tells me you were an independent spirit."

"Haven't changed, it's so. I've lived most of my life as a . . . Bohemian, I guess, best describes it. I'm an obsessive writer. I'm indifferent to competitive consumption. I love to travel." I stop. "Well, yes, I have changed. We all do." I look at him, trying to think of a good way to express my way of looking at the world. "Have you ever lived abroad for any period of time? I mean for years, not weeks or months."

He shakes his head no.

"I've recently come back from Asia after my last stretch of exile. Amost five years. When I returned, I found the country had changed dramatically. The Internet is everywhere. Television is far more violent and crazy than it was when I left. Young people are getting tattoos and having themselves pierced with rings. Cigars are fashionable. Congress is on C-SPAN, and what was once serious because it was remote is revealed to be a circus of competing egos. Turns out congressmen and senators are no different from the grasping assholes in city hall or the county seat. This shouldn't have surprised anyone, but it was more public myth shattered. It's as though we're edging closer and closer to Anthony Burgess's vision in *Clockwork Orange*. You ever read that novel?"

Again, he shakes his head.

"I left one country and came back to another. It's the same culture, but far, far different. People evolve in much the same way, if you think about it. When you stand in front of the mirror each morning, you see the same face. It changes day by day, but you can't recognize the changes. They're too small. If you look at a picture of yourself when you were younger, you can appreciate the difference, but not from day to day. From day to day, you're the same, or think you are. We're all the same as when we were young, but different too, both on the exterior and in the interior."

I hold up the newspaper clip. "For example, this kid Jeremy Inskeep is the son of an old friend of mine. They still stomp mice in Umatilla, which is why I smiled, but potato fields have scarfed up almost all the old desert. The skull Jeremy flattened was a good five miles west of our old stomping grounds. You see what I'm getting at? Umatilla in 1957 was a forest ago and then some. It remains that still."

"A forest? I thought it was semiarid desert."

Angie is watching me, remembering the adolescent foolishness of our reading Camus and Sartre. "I mean in a metaphorical sense. A dark woods of constantly dividing trails. Choices. Each fork is a choice. We're faced with multiple forks every day of our lives. We create our identities by the forks we take. We take some of these forks on purpose, but others are accidents over which we have no control. Easy to track in circles just like your questions and answers." Or if you're in a sandstorm like the dazed, bleeding Billy Karady, I think. I like Feuer. He's an okay guy. Angie has done well for herself. Good for her. "Angie was my girlfriend back then. Did she tell you that?"

"Yes, she did."

I glance at Angie.

She says, "Go ahead, tell him. He's probably already figured it out."

Tell him what? What has he figured out? I smile at the ambiguity of my dilemma. It, she says. Figure it out. What the fuck is *it?* I want to give Angie a lecture on the precise use of language.

I get a stoned flash of the naked Angie and I on the rear seat of the Wheeled Turd, daring the train to run over us if it would. How long I had sat there without replying, I can't say. Losing track of time is part of being stoned. Seconds? Half a minute? A minute? It was impossible to judge the length of such interior action. I say, "Angie was the girl in the willows."

"I figured that out, then Angie confirmed it," he says.

"But at first, you didn't know for sure."

"You and Angie were sweethearts. Tom Agnopolous was dating your sister. It was obvious from his reports that he wasn't telling everything he knew."

I say, "Have you talked to Tom about the case?"

"Yes, I have. Several times. He says he has no idea what happened. It's always been a mystery to him."

Good old Tom. He wouldn't want to rake up the mud after all these years. What was the point? Was he going to be responsible for putting his brother-in-law in the slammer? Gracie would skin him alive. I say, "So tell me, if you think the stomped skull is Billy Karady's, who do you think killed him and why?"

Feuer, watching me, says nothing for a moment. Then, he says, "Brian Mungo is a possibility. He had a motive. He was in love with Karady. He was jealous that Karady was obsessed with a high school girl. It's possible that he had a lover's quarrel with him, killed him, and buried his body in the desert. Easy to do. Just scoop some sand over the corpse."

I say, "So what it boils down to is that you don't have any idea whether or not the skeleton belongs to Billy Karady, and if it is him, you don't know how he died."

"That's about it," he says. "We can only speculate."

I think about that. The *K* killer had struck twice in Kennewick, once in Hermiston, then in Tucson, Arizona. Who in the hell was *K*?

THREE

DAVID FEUER SUDDENLY SLIDES off the bar stool and stands. "If you'll excuse me, I better go recirculate some of this alcohol. I suspect the old prostate is getting bigger."

I say, "Happens to most of us, if the statistics are correct."

Watching her husband head for the john, Angie leans over and murmurs in my ear; her breath is warm. "I once loved you more than life itself. I will never forget it. Never."

"Nor will I. But that kind of passion can never last, I suppose. It's incandescent. It rushes up and bursts in brilliant colors and is gone. Not a bad thing, however. The memories are wonderful."

She smiles. "They are for a fact. I agree."

"I think about you all the time. If it hadn't have been for you, I'd never have had the courage to ask Brenda Lee for a dance. And remember the trip to Walla Walla to buy the rubbers?"

"And the night we dug the grave by the right-of-way?"

"We might have been flattened by a freight train. God, how could I forget that?"

We're silent for a moment. Then, I say, "I like your husband. He seems like a good person."

"Thank you. I thought you'd like him. He's treated me well."

"Does he think we killed Billy Karady?"

"He says it was most likely Coach Mungo."

"I know what he says. I want to know what he thinks. He knows Billy tried to rape you. He knows you were my girl-friend. He's talked to Carl, so he likely knows we complained about Billy, but nothing was done. We had a motive."

"I don't know whether he suspects us or not, but I don't think it makes any difference," she says. "He loves me. He's just curious is all. You have to understand the Tucson K murder happened on his watch, and he wasn't able to catch the killer. After all these years, it still grinds at him. For him, the mystery is the thing. He's just as interested in closing the mystery as he is in justice."

"Did you catch the way he circled the possibility with his questions? He was curious about how much I would hold back." She sees David coming back from the john. Quickly she hands me an envelope under the table. "This is for you. I want you to look at it later, when you're back in your hotel."

I quickly slip the envelope into my jacket pocket, wondering what it is.

When he's back in his chair, I say, "By the way, David, did you know Paul Remillard was at one time a pitcher for the Walla Walla Bears?"

Feuer looks puzzled. "A pitcher? He was?"

I know he doesn't see what I'm getting at. "The night of my first date with Angie we were talking in his living room; he told me he had trouble with a hanging curve. Said he had a good fastball and forkball and an okay change-up. If he'd had a decent curve, maybe he'd have made the show. The Bears were then a Class-A farm team of the Yankees. He said in those days all the Yankee scouts wanted all their pitchers to be like Whitey Ford. They had to have everything—the full repertoire of pitches. They didn't want Bob Fellers, all heat and nothing else. Do you know how a baseball scorer records a strikeout?"

Feuer thinks for a moment. "With a K."

"That's right, *K*," I say. "A pitcher's favorite letter. Think about it for a moment. Remillard was living in Umatilla when the girls were killed in Kennewick and Hermiston. He moved to Tucson, and the *K* killer struck there. All this time I thought it was Billy Karady who had followed Angie south. Then Remillard raped Angie. What if that wasn't his first rape? If he'd followed *K*'s MO, he might have killed her . . ." I take a sip of my Heineken, thinking. "Maybe he thought that because Angie was his sister-in-law, she'd never press charges. He was safe. No need to kill her. In fact, it would be downright dangerous to scratch his trademark *K* on the chest of his dead sister-in-law. The police would immediately make the connection between Kennewick and Tucson."

"You think Remillard was the *K* killer?"

"I don't have any idea. A matter of circumstance, I know. When he went to the slammer for raping Angie, the *K* killings stopped, didn't they?"

"Yes, they did," he says. "Definitely suggestive. *K* for strikeout. I hadn't thought of it."

"Also think of the baseball expression, 'grab some pine,' meaning take a seat on the bench. If you strike a player out, he grabs some pine. I remember my dad always saying, 'We're all gonna rest in pine some day.' Meaning what?"

Feuer says, "A pine box. A coffin. We'll all be dead."

"There you go," I say. "Pine is a soft wood, easy to work, and the most available on the frontier. Out west coffins were made of pine, not fancy hardwood. That's what the killer was doing, wasn't it? Sending those girls to the pine. Then he marked his strikeout on his victim's chest with the traditional *K*—perfect for the frustrated pitcher who never made it to the bigs."

"Maybe you should have been the detective, not me."

"Pot flash," I say.

He laughs.

We sit in silence for a moment. Even if Paul Remillard was

the *K* killer, that left the question of Billy Karady's fate unanswered.

I say, casually, "If Billy Karady was dead in the sand back in Oregon, he couldn't very well have raped and murdered anybody in Tucson." The envelope in my jacket is burning a hole through my shirt. I can hardly restrain myself from ripping it open to see what the hell is in it.

Angie nudges my ankle with her toes.

What the hell? I catch her eyes. She uses her eyes to direct my attention as I had once told the Fossil linebacker which hole Billy Karady was coming through next.

I look. I'm astonished.

Billy Karady, or a man who looks just likes him, a doppleganger, his double, is sitting with his wife or girlfriend at another table. The woman's back is to us. The man's left eye looks a trifle odd. Whether it is a glass eye or slightly misaligned is hard to tell. It's also difficult to tell whether or not he's actually looking at us. Maybe so. Maybe not. Maybe he's just talking to his companion. He sure as hell looks like Karady, but forty years is a long time. Maybe he just looks like him.

I glance at Angie. She too is shaken. It's obvious she too doesn't know what to think. Is the man Billy Karady? If he is, he's not in the French quarter to sample Cajun food and listen to jazz.

"Well, I'm hungry," I say. "Time to eat, do you think?"

"Good idea," Feuer says.

I take another look at the man out of the corner of my eye. It is Karady! There's something about him. That long face of his. That jaw. That chin. Even with his bad eye, he has a familiar look about him. I've seen that face many times before—glaring at me out of the huddle at Fossil, studying me from the interior of the Cunt Wagon, staring up at me in pain at the stomping grounds. Billy Karady risen from our past to haunt us. Shit!

Then I think no. My imagination is playing tricks.

Then yes. It's him. No question. Billy Karady is back. I've returned to the United States and published a novel under my own name and with my photograph on the dusk jacket. Face him if he's there, I told myself.

FOUR

LATER, BACK IN MY hotel room, listening to the distant honk and beep of traffic on the street below, I do another hit of sticky green. I open a can of Heineken from the small refrigerator in my room. The pot makes the beer taste extra delicious; I savor it in my mouth. I take the envelope out of my jacket and lay it on the bed. I stare at it, but I don't open it. I decide to treat the envelope like the possibility of the oncoming train all those years ago. I will leave it there unopened. How long will I be able to refrain from looking?

I have spent the last forty years living in the eye of a massive typhoon. With the appearance of Angie and her husband, a cop poking around in the past, followed quickly by Billy Karady, or a man who looks just like him, I know the calm is up. I face the backside of the whorl.

When I got back from Asia, I read about an author who had written a memoir in which he purported to have been brutally abused by a guard in a prison for wayward boys. He was in this awful place for a year, he said. When he grew up, he and some friends who had likewise been abused conspired to murder the guard, and they got away with it in a clever courtroom ruse. It turned out that this story was bogus. In wasn't a memoir at all; it was fiction. In fact, as a youngster the writer had been missing from school for only nineteen days, not an entire year. No record could be found of the court case or anything even resembling it.

Did the cowboy publisher receive public censure for having perpetrated a fraud? Why, certainly not! Owing to the generosity of the First Amendment there are no consumer's rights in the publishing world. The ruse of fiction marketed as nonfiction was considered a triumph. The herd, by nature a lover of the bogus and inauthentic, had responded predictably. The book was a best-selling stampede. The publisher made a bundle. The author got rich. His next book would be written about in the news magazines whether it deserved it or not. A movie was made. Everybody was happy.

I get up with my can of Heineken in hand. I look down at the street below. The sidewalks are full of celebrants on their way to Bourbon Street. The Heineken tastes delicious. On the sidewalk, a man standing beside a matronly woman in her fifties looks up in my direction. This is the Billy Karady look-alike that Angie spotted in the bar. He *is* Billy Karady. Has to be. Or is he? Is this just my imagination working overtime—fueled by fear and guilt? He turns his head before I can be sure. He and the woman continue on their way. Shaken, I return to the single comfortable chair in my room and take another hit of pot.

Sitting there, I decide to bring this episode of my life to some kind of conclusion. I decide to write a novel about a murderer who becomes a writer and later, as a form of tempting fate, twists the facts of his crime into a manuscript that is a form of confession. My confession will say to David Feuer and to any officer of the courts in Oregon who might be curious that, yes, my high school girlfriend and I attempted to commit murder one cold and windy night, but they need to know the context. The larger story is more than the details of means, motive, and opportunity, and that is where the tools of fiction come in.

I open a file on my notebook computer. I sit there, stoned,

my hand on the mouse. I watch the blinking cursor, a baton conducting my heartbeat, the opening and closing of mortal valves. The cursor is blinking to the ticks of the Timex on my wrist. I bought the Timex in Kuala Lumpur, and when it's totally quiet, I can hear it ticking. I think of the Native Americans, whose *ba-bump, ba-bump, ba-bump* drumbeat also matched the heartbeat.

To grasp the full meaning of what happened, I decide my readers should also know what happened in the future, which I will tell in a series of short flash-forwards whose meanings at once enlarge on the story and loop back. These will be Albert Camus' existential backdraft—the wind forever blowing from the future.

What is the worst that can follow if I tell the truth? Will the state of Oregon reopen the case and charge Angie and me with murder? I'll simply say my novel is fiction based on an old case and any resemblance between my characters and real people is strictly coincidental. I'm just an opportunistic, lying writer, part of an honorable, crass tradition. What do I care about meaningful labels and the accuracy of language? Yes, I was there at the time. Yes, my name figured in police reports of the investigation, but nobody can prove the shattered skull belonged to Billy Karady, much less that he had been murdered. They might build a circumstantial case against Angie and me, but they can do the same for Coach Mungo. Maybe Coach killed him, then ran off.

Will the prosecutor have enough evidence to convince a jury beyond a shadow of a doubt?

My phone begins ringing. It could be my wife. I hope it is. I love her, and I miss her and my daughter. It could also be Angie or her husband. Or it could be Billy Karady.

Looking at the unopened envelope, I let the phone ring. One, twice, three times. It continues ringing. Four times, five, six. Then it stops.

I pick up the envelope and start to open it, then think no.

I've got more discipline than that. I put it down.

It wasn't as though Angie and I murdered, or attempted to murder, Billy Karady as a form of blood sport. At the time we thought we were acting in self-defense. The state and all its fancy laws had clearly failed us, and the question remained: did we not have the right to defend ourselves? It was stomp or be stomped, so we stomped. We really didn't know whether we killed Billy or not. We tried. That's true. We did our best to put him under. But we never actually saw him dead. He might very well have survived the night, as I thought he had after the *K* murder in Tucson. Let Oregon and Washington readers with a memory be teased a little. Let them wonder. Let them check old newspaper stories if they want. Let them pore over old police reports. Let them add and subtract possibilities.

I reload my pipe and take another hit.

Billy Karady has become a form of jack-in-the-box for me. He has popped up as the villain again and again in my stories. Each time I knock back the evil son of a bitch, but he lurks in my subconscious with his eye popped half out of his head. I started out as a farm boy and remain one, so I've most often put him in shined shoes and given him a neatly knotted tie, but it's always been him, the confident, willful Billy Karady, forever rumbling through the byways of my imagination in his sleek black Cunt Wagon.

I can't stand the unopened envelope any longer. I rip it open. There is a photograph inside. The photograph is of a man, my obvious clone, who is sitting in a room filled with people working at computers. I immediately know this is the city editor of the *Denver Post*. I turn the photograph over, and Angie has written me a short note:

David knows you are the father. You should expect Richard to come calling. Love always, Angie.

I stare at the picture. I remember our passionate screw as the Wheeled Turd glided along the rails. On that night alone I did not use my Walla Walla rubbers. Richard was the issue of that crazed union. Now I know why Angie is not worried what her husband might conclude from the past. She should have named the baby boy Freight Train.

I jump up, but refuse to go to the window.

If the man in the bar and on the sidewalk was Billy Karady, whose bones were those found in the desert?

When I start a new novel, I like to name my files after the title. What should I name this file? I remember the mouse running through the cow's bones on the night I discovered that Billy Karady was a soda popper; that is, he was completely devoid of honor or sense of fair play. I see Billy's bloody face looking up at me. Now Billy Karady, or the possibility of Billy Karady, is like a raised foot ready to drill me into the ground.

Stomp!

Stomp was all I could think of then and is all I can think of now. I open a file. I change the ten-point type to twelve-point so it's easier to see while I write. I tap the save icon on the tool bar. I name the file STOMP. This will be my master file, where I keep summaries of my chapters as I write and rewrite them. I close STOMP. I open a new file for the first chapter. I name this one STOMP 1.

Somebody begins knocking at my door. It's possible to see my window from the street, so whoever it is must suspect I'm in. Who is it? The same person who tried to call, most likely. As far as I can deduce, there are three possibilities: Angie, David Feuer, or Billy Karady.

I don't want to talk to Angie until I've had time to digest news of my son. Neither do I want to go through any futile, doomed attempt to re-create the past. Angie and I are both different people than we were in 1957. Better to treasure the memory of what we once were and the passion we once shared.

Is it David Feuer, arrived to tell me that he's certain Angie and I murdered Billy Karady? I don't want to talk to him either.

If it's Billy Karady, he's almost certainly bent on tearing me limb from limb for the loss of one eye and having to wear dentures since he was a teenager. I'll pass on a chat with Billy.

The knocking continues, insistent, just like the ringing of the phone. I quietly retrieve another Heineken from my refrigerator and twist off the cap. I take another hit of pot and listen to the knocking.

Knock, knock, knock!

I remember the lyrics of a song.

Knock, knock, knock! Who's that knocking at my door?

The end of my story? Is this knocker the end of my story? I look at the picture of my son. He's a good-looking man. A city editor! The *Denver Post* is not a bad paper.

I think about the man who looks like Billy Karady. Karady could have read about the ABA convention in the newspapers and learned of my appearance on the convention's Internet website. For all I know, he could have been eyeing me at a discreet remove on the floor of the convention hall.

The insistence of the knocking momentarily convinces me that it is Karady.

Knock, knock, knock!

I think: wait, what if there's a fourth possibility? What if the person at the door is Richard, come down from Denver to meet his biological father? Am I to choose between meeting my son and opening the door to a maniac bent on beating my brains out? It's a terrible choice.

Then, mercifully, the knocking stops.

If the knocker was Karady, I know he's not going away until he gets his revenge. The cops begin a murder investigation with motive. The least I can do is finger him with the truth from the past. I'll take him under from my grave. I'll use the truth to do what I failed to do with a baseball bat.

I decide to set the tone in the first paragraph with a truth that will be recognized immediately by all males and probably suspected by all females.

Years later, I read in the Oregonian *that an adolescent male spends 80 percent of the time in the classroom thinking about sex: I believe that. In the classroom and out. The summer of 1957, the break between my sophomore and junior years at Umatilla High School, was a hormonal time for me, that's for sure. I was flat addicted to the nudist colony magazines in Anderson's Market, and there were days when I felt compelled to lope my goat four or five times a day in pursuit of elementary relief.*

Knock, knock, knock!

I look at the door. I sigh.

Knock, knock, knock!

Aw crap!

I can't stand it any longer. The uncertainty is too damn much. I've borne the burden of my secret for decades. I feel intuitively that I can have resolution by answering the door and taking my chances. Anything is better than prolonging the happy horseshit of not knowing. I'm tired of it. Dragged down. Weary. If I'm to have my brains beaten out, it might as well be now as later.

I pop up and throw open the door.

FIVE

It's him. Billy Karady! Standing there with his woman friend. Karady has thickened over the years. He's bald, with only a slight fringe of hair around his neck, and this has been cut so short that he almost looks like Kojak. He's wearing a plaid, long-sleeved cotton shirt with one of those western string ties around the neck. He's wearing charcoal slacks that look suspiciously new and is packing a hefty gut that hangs slightly over an overworked belt. His serviceable, but unfashionable, black shoes are polished to a sheen.

But my eye passes right over these details. They're nothing compared to a couple of mind-boggling realities.

The first is that I'm now larger than he is by three or four inches, and I'm heavier and more robust. After all these years of being pursued by a looming, athletic Billy Karady, it's hard for me to adjust to this stunning physical reversal. He may have been one hell of an athlete in high school, but he doesn't look big now.

The second reality is that Karady has a baseball bat! He's holding it by the knob with his left hand, the end resting on the carpeted floor of the hallway. It's like he's in the hole—just two batters away and waiting his turn at the plate.

My stomach flutters wildly. Talk about adrenaline! Just give me some stainless-steel earmuffs, and I'm ready to go twelve rounds with Mike Tyson. But Karady, strangely to my mind, does nothing. If I had been in his shoes, I would have splashed a few writerly brains about the room. But no. None of that. Far from looking aggressive or mean-spirited, Karady appears slightly embarrassed.

So does his companion. "Excuse me, Mr. Hawkins," she begins. She has a soft voice and a southern drawl. I only saw the back of her head in the bar. Now that I see that's she's middle-aged, thickened out a trifle and with a largish bosom, but attractive in her way. She has large brown eyes and a round face. In her youth she would have been a real flower.

It's almost impossible to take my eyes off the bat. Is Karady going to take my head off now or later? "Yes?" I say. The only thing I can think of is to keep calm.

She says, "My husband and I hate to bother you this late at night, but it's very, very important that we talk to you. It will only take a minute."

Karady sees me eyeing the bat. "It's supposed to be autographed by Johnny Bench. Neat huh? I saw it in one of those shops full of collectibles on my way over here."

"Mr. Cheapskate of the Gulf Coast." The woman rolls her eyes. "Then he goes and pays three hundred dollars for a stupid baseball bat." She shakes her head in disgust. "You have to understand, Hawkins. Peter is obsessed with baseball bats. He collects them. He's got more than two hundred of them."

"All of them are autographed," he says. "I've got Mickey Mantle, Roger Maris, Roberto Clemente. All the great sluggers. Some day those bats will be worth a fortune, then you'll laugh. A good honest, *crrrrraaaack* when it hits the ball. Not that awful ping sound of an aluminum bat. That's not baseball as far as I'm concerned. I may even let my grandson hit a few balls with this one. Let him know what it feels and sounds like."

She looks horrified. "You're not going to let him actually play with that bat, are you? Three hundred dollars!"

"Why not? He won't hurt it any." He grins broadly.

An obsession with baseball bats. Right. Looking at him, with adrenaline coursing through my system, it's difficult to imagine that he was once a terror as a tailback ripping through the line. But the soul lies in the eyes, and even though his left eye is obviously artificial, this is Billy Karady, there is no doubting that. Is all the palaver about baseball bats just nervous talk, delaying the real reason for their visit, or is Karady planning to lay into me with his Johnny Bench special? "And this visit is about?"

She says, "My husband saw your novel in the window of a bookstore. He thought he remembered your name, so we went inside to check it out. When he saw your picture on the dust jacket, he was sure of it. Ray Hawkins, who grew up in Umatilla, Oregon."

"I know you. I'm certain of it," Karady says.

"From his past," she says.

"Please," he says.

"He's only able to remember fragments. Bits and pieces," she says.

"I have these nightmares," he says. His face is earnest in the extreme. He's all but begging me to hear him out.

"This is truly important to him," she says. "You just have to understand. We know it's late, but we have to drive back to Alabama tomorrow. I have to be at work Monday morning. I'm a court reporter. We have an important trial coming up."

"We saw you up here in the window, looking down," he says.

"I didn't answer the knock because I'm beginning another novel. I just wrote the opening paragraph." It's impossible to relax completely with Karady standing there with that damn bat. But the woman is both sincere and disarming. I suppress the urge to slam the door shut. Maybe it's possible to talk my way out of this jam. Also, the reversal of our physical stature has given me a strange new confidence. I step aside. "Won't you come in? A few minutes won't hurt me. Maybe I can help you out."

"Maybe it'll be something you can use in a book," he says. He laughs. "My name is Peter Bounds," he says. We shake.

"And I'm Agatha Bounds," she says. I shake her hand too. "Thank you, truly."

I say, "I don't have a lot in the way of furniture, but please, do take a seat." I gesture toward the two soft chairs by my small table. I sit on the bed.

They step inside. Karady walks with a pronounced limp. This was almost certainly caused by my teeing off on his knee-cap forty years earlier. They sit in the chairs, looking uncertain. Karady lays his bat on the carpet.

I want to throw the damn bat through the window, but I resist the urge. "Would you like something to drink?" I say. "I have some cold cans of Heineken in my little refrigerator." Peter Bounds? What the hell is this?

"Nothing for me, thanks," he says. He would say yes at a friend's house, but I'm a stranger and an author. He's doing his best to relax, but is still awkward.

"No, that's okay," his wife adds.

"Sorry, I don't have a Coke or anything like that," I say.

Peter Bounds, as Karady calls himself, clears his throat.

Agatha reaches over and gives her husband's hand a squeeze. She turns to me. "It's always been difficult for Peter to tell his story, so let me start it for him. When Peter was a young man, he was taken off an empty boxcar in Boise, Idaho, with no identification and severe injuries that cost him the sight in his left eye, his hearing in his left ear, and most of his teeth. His skull was fractured, and his jaw was broken in two places. That's not to mention his smashed left kneecap. You can see he still has the limp. His hands and the calves of his legs and his thighs were cut in numerous places, and his clothes were in rags. He was nearly dead. He didn't know who he was or where he had come from."

"I couldn't remember anything at all," he says. "Or hardly anything." He bunches his face. "All I have are the nightmares. I know they're the key, but I don't know what they mean."

Agatha says, "The police assumed he had been mugged by a hobo. The doctors said his memory was likely lost forever."

"Permanent brain damage," Bounds says.

"An Idaho social worker named him after her nephew who had drowned in a swimming accident in the Snake River. After he recovered physically, the state of Idaho declared him to be nineteen years old and sent him to a community college, where he learned to repair air conditioners and refrigeration systems."

"I eventually got a job in a refrigeration and air-conditioning shop in Mobile that was owned by the brother of my teacher in Boise. At the time, Alabama seemed like a foreign country, but I came to like it, and I've been there ever since. I wound up owning the shop. Good business in the summertime."

Agatha says, "The people in Idaho gave him extensive therapy, including hypnosis intended to restore his memory. But he could never remember anything except a few flashes."

"It seems like I've been over those nightmares tens of thousands of times, and they still don't make any sense. But the images I do have are clear enough." He picks up the handle of the bat and begins playing with it.

I suppress the urge to tell him to leave the fucking bat alone. Now we're getting down to it. I hope the images in his nightmares aren't too damn clear. "Are you sure you won't have a Heineken?" I say.

He grins. He's more relaxed now and comfortable. "Well, sure, thank you. I believe I will have a beer."

Agatha gives him an encouraging pat on the hand. This is obviously a big moment in his life. "None for me," Agatha says.

I get up from the bed and retrieve two cans of Heineken from my little refrigerator. "You have kids?" I say over my shoulder. I grab a glass.

"A daughter who's married to an insurance agent. Agatha and I are grandparents."

"A little boy who's eleven, and an eight-year-old grand-daughter," Agatha says.

"That's right, the little slugger in the making." I give him a Heineken and a glass and return to the bed. I have to know what's in those nightmares before I say anything more. "So what is it you remember?"

SIX

PETER BOUNDS PUTS THE bat back on the floor, rips off the tab of the can, and pours a glassful of beer. Hard for me to match Billy Karady with Bounds's face, fractured and aged as it is, but this is him, no doubt, evil Billy, maximum asshole. I even recognize the pitch and timbre of his voice. For my own safety, I need to remember that whatever he is now, he was once an obsessive stalker. "Shame to drink good beer out of a can," I say. "Tastes better out of a glass for some reason." I want the bat to stay on the floor.

He takes an appreciative sip of beer and leans forward, earnest in the extreme. "Something happened to me in a terrible storm," he says. "I remember blowing sand. I was someplace where there is wind and sand."

"We think it could have been a hit-and-run driver," she says.

He grimaces. "I remember the wind. It was freezing. It's difficult to imagine having cold nightmares, but I do. This was a cold, hard wind."

"He was found in early December," she says.

"That's one dream. The wind and the cold and the pain. In a second dream, it's still cold, but the wind is gone. I'm hurting. I have a terrible headache. A good friend finds me, but he's furious at me for some reason that's not clear. He's chewing me out about something. Yelling at me. I'm hurting. I don't want to hear whatever he's saying. I tell him just get me to a doctor, and we'll deal with that later. But he won't shut up. I get madder than hell. Furious. 'Shut up!' I yell. He snarls at me. I pick up something, a rock, I think, and hit him with it. I . . ." He stops. "I wasn't thinking. I hit him a real solid blow, that much is clear." He puts his glass of beer on the coffee table. He picks up the bat again and starts playing with it.

I think, *Forget the fucking bat, drink your goddam beer!*

"For years, Peter has thought he likely killed this person," Agatha says. "You can understand how this would eat at him."

"Sometimes I can see him lying there on the ground. I can see blood. He doesn't move. What you have to understand is that this scene never repeats itself in exactly the same way. And it's scrambled and confusing. I've had this nightmare for decades, and I've never had any idea just what it is that's got him so pissed." He thumps the end of the bat on the floor.

"But maybe Peter didn't actually kill this person. Maybe he just knocked him down. You can understand why Peter wants to learn the truth."

He leans forward, chewing on his lower lip. "Hard as I try, I just can't remember. I think I might have scooped sand over his body. It was morning. I see a train stopped on the tracks. For years, I had no idea who this person was until I saw your picture on the cover of the book. Then I thought I knew. I had a fight with you."

"Me?"

"Yes, you. I knocked you down. You're the friend in my nightmares. I recognized your face. The only problem is that I thought you'd be smaller. I remember you as being small."

"I was a late bloomer," I say. "Everybody matures at a different rate. When I was a freshman in high school, I was five foot two inches tall and weighed ninety-six pounds. By the time I was a freshman in college, I had grown nine inches and gained eighty pounds."

Agatha says, "But if it was you, and you're still alive, then Peter didn't kill anybody. That's a relief."

"It was you. I know it." He looks at me, and for a moment I believe him completely. He's desperate for the truth. Peter Bounds's only connection with Billy Karady is memory, and that, save for a few threads, has been destroyed.

I think for a moment. The morning Coach Mungo disappeared, a railroad engineer saw what he thought was a grave in the right-of-way. He stopped the train for a few minutes to take a look. The cuts on Karady's hands and thighs likely came from climbing the barbed-wire fence between the stomping grounds and the stalled train. If there's anything else that's been welling up in his subconscious, I want to know about it. I want it out now, not later. I want all this behind me. "What else do you remember? There must be something."

"I think you might have had a girlfriend who I admired. Maybe that's why we had the fight." He glances at his wife and gives me a rueful grin. He puts the bat back down and takes another sip of beer.

"Can you help Peter out?" she asks. "He needs to put the past to rest. It doesn't have anything to do with who he is now. We both understand that. But it's there, and it bothers him."

I say, "I don't know who you had the fight with, but it wasn't me. Yes, looking back, I think you probably did admire my girlfriend."

He looks at his wife. "See! I was partly right at least."

I say, "Your real name is William Karady. You were a star athlete in the high school in Umatilla, Oregon. That's in the eastern part of the state by the Columbia River. You were called Billy. You were very well liked, and yes, we were friends. You disappeared the week of a state quarterfinal football game, which caused us to lose. By us, I mean the Umatilla Vikings. You were probably eighteen years old when you were found, not nineteen. Your disappearance was a mystery that was never solved." Very well liked! That was laying it on a bit, but I figured what the hell. What did it hurt?

"Really?" Peter Bounds appears overwhelmed. His wife embraces him. At last, he has found a clue.

I pop up and put my arm around one of his shoulders and give him a squeeze. As I do, I can feel the bat against the side of my foot. I give it a little nudge to make him reach for it if he develops a sudden, untoward urge.

"Thank you," he says. "Oh, thank you. At least now I know who I was."

Then Agatha gives me a hug. "My husband is a kind and generous man, Mr. Hawkins, but you have no idea how this has been gnawing at him. The business of not knowing. Of having appeared out of a vacuum, found near dead on a freight train with no identity whatsoever. He's been haunted."

He says, "Billy Karady. Not a bad name, but it sounds strange on me." He mops his eyes with his forearm. "Billy Karady." He's found his past. He grins broadly.

"You're Peter Bounds, dear. Billy Karady is dead. We're burying him tonight. You promised if you found out, you'd put it to rest."

She's right about that, I think. Smart woman.

"Maybe the nightmares will stop," he says.

She gives him another hug and pats him on the back. "Let's all hope so."

I say, "You were an only child. Your parents moved to California early in your senior year. You moved in with the high school football coach so you could graduate from Umatilla." I stop. I understand the likely identity of the friend who was angry at Billy. Coach Mungo had been enraged that night when he showed up at the barn. He had figured out that Billy had likely followed us to our parking spot in the stomping grounds, and that's where he went the next morning—the day he disappeared. Mungo and Billy Karady were more than coach and star athlete. They were lovers. Coach had somehow found Billy, and they had likely quarreled, and Billy killed him. Hadn't the forensics examiner concluded that the bones belonged to a male between eighteen and thirty-eight years old?

All those years later, Jeremy Inskeep had stomped on the skull of Coach Mungo's skeleton. Had to be.

Bounds can see I've thought of something. "What else?" he says. "You just remembered something. What is it?"

Should I tell him about Coach Mungo? I figure there's no point in that. The asshole who had tormented Angie and me all those years ago is dead. I had literally beaten the Karady out of him with a baseball bat. The murderous Billy was in the past. "Nothing," I say. "I was just trying to remember. When I say we were friends, I mean more like an acquaintance. We didn't hang out together or anything like that. My closest friend was a kid named Buddy Inskeep. You remember that name?"

He shakes his head.

I raise my glass for a toast. "I guess none of it matters now, does it? Here's to gentle breezes and pleasant memories."

"You got that right," he says. We tap glasses.

I say, "It looks like you've done okay by yourself. You'll never know what would have happened if you'd lived your life as Billy Karady. Maybe it wouldn't have turned out so well. The loss of your eye wasn't good, but still . . ."

His wife likes the sound of that.

"I know what you're saying, but I still wanted to know," he says.

I say, "I was just thinking. You mentioned my girlfriend. That was her with her husband in the bar tonight. They're from Tucson, Arizona."

He grins broadly. "I thought so. See, Agatha, didn't I tell you? That was her." He looked at me. "I wasn't as sure about her as I was about you, but there was something familiar about her."

He recognized Angie too? His memory is improving too damn much for my taste. I'm on an emotional roller coaster. Just as I begin to believe his story and start to relax, I have second thoughts. What if Bounds and his wife have already pieced together his past? What if they're out for a measure of revenge and justice, as Angie and I had been that long-ago night? Agatha obviously loves her husband. He suffered permanent injuries from a terrible beating from a baseball bat. So they concoct a story about his collecting baseball bats, and here they are, ready to take me under. So what does it hurt if he all but admits murdering Coach Mungo? What difference will it make if they walk off leaving a corpse behind?

What I need now is a third party to help cool this guy down if he has vengeance on his mind. David Feuer, a savvy old cop! That's it! "Would you like to meet her too?"

He says, "Well, sure, if it isn't too much trouble."

"No trouble at all. She and her husband are staying in a hotel just down the block."

There's nothing to do but play out my hand and see what happens. I pick up the telephone directory and find the number of the hotel where Angie and David are staying. I punch it up and get the desk operator. She puts me through to the Feuers' room.

SEVEN

ANGIE ANSWERS WITH A hello. Her voice sounds somehow expectant. Is something wrong? I say, "Angie, there's an extremely pleasant gentleman in my room whom I think you might be interested in meeting. I know it's late, but you and your husband might want to drop by my room for a few minutes. Ordinarily I would wait until tomorrow, but he and his wife have to drive back to Alabama in the morning."

She hesitates. "An extremely pleasant gentleman?"

I know she must be thinking of Billy Karady. Extremely pleasant doesn't fit the Billy we knew.

"Who would that be?"

I say, "His name is Peter Bounds. You have to understand, he's had his problems. He's uh . . ." I pause, searching for the right phrase. I want Angie to know what has happened, but I can't tell her too much. I don't want to jar any ugly truths from Bounds's subconscious.

"Memory impaired," Agatha says. She's holding her husband's hand, pleased for him.

That's it! "Memory impaired," I say. "He got hit by a car or something in a winter storm. He's burying the past. He used to be Billy Karady. You remember Billy? The athlete."

Bounds watches me with an odd look on his face. He recognized my name in a bookstore window. He somehow remembered Angie's face when he saw her at the bar. What else was welling up from the murkiness of his past? Was it all coming back to him in a rush? Jesus!

"He wants to see me?" Angie says.

"The kid who disappeared," I say. "He can't remember what happened to him. He has nightmares with flashes that he doesn't understand."

Listening to me talk to Angie, Bounds is obviously struggling to fight through the darkness of damaged synapses. The root of the word *circulate* is *circle* from the Greek *kirko*. Ultimately blood, water, and wind all circulate. They move in circles. Blood through arteries and veins. Evaporation and rain. Growth and decay. The jet stream. Typhoons. Themes of the human condition. Angie and I have a son in Colorado. As I talk to Angie, Peter Bounds picks up the bat again. Studying me, the man who had once been Billy Karady quietly thumps the end of the bat on the floor. He's now on deck.

If he's scamming me, he's one hell of an actor, I'll give him that. I hear Angie saying, "David's not here. He went out for a *New York Times* and some pipe tobacco, and he hasn't come back."

Bounds stands, bat in hand. Is he Billy Karady on deck, studying my head as a batter would a pitcher's stuff before he steps up to the plate?

"He's been gone for more than two hours," Angie says. "It's not like him to just take off like that without calling. I worry. He knows that."

"Well, it's up to you."

Angie says, "I . . . I'll come on over. David probably just dropped into one of those girlie joints and can't bring himself to give it up and return to the old lady in the hotel. He likes those places. Watching never hurt anybody, so I've never cared. He knows that."

"So what do you think, not tonight?"

She pauses for a moment. "No, I think we should get it

over with. We have to put Billy Karady in the past once and
for all. He's been hanging over us far too long."

Isn't that the damn truth? I want to tell her to bring a New
Orleans swat squad, but I can't. I don't have proof of anything,
just paranoia. Maybe Bounds and his wife have already taken
care of Angie's husband, and we're next, or maybe he's just a
bewildered survivor hungering to understand his past. The ambiguity is terrifying. The worst part is I can't talk freely with
Bounds listening in.

"Later then," I say.

"I'll make one last effort at finding David before I come. If
not, I'll leave him a note."

"*Good* thinking," I say, hoping she'll pick up on the emphasis. I hang up. Did she understand?

Bounds has been reading the paragraph on the screen of my
laptop. "Is this the beginning of your new novel?" he asks.

Who in the hell asked him to read my stuff? I hate it when
people read my fiction before it's finished, but I suppress my
feelings. "As it stands now," I say. "I'll probably rewrite it ten
or twelve times before I'm finished." Paul Remillard had said
he had failed with the Walla Walla Bears because his curveball
hung on him. If ever there was a hanging curve, it's my skull
at this moment, sitting atop my neck like a volleyball waiting
to be blown through the window—a form of human tee-ball.

He rereads the paragraph "Mmmm. Set in 1957. Say,
what's it called?" He cocks the bat. He's now at the plate, eyeing a pretend pitch. He holds the bat at the very end, in the
manner of a power hitter. He has slugger's wrists and forearms.
He waggles the barrel menacingly, waiting for the pitch. Is he
just a playful manchild pretending he's Johnny Bench facing a
Dodger on the mound? Or does he have something more terrible in mind?

If I'm able to conclude an amiable chat with Peter Bounds
without stirring up the details of the past, I will have dodged
the cocked bat of memory. I worry that my eyes shine with guilt

as those of the long-ago mice reflected the headlights of our pickup. I say, *"Stomp!"*

"What's it about?"

I have this spooky feeling that he's suddenly remembered everything. He knows the reason for his obsession with baseball bats. He remembers the night of the terrible wind. He can see me teeing off with my Nellie Fox special. I can't take my eyes off his Johnny Bench model. My blood is fairly exploding through my body. I suppress an urge to bolt for the door and make a run for it; if he's here to put me under, I wouldn't get two steps. "Passion," I say.

He takes another look at the computer screen. "I was in Umatilla High School in 1957, wasn't I?"

I nod my head yes. "Yes, you were."

He takes a couple of practice swings. He cocks the bat. "What else will your novel be about?"

"As I see it now, it will be a story about snapshots of people, one after another—a lifetime of them so that they run together like frames on a strip of movie film."

"Snapshots. Like in photo albums?"

"In photo albums, sure. These frames move so fast that we're all fooled into thinking we never change."

He looks puzzled.

I say, "The outside of us changes, of course. We all eventually sag and the rest of it. The inside changes too, but the core of us remains pretty much the same unless we suffer serious trauma like you did."

Hmmmmm. He thinks about that.

"It will be a story about fluids too and current and the wind."

"Fluids. You mean water? Blood?"

Blood? *He knows.* "Water, yes. Blood, too. Blood is mostly water, if you think about it. We're all walking bags of water with some chemicals and a few elements thrown in for good measure."

He steps back, like a batter calling time out. He watches me with renewed interest. "Walking bags of water. That's good!"

"I want it to be about decisions and consequence." If the skeleton whose head Jeremy Inskeep stomped belongs to Coach Mungo, the army will likely be able to identify it. Coach spent the war in a Japanese prison camp. After the war, the army would have taken him to a hospital for examination and treatment for malnutrition. There should be all kinds of medical and dental records on file. There is no statute of limitations on murder.

"Sounds like a good story." Bounds steps up to the plate and cocks the bat again. He seems cheerful, if not downright playful. If he's toying with me, that's understandable. He's found out who he is, and he's feeling good. I also remember Billy Karady staring at Gracie with that same knowing smirk on his face, scaring the daylights out of her and tormenting me just for the hell of it, or laughing at Angie and me after he tried to knock us into the Umatilla River. Ha, ha, ha.

Tom Agnopolous said he had lifted Billy's prints from the door handle of his Cunt Wagon. By now Bounds has left his prints all over the room. If he drills my head through the window with his bat, maybe there'll be a cop out there somewhere who will have brains enough to figure everything out—David Feuer, if he's still alive.

I can't afford to make the fatal error that this is a benign Peter Bounds. For my own protection, I have to assume the worst. Billy Karady was a soda popper. Despite his incarnation as Bounds, it is difficult to believe that his shocking lack of honor, like his memory, was totally a thing of the past. I have to regard this enigmatic figure as Billy Karady, bat cocked, eyeing my skull. If it is only Bounds, curious about my novel, no harm done.

I make my pitch:

"But in the end, it will a story about the identity and fate of a skeleton of a male found a couple of days ago in the desert just southeast of Irrigon, Oregon—dead about forty years, they say. The wind had apparently uncovered the bones, which were found near a place that Umatilla's coach abandoned his pickup a couple of days after you disappeared. He vanished too. The question is, whose skeleton was that? Did it belong to the missing coach? A retired cop who has been working on the case for years has agreed to share his notes with me." A little bluff there at the end, but I figure what the hell, when David Feuer learns that Billy Karady is still alive, he'll help me all he can.

"Tell me about the coach."

"Coach Mungo. As it happens, you were living with him at the time of your disappearance. Your parents had moved to California, but the rules then permitted you to live with somebody else so you could finish the school year."

He glances back at the computer. "This will be a murder mystery, then?"

"A mystery without a doubt. Possibly a murder too, depending. The forensics people need time to establish the cause of death. Coach Mungo had been a prisoner of the Japanese during World War II, so investigators are betting the army will be able to identify the remains." "Investigators are betting" was a verbal knuckleball. Knuckleballs have no spin; they hop and jump as they cross the plate, leaving the batter guessing. Catchers too, for that matter. "Coach was extremely fit. He lifted weights. Difficult to believe he died of natural causes."

"Investigators? You mean the retired cop?"

I deliver a fastball, high and inside: "I mean the Oregon State Police. If somebody finds a skeleton, it's their job to find out who it is and how he came to be there. If it is Coach Mungo, and he was murdered, then who did it? Why would anybody want to kill him? The motive is there somewhere. Difficult to say at this point where the story will end up."

Bounds pauses, as well he should. "Will I be in the book?" he says. "The old me, I mean, Billy Karady?"

I think, *If you know you murdered Coach Mungo, you also know you got what you deserved, don't you? Nobody went unpunished—not you, not me, not Angie. Better to play it smart and just fade into the night. Go back to Alabama, and enjoy your new identity and your family.*

Before I have time to answer his question, somebody knocks at the door. Angie. I hope she had the presence of mind to bring somebody with her. Her husband. A cop. Any third person will do.

I head for the door. Over my shoulder I throw him a change-up. "Sure, you'll be in the book. Record-setting halfback. All-around athete. You had this fabulous black Mercury coupe. It was lowered and had flipper hubcaps and a chopped roof. The engine made a low, rumbling sound when you dragged the gut. The Cunt Wagon we all called it, begging your pardon, ma'am."

The Cunt Wagon. Peter Bounds grins. He had been a cocksman as a kid! Famous for it. Glancing at his wife, he steps out of the batter's box. If he has remembered the past, the news that a cop is working on the mystery has to be disconcerting in the extreme. I haven't sent Billy Karady to the pines just yet; I don't have any idea which of my pitches were balls and which were strikes, but I'm convinced I'm working with a pitcher's count.

His wife sighs heavily. Whether this is because of mounting or dissipating tension is hard to tell.

I put my hand on the doorknob.

Behind me, Billy Karady yells, "Hey, Skeeter!"

His wife moans.

The wind!

I throw open the door and hurl myself past a startled Angie. On the way by, I grab her hand and almost yank her off her feet. I yell, "Run, run, run!"

I glance over my shoulder at Billy Karady, hobbling after us with his Johnny Bench special. He can't begin to run. He lurches, poor bastard.

The watcher, Skeeter Hawkins, is long gone too. I'm Ray Hawkins, Miss Davis's favorite turned intellectual and author, and I've returned to reclaim my life from the grip of fear. I'm bigger and stronger and faster than he is. Who would have imagined this physical reversal?

I pull Angie into an open elevator and punch the down button. The door closes. The elevator moves. I hold her tightly. We say nothing. I think, momentarily, of waiting for Billy Karady on the ground floor and taking him on *mano-a-mano* in the manner of Sylvester Stallone or Arnold Swartzenegger. My advantage in speed and size is such a dramatic reversal of the way we once were that it's hard to get used to. I realize that if I wanted to badly enough, I could take Billy Karady's stupid bat away from him and jam it halfway up his rear end. Stomp the evil bastard to within an inch of his life. But no, I think, we've both suffered enough.

I feel my confidence returning. I will weather this long-enduring storm. One day the wind will take me under, but not this time, thank you.

Angie and I hurry across the carpeted lobby and onto the sidewalk. We have faced the reckoning, and we're still alive. Saying nothing, we join the people headed for the eternal celebration on Bourbon Street. Liberation! Each day survived is triumph.

We see David Feuer coming our way on the sidewalk. He can see by our faces that something dramatic has happened.

"What's up?" he asks. He cocks his head. He's curious.

"I think we should all go have a drink and listen to some jazz," Angie says. "Where have you been?"

He looks foolish.

She laughs. "Ahh, watching the ladies, eh? They have some good ones?"

He grins.

At that moment Billy Karady and his wife come out of the hotel door. Billy sees us. He walks toward us, bat hanging down. He stops by a lamppost ten feet away. He carefully leans the bat against it. He looks at me catching my eyes for a heartbeat. His face is a mask. He turns and walks away, joining his wife.

I watch them disappear into the crowd of tourists on the sidewalk.

I pick up the bat. No Johnny Bench signature.

Feuer says, "Who's that?"

Angie ignores him. She says, "David, I want you and Ray to take me to one of those places where the girls dance. I've never been in one of them."

He leers mischievously. "Sure! No problem!" he says. "Ray and I like to watch naked ladies. Right, Ray?"

"Absolutely," I say. "By the way, we've solved your mystery."

He looks confused. "Oh?"

"About Billy Karady and Coach Mungo and the *K* killer. It's a long story. We'll tell you all about it."

Angie says, "What do you think, Ray, tell him about the incident on the railroad track too?"

"I don't know why not. He'll get a kick out of it. Freight train, freight train, don't look back."

Angie laughs. "Existential sex! Nothing like it." She takes her husband by the arm.

Existential sex? He doesn't understand that either.

"Another long story," she says. "You had to be there to appreciate it."

It's a warm night. A gentle breeze stirs, carrying with it the murmur of celebrants, the bluesy wailing of a saxophone, and the sweet, dank, wormy smells of the Mississippi River. River smells always make me think of the Columbia River and those long-ago days when I was Skeeter Hawkins, the watcher who cleaned the toilets at the bus stop in Umatilla, Oregon. Awful job. Fun memory.

▶ FOL ◀

SEP 0 4 2024